Carry Me Down

Also by M.J. Hyland

How the Light Gets In

M.J. Hyland

Carry Me Down

HarperCollins*PublishersLtd*

Carry Me Down

Copyright © 2006 by M.J. Hyland. All rights reserved.

Published by HarperCollins Publishers Ltd, by arrangement with
Canongate Books Ltd., Edinburgh.

First Canadian Edition

No part of this book may be used or reproduced in any manner
whatsoever without the prior written permission of the publisher,
except in the case of brief quotations embodied in reviews.
HarperCollins books may be purchased for educational, business,
or sales promotional use through our Special Markets Department.

HarperCollins Publishers Ltd
2 Bloor Street East, 20th Floor
Toronto, Ontario, Canada
M4W 1A8

www.harpercollins.ca

Library and Archives Canada Cataloguing in Publication
Hyland, M. J. (Maria Joan), 1968–
Carry me down / M. J. Hyland
ISBN–13: 978-0-00-200738-2
ISBN–10: 0-00-200738-X

I. Title.
PR9619.4.H94C37 2006   823'.92   C2005-905569-3

HC 9 8 7 6 5 4 3
Printed and bound in the United States

For
Stewart Andrew Muir
(if only there were more like you)

I

It is January, a dark Sunday in winter, and I sit with my mother and father at the kitchen table. My father sits with his back to the table, his feet pressed against the wall, a book in his lap. My mother sits to my right and her book rests on the table. I sit close to her, and my chair, which faces the window, is near the heat of the range.

There is a pot of hot tea in the middle of the table and we each have a cup and plate. There are ham and turkey sandwiches on the plates and, if we want more to eat or drink, there is plenty. The pantry is full.

From time to time we stop reading to talk. It is a good mood, as though we are one person reading one book – not three people apart and alone.

These kinds of days are the perfect ones.

Through the small, square window I can see the narrow country road that leads to the town of Gorey and, beyond the road, a field of snow. Beyond the field of snow, although I cannot see it now, is the tree I pass every morning and two miles beyond the tree is Gorey National School, where I will return at the end of the Christmas holiday.

On the corner of the road, to the left of the front gate, there is a post with a sign pointing to Dublin and another, smaller sign beneath it, pointing to the cemetery. For two more days we will be together, the three of us, and that's what I want. I don't want anything different.

* * *

When I see that my mother is near the last page of her book, I take a pack of playing cards and move it towards her elbow. Soon, she will put her book down and offer me a game. I look at her face and wait.

Suddenly, she closes her book and stands.

'John,' she says, 'please come with me.' She is taking me out to the hallway, away from my father. She is taking me out of his sight as though I am the rubbish. 'Come now and leave your book behind,' she says.

We stand at the base of the steep and narrow stairs that lead up to my parents' loft-bedroom – the only room upstairs – and she leans against the banister with her arms folded across her chest, the skin on her hands cold and white like chalk.

'Do I look different today?' she asks.

'No. Why?'

'You were staring again. You were staring at me.'

'I was only looking,' I say.

She moves away from the banister and puts her hands on my shoulders. She is 5 feet 10 inches tall and, even though I am only one and a half inches shorter, she bears down on me until I sink lower. Her body hunches over and her bottom pokes out.

'You were staring at me, John. You shouldn't stare like that.'

'Why can't I look at you?'

'Because you're eleven now. You're not a baby any more.'

I am distracted by the cries of our cat, Crito, who is locked in the cupboard under the stairs with her new kittens. I want to go to her. But my mother presses harder.

'I was only looking,' I say.

I want to say that there is nothing babyish about looking at things, but my body shakes beneath the weight of her arms and I am trembling too much to speak.

'Why?' she asks. 'Why do you have to stare at me like that?'

She is hurting my shoulders and her weight is surprising. She looks lighter and smaller and more beautiful when she's sitting at the table or at the end of my bed, talking to me, making me laugh. I'm angry with her now, for being tall, for being so big, so heavy and for making me so big, far too big for my age.

'I don't know why. I just like it,' I say.

'Maybe you should get out of the habit.'

'Why?'

'Because it's unnerving. Nobody can relax when you stare at them like that.'

'Sorry,' I say.

She stands up straight now and releases me. I lean over and kiss her near the mouth.

'All right then,' she says.

I kiss her a second time, but when I put my arms around her neck to pull her in closer so that we can hug, she pulls away. 'Not just now,' she says. 'It's cold out here.'

She turns and I follow her back into the kitchen.

My father's dark, curly hair is messy and his fringe has fallen down over his eyes. 'Shut the door,' he says, without looking up from his book.

'It's already shut,' I say.

'Good,' he says. 'Keep it shut.'

He smiles in the direction of his book: *Phrenology and the Criminal Cranium.*

My father hasn't worked for three years, for as long as we've lived here, in his mother's cottage. Before we moved in with my grandmother, he worked as an electrician in Wexford, but he hated his job, and said so every night when he got home. Now, instead of going to work, he reads. He says he is preparing for the entrance exam at Trinity College, and that he shouldn't have too much trouble passing because last year he sat the Mensa test and passed with flying colours.

'Look out the window,' I say to my mother. 'It's snowing sideways.'

'So it is,' she says. 'Doesn't it look like flour coming through a sieve?'

'Flour doesn't go sideways through a sieve,' I say.

Her tongue comes out to lick the corner of her mouth and it stays out. I lean across the table to touch it.

'Your tongue is cold,' I say.

My father looks at us, and my mother's lips clamp shut.

'I'm like a lizard,' she says.

She smiles at me, and I smile back.

'A strange pair,' says my father.

Crito is quiet now. She's probably glad to hear us talking and to know we are near by.

I return to reading the *Guinness Book of Records*, my favourite book. I own every edition with the exception of the 1959 edition and it is one of my Christmas presents every year.

I have a few pages left to read of the new edition for 1972, and I have almost finished reading the Human World section for the fourth time. The *Guinness Book of Records* is full of wonders, like the Chinese priest who holds the record for the longest fingernails. It took him twenty-seven years to grow nails twenty-two inches long and in the photograph they are black and curled, like a ram's horns.

Best of all are the escape artists and men like Blondin, who crossed Niagara Falls on a high wire, and Johann Hurlinger, who walked on his hands for more than fifty days. He walked for 871 miles on his hands.

One day I will be in the *Guinness Book of Records*, along with all the other people who do not want to be forgotten or ignored. I will break an important record or do a remarkable thing. I don't see the point of living unless there is something I can do better than anyone else can or unless I can do something that nobody else can do.

I fold the picture of the shortest woman in the world so that she's up against the tallest man. His name was Robert Pershing Wadlow, and he was 8 feet 11.1 inches. By the age of eleven he was already 6 feet 7 inches tall.

I used to wonder if his voice started to break early the way mine has. I used to wonder whether I would become a giant. I still worry about these things but less now that I have decided that I won't end up in the *Guinness Book of Records* for being a freak. I will get in there for a much better reason.

The shortest woman was Pauline Musters, and she was 1 foot 11.2 inches. When I fold her picture against the tallest man, she looks like something that has fallen from his pocket, not like a person at all: a person does not stand next to another person and reach the bottom of that person's knees.

'Look,' I say to my mother. 'This midget looks like an ormamint.'

I already know what she is going to say.

'Ornament,' she says.

'Don't bend your book,' says my father.

'OK,' I say.

'And you've hardly touched your sandwich,' he says.

'I don't want to touch it,' I say.

My mother taps my hand. 'Did you leave half your sandwich uneaten just so you could say that?'

'No.'

'Then eat it.'

But the bread is stale now and it's six o'clock, time for tea. My mother stands up and looks out the window. The snow has stopped falling. She wipes her hands on her jumper and puts a pot of water on the range. She opens the fridge and removes a package.

'Do you want this?' she asks my father.

He rubs his chin and doesn't answer. He shaved his beard off yesterday and his shaving has revealed a dimple; a dark vertical slot in the flesh on his chin. He has been rubbing at it all day as though he hopes to flatten the crease.

'Michael, do you want this for tea or not?'

He looks at the package. 'No,' he says. 'I'd prefer kippers.'

'We have none,' says my mother. 'We have no kippers.'

My mother hates to cook.

'Then I'll have that fish 'n a bag,' he says.

'That you will, then,' she says.

They smile at each other, with a smile that is different from the one they use for me. What my father calls fish 'n a bag is a meal cooked in boiling water: a square piece of fish in a clear plastic bag full of white sauce.

'Can I hold it?' I ask.

'If you really want to,' says my mother.

I take the bag from her and squish the plastic, which is soft, like wet felt. 'It feels like that goldfish I won at Butlins,' I say.

'Come here to me,' says my father, and he hugs me, but his arms are pressing hard against my neck, and his grip is too tight.

'Stop hugging my neck,' I say. 'It hurts.'

6

'Give the bag of fish here,' he says.

I give him the fish 'n a bag and he fondles it. 'I'm going to have to disagree with you,' he says. 'This bag feels more like a bag of snot than a goldfish.'

My father laughs, and I laugh, although I don't like it that he has compared my dinner to snot.

My mother confiscates the fish and puts it in a pot of water. I face my father.

'Da, can you tell me a story?'

'What kind of story?'

'Any kind.'

My father clears his throat and sits up taller in his seat before he begins. 'Very well. Here's the story of Tantalus, who was sentenced by the gods to stand in water up to his waist. In winter the water was cold and in summer it was too warm. When Tantalus got thirsty and his mouth was very dry, he bent down to the water to drink and the water evaporated, and when he got hungry and reached up to the branches which were laden with delicious fruit, the branches lifted the fruit, and both food and water remained out of his grasp. And this happened to Tantalus for . . .'

'A few days,' says my mother, 'as punishment for not washing his hands before tea, and then he sat down to a feast of roast chicken and chocolate ice-cream and he never went hungry or thirsty again.'

He smiles and says, 'Wash your hands.'

As I wash my hands I see Tantalus licking his lips as he reaches down for the water. On the way back to the kitchen I go to the big bookshelf in the living room where my father keeps his reference and textbooks. I look in the encyclopaedia until I find the pages I need. There is Sisyphus with a red exclamation mark next to his name. I put that mark there last year. I go back to the kitchen.

'Tantalus is a lot like Sisyphus,' I say. 'You could say that both of them suffer in the same way.'

My father laughs. 'Did you remember that while you were sitting on the toilet?'

'I wasn't on the toilet. I was only washing my hands and that's when I remembered.'

I look carefully at his face. He is not laughing at me, so I join in.

'Yes,' I say. 'I could clearly see Sisyphus pushing the boulder up a big hill and the boulder rolling straight past Sisyphus and back down the hill. I could see Sisyphus standing there, watching the boulder roll down, all sad and silent, and then pushing the boulder back up and the boulder rolling back down where it came from, over and over again. I think he must feel just like Tantalus.'

'Straining to get the big brown thing where you want it to go,' says my father, laughing until there are tears in his eyes.

Now my mother is laughing. 'Good God,' she says, 'somebody get the poor man a glass of water.'

I jump up and get a glass of water for my father and when I sit back down my mother kisses me on the nose to thank me. 'You're nice to have around,' she says. 'I think we'll keep you.'

'Good,' I say.

When my father has finished with the water I see that the buttons of his jacket are done up the wrong way. He does this on purpose, and it's often a sign of good humour. I lean over and reach for the top button.

'May I fix your buttons?' I ask.

'No, no!' he laughs. 'You'll ruin my crooked and disarming looks.'

He's in the mood for button-fixing and so I go around the table and grab for the second button. He shouts and laughs.

'Get off me, fish face! Get off me!'

'Only four buttons left!' I shout in return.

I manage to undo one more button and then he gets up and goes to the window. He stand and looks out, his face suddenly serious; no more playing.

'Christ almighty. I thought she was back early.'

'Is she?' I ask.

He's talking about my granny, his mother, who'll be back from the Leopardstown races on Tuesday. I've only two days left alone with them.

'No,' he says. 'A false alarm.'

We sit down and he returns to reading.

I face the dresser so that I can look at the black-and-white portrait taken on their wedding day in 1960. My father was twenty-seven then, and even more handsome than he is now because his hair was longer. My mother was twenty-six. She is just as beautiful now.

Nearly all of Wexford parish knew of my parents' courtship and the way each broke off an engagement to be with the other. I've heard that there was nobody who did not stop to stare at them as they walked down the street: they were like movie stars.

They look happy in the photograph, my father behind my mother, four inches taller than she is and making her smaller. I like the way they cut the cake together, my mother's hand over my father's, both holding the long, white-handled knife.

I'm not handsome, too lanky, and my nose is already too big for my face. It must be hard for my parents to look at me, wondering whether there's any hope that I'll turn out to be as good-looking as they are.

I return to the *Guinness Book* and read on page 398 that the record for being buried alive in a 'regulation'-sized coffin is held by an Irishman by the name of Tim Hayes. He was buried for 240 hours 18 minutes and 50 seconds. He came up for air on 2 September 1970. I'm surprised I haven't heard of him. Perhaps I could meet him one day.

It is nearly seven o'clock and I'm getting bored. I put my foot on top of my mother's foot and she pulls her foot out from under mine and puts hers on top. We go back and forth until my father looks at us and shakes his head. I don't let him see that I've noticed, but this slow head-shaking stops my mother straight away and she stands up and looks at her watch.

'You'd better get it over and done with,' she says to my father. She's talking about Crito's kittens, who must be killed before my grandmother returns.

'In a minute,' he says.

'Please do it before somebody starts giving them names,' says my mother. 'And, John. You stay here with me.'

'I don't care,' I say. 'I'm going to help this time.'

'I don't care either,' she says. She looks at my father now. 'Just get rid of those things before your mother gets back or we'll never hear the end of it.'

My father named our cat Crito after Socrates' closest friend, who cried the most at Socrates' deathbed. I like Crito's black-and-white face and her long white socks.

My mother shakes her head at my father and he stands. 'Come on then,' he says. 'Let's see what the boy is made of.'

I follow him to the cupboard under the stairs. He crouches in the sooty dark, between the Hoover and the shovel. He tells me to turn the light on and then he pulls six kittens by their tails to remove them from Crito's teats. He puts them in the pouch he has created by tucking his jacket into his trousers.

'It's okay,' I say to Crito, 'we're taking them for a walk.'

'Are you sure you're ready for this?' my father asks.

'Yes,' I say.

'Then go and get the sack from the coal-scuttle and bring it to the bathroom. I'll meet you there.'

He makes it sound as though we're going somewhere far away, but the cottage is a small place and nobody could ever get lost in it: you walk in the front door and stand in the hallway, and if you turn right, you go through the kitchen, and from the kitchen you can either go back into the hallway, or you can go into the living room. The living room has two doors and you can go out again to the hallway where you will face the door to the bathroom and then take a few steps and you'll see my bedroom door and then, at the back of the cottage, you'll find my grand-mother's bedroom. And at the very end of the hallway is the back door, which leads to the small garden. The only adventure is going up the narrow wooden stairs to my parents' bedroom.

I put the sack down by my father's feet.

'Right. Pop them in here for me.'

I take the kittens — all of them black and white like Crito — from the pouch in my father's jacket and put them into the sack while he runs the bath with hot water. The steam makes my face sweat.

'They're not wriggling very much,' I say. 'It must be cosy in the sack.'

'Don't be soft,' he says. 'Grab that chair for me to sit on, and grab that stool for yourself.'

He pulls his chair near to the bath, and I sit on the stool by the taps, in case he needs more water. He lowers the sack into the hot bath. The sack floats for a moment, then sinks to the bottom. As the kittens move around inside, the sack moves with them.

'How long does it usually take?' I ask.

My father shrugs. 'That depends.'

We don't speak. His leg is jumping up and down and air bubbles float to the top of the water. I'm unstable on the stool and there is nowhere for me to hang on. I'm going to fall off and I want to get down, but I don't say so.

'God, Da,' I say. 'They're moving around a lot. Maybe we should've given them some kind of injection or something.'

He doesn't answer. He stares at the water and chews the inside of his lip. The heads of the kittens are straining against the darkened cloth of the sack.

Now there are fewer bubbles.

'It's taking a very long time,' I say.

He turns on me. 'Are you able for this or not? If you're not, then go and help your mother in the kitchen.'

My mother is not in the kitchen; she's in my bedroom next door. I can hear her singing.

'I am able for it,' I say.

There are certain things my father says, when we are alone, that give me a feeling that is a mixture of excited and sick.

'Feck it,' he says. 'The water mustn't've been hot enough.'

He gets up from his chair and lifts the sack out of the water. I climb off the stool and watch as he struggles to undo the knot in the sack. The kittens are still moving.

'Quick,' I say. 'Let them out.'

The knot is hard to loosen, but at last the sack is open. My father is red in the face and neck. He empties four of the kittens onto the floor and they wriggle and climb on top of each other. Their small ribs heave up and down under thin strands of wet, dark fur. If not for their mewing, they wouldn't seem like kittens at all.

'I knew you'd let them out,' I say, 'I knew you couldn't kill them.'

My father turns to me, takes a kitten in his hand, swings it over his shoulder, and smashes its head against the edge of the bath. The sound of the skull cracking is loud and sharp; like a ruler being snapped in half.

'You stupid, soft little bastard,' he says.

He holds the bashed kitten by the tail over the bath. I want it to live and I still hope it might but blood drips from its skull and ears and it doesn't move. I know it must be dead.

There's not much blood but there's enough to drip down the inside of the bath, enough to turn the water pink near the surface. The blood sinks, then fades. I don't look at my father and then, without warning, he lifts another wet kitten from the floor and bashes its head against the side of the bath. His face is redder than I've ever seen it and, as he reaches for the next kitten, his hand shakes.

'Stop it!' I say. 'Please stop.'

He looks down. The kittens still in the sack have stopped moving.

'It's only nature,' he says, his chest rising and falling. 'You've got to learn that it's only nature.'

I look at him. 'Don't you feel sad?' I ask.

'Why would it make me feel sad?' He stands up. 'It's only what the farmers have to do every day of the week to get the food on your table.'

I look carefully at him and something happens. I know – I am certain – he is lying. There is something in his face, a flash, a momentary smirk, and then a frown. There is also something false about the way he said, 'it's only what the farmers have to do every day of the week' (something he has never said before). He's lying about not being sad.

'Do you really not feel sad?'

He stares at me and, as I stare back, his hazel eyes turn black.

'No, not a bit. They don't even have a soul yet. It's about time you toughened up.'

'But you bashed their heads. Doesn't that make you feel sorry for them?'

'No, sure I told you. There's nothing sad about it at all. They're only grubs with fur.'

'You're brave,' I say, and as soon as I've said it I am sick.

I vomit, without warning, on the bathroom floor, a few inches from a kitten's head and an inch from my father's foot. It is as though a bucket of yellow poison is coming out of me. He lied to me and it has made me sick. He stands back and calls out for my mother. 'Helen, come help us with this mess.'

I move my shoes away from the pool of yellow vomit and vomit a second time. I look down so that he won't see my face.

'Jesus,' he says. 'You poor, soft lad.'

My mother comes in with a dishrag in her hand and looks at my sick on the bathroom floor. 'Michael? What's wrong?'

'He was sick,' says my father.

I look at her shoes. They are my father's shoes. She shouldn't wear his shoes.

I want her to say something, but she stares at my sick and does not speak to me. I walk towards her and still she says nothing.

'They're all dead,' I say, as I squeeze between my mother and father and walk out the door.

My mother comes to my room at half nine and sits on the end of my bed. 'John, come and say goodnight to your father.'

'What about a puppet show?' I ask.

Some nights, before I go to sleep, my mother performs a finger-puppet show for me. There's a cardboard apple-box with curtains painted on it and holes in the side for her hands to go through.

This box stays in my room, near the foot of my bed, and the puppets are stored in my cupboard.

'I don't think so. Not tonight, John.'

She stands up. 'Come. You need to say goodnight.'

My father is in his armchair by the fire. Usually when I come to him to say goodnight, he parts his legs, or uncrosses them. And even though I'm too big, I sit on his knee, just for the play of it, and he asks me whether I've combed my teeth, the same joke he makes every night, and we laugh.

But when he sees me walk into the living room, he keeps his legs tightly crossed, and looks at me as though he has never seen me standing by his chair before. He has swept his fringe away from his eyes and the artery on his left temple pulses in time with the grandfather clock; it looks like mercury pumping inside sausage skin, ugly and hot.

'Goodnight, Da,' I say.

'Goodnight then,' he says.

'Goodnight,' I say again, but he pretends not to have heard.

I go back to bed and read for a while.

My mother comes in. 'OK?' she asks.

'OK,' I say.

'Read for a bit longer tonight, if you want to,' she says.

She's wearing a pair of my father's pyjamas, and the hems drag on the floor.

'Why was everything different today?' I ask.

'Nothing was different today, John.'

'Oh,' I say. 'Are you sure?'

'Yes, darling. I'm sure.'

She steps closer to the bed. I sit up and lean forward. Instead of kissing me, she touches the collar of my pyjama top.

'Sleep well,' she says to the wall behind me. But her voice is kind, and after she leaves I am happy for a while, until I realise that there is something stuck in my throat and that the feeling is getting worse.

I can hear the melted snow trickling into the drain outside and I'm afraid of something, although I don't know what. I wonder what it means to be sure that a person has lied. I will check the *Guinness Book of Records* tomorrow to see if there is an entry for lie detection.

2

My mother is outside in the car, waiting to take me for a drive with her into town to buy some new trousers. I've outgrown my old ones.

On the way out through the kitchen, I pass my father, who is reading at the table. During the night he buried the kittens in the back garden and put a rock over them. The window in my bedroom looks out over the side of the house and, when I stand up, I can see over the hedge to the small road that leads to the cemetery. And although I didn't see outside last night (I was under the blankets, keeping warm), I knew by the kicking noises my father made that he was looking for a rock.

'Hello,' I say.

There's a plate of half-eaten black pudding in front of him. I move towards him and ask, 'What's the book about?'

He looks up at me. 'The same thing it was about the last time you asked.'

'Oh,' I say.

'Criminals and criminology,' he says, rubbing his knee.

'What kind of criminals?'

'Lombroso's born criminals. Criminals who can't seem to help but break the law.'

His dressing gown is too short and his knees and his hair white calves poke out from under the table.

'Like robbers and murderers?' I ask.

'Your mam's waiting. I'll see you later. And I'll have a present for you.'

'Last time you forgot.'

A gust of wind slams the door shut and he looks up at me as though it is my fault. 'I didn't forget,' he says. 'But this present will be a very good one. You'll see.'

He looks back at his book and I look at his wide mouth. I wonder what would happen if I walked to the end of the table and kissed him goodbye. He might like that, or he might be irritated. I can usually tell whether he's in the mood to be kissed, but today he seems both to want and not want me near him. I watch him carefully.

He rubs his knee again, then he looks up. 'What are you staring at?'

'Nothing.'

'Goodbye, son. Have a good day with your mam.'

I walk away.

My mother is wiping the inside of the windscreen with the sleeve of her coat. I get in. 'What kept you?'

'I was talking to Da.'

It's cold today and even colder in the car. I put my fingers against the palm of my hand and wonder how my palm can be warm when my fingers are already so cold they feel bruised. I fold my arms tight around my body and make myself rigid.

I want to ask my mother whether she thinks my father will go to university and, if he does, whether we will move to Dublin. I like it here, but I like Dublin too, and it's only two hours away. It might be easier to meet with the people from the *Guinness Book of Records* in Dublin.

'Are you looking forward to going back to school next week?'

'Not really.'

She uses the same sleeve she used to wipe the windscreen to wipe under her nose.

'Do you want a hanky?' I ask. 'I've one in my pocket.'

I wipe her nose with my handkerchief while she drives and I wonder where the pink hanky I gave her for Christmas has gone. The end of her nose is red and there's a thin blue vein around the edge of her nostril. I don't remember seeing this vein before or the dark mole near her knuckle with three black hairs growing from it.

'When did they last measure you at school?' she asks. 'I thought maybe we should talk to the doctor again?'

'I'm an inch and a half shorter than you,' I say. 'I'm exactly five foot eight and a half.'

'We want to keep an eye on things. That's all. Wouldn't you be happier talking to the doctor about these things?'

'There's nothing to talk about. I'm just tall. That's all.'

'What about other things?'

'There are no other things! I'm just tall.'

She clears her throat and slows the car. 'What about puberty? It might begin early for you.'

'Well, it hasn't. So what's there to talk about?'

'But look at your legs,' she says. 'There's barely room for them in the car. And your hands! As big as rubber boots.'

'I've been this size for weeks. They've been like this for at least three weeks.'

'Well, then. You've had another growth spurt. Maybe we should talk to the doctor? What do you say?'

I don't know why she's talking to me about this in the car. Perhaps it's so she doesn't have to look at me. But she's going red in any case. Maybe she talks about this in the car so I won't be able to see how worried she is. Still, I won't talk about this no matter at school. I feel more nervous and, although I don't like it, I am used to it.

I have only one friend at school. His name is Brendan and I made friends with him on my first day at Gorey school. He asked me if I knew how to make a paper helicopter and at break-time we sat down on the floor in the classroom and tried. Most of the other boys don't like me because I don't say much, and don't play sports or games with them.

My class teacher, Miss Collins, doesn't much like me because I'm doing poorly at Irish when she knows that, if I wanted to, I could do well enough. I'm not a brilliant student; third, fourth and sometimes as low as fifth place in tests, but I'm not stupid.

I'll admit that I'd like to be smarter than I am and that it would be good to excel in tests with less effort. But I know I'll discover how to stand out and make an impression in the world, in ways that will matter much more than being clever.

My mother doesn't want to let the subject rest. 'John, please listen when I ask you a question. Are you teased about your height? Do other children tease you?'

'No,' I say. 'They don't even really notice.'

They do notice. They sometimes call me Troll, after the fairy-tale monster who lives under the bridge in 'Three Billy Goats Gruff'. And, before Christmas, when my Uncle Jack and Uncle Tony came to stay for a few nights, and played cards with my father, Uncle Jack came into the bathroom when I was washing before going to bed.

Uncle Jack has bits of beard on his cheeks and he's shy and often has a frog in his throat; the words get stuck and he is some-times unable to speak at all. But he must have had a few drinks that night because he seemed happy. He gave me a quid, and asked me about school.

I talked to him for a while and he said, 'Talking to you is like watching a ventriloquist's dummy with the ventriloquist nowhere to be found.'

Later, when I put the quid he gave me in my piggy bank, I wished I hadn't talked to him at all. Talking to somebody who's drunk is like talking to an animal.

My mother wipes the windscreen while we wait at the corner for some children to cross the road. When she's finished wiping, she turns to me. 'If you ever want to talk to Dr Ryan or Miss Collins, let me know. Your father and I love you very much.'

'OK,' I say, wondering if there's anybody crossing the road who can read lips.

'Darling boy. Will you talk to Miss Collins if you need to? If there's any trouble?'

'I already have,' I say. 'Everything is fine.'

I haven't talked to Miss Collins about my height or my voice. I want to get on; that's all I want to do.

We drive down the dip in the road and enter the small and busy town where we shop for my new trousers. When we have finished in the shop, I go to the library around the corner, while my mother goes to the chemist. I borrow a book about lie detection and the librarian helps me to order another book from the Wexford library, which is much bigger. I tell her I'll pick it up on my way home from school next week.

finished in the shop, I go to the library around the corner, while my mother goes to the chemist. I borrow a book about lie detection and the librarian helps me to order another book from the Wexford library, which is much bigger. I tell her I'll pick it up on my way home from school next week.

3

It is Tuesday, late afternoon and I am sitting on my bed eating a banana and reading a book when her car pulls into the gravel driveway. My granny is home from Dublin.

I get up from my bed and listen at the door. She is on the front doorstep, talking to Joseph, whose caravan is parked with five others by the side of the road, two miles from here. He must have been waiting for Granny to come back. She gives him some money and he says, 'Thank you, Mrs Egan. You're my truest friend. Would you have an apple for Neddy?'

Neddy is Joseph's piebald horse, who stares at me and snorts whenever I see him. My granny goes to the kitchen, gets an apple and gives it to Neddy.

'You're a fine horse,' she says.

She closes the front door and I go back to my bed where I listen as she goes to her bedroom and then to the kitchen before she makes her way to me. I wish she would leave me alone. When she comes to my room, I often want to pull a blanket over my head, hoping that I might create a blackout and wake when she's gone.

'I'm back,' she says as she barges into my room and looks me up and down with the big, gaping eyes of a deep-sea fish.

'Hello,' I say.

'Did you miss me?'

'Yes,' I say. 'Did you have a good time at the races?'

'Oh, yes. And I saw your Aunty Evelyn in Dublin, too.'

'That's grand.'

'Will I tell you a story, about a mouse in Gorey? Will I begin it? That's all that's in it.'

I hate this riddle. 'Go away,' I want to say, but I can't. This is her cottage and I prefer living here. When she sits on my bed, and grabs hold of my hand, I don't stop her.

We used to live in a two-bedroom flat that had pale green walls and smelt of mould and mouse urine. But when my father lost his job, my mother's pay wasn't enough for the rent and so, a few months later, my grandmother invited us to live with her.

My grandfather owned a jewellery shop and left it to Granny in his will. He died when I was seven and Granny sold the shop and all the jewellery in it. As far as my father is concerned, some of the money from the sale of the jewellery shop should be his.

'Tickle, tickle, tickle,' she says, as she lunges at me, putting her cold fingers under my right armpit, digging her nails in.

'I know where you're ticklish,' she says. 'I know where! Under there!'

I thrash and move away. I want her to tickle me but I know it will start out feeling good and end up feeling bad.

The more I move away, the more she digs under my armpits. We don't speak and I pretend to laugh, pretend to be enjoying myself, and the silence during these episodes makes them stranger, as though we both know I'm pretending.

She stops.

'Can I've some sweets now?' I ask.

'Maybe,' she says. 'Maybe not.'

'Please?' I say. Before my grandmother has time to answer, my mother throws the bedroom door open so hard that it hits the wall. Perhaps she didn't mean it.

Her face is flushed, down to her neck, and her eyes are wide and blue. She looks nicest when she comes home from working on her puppet shows, and I know that she will never get too old or ugly and will never look like Granny.

When my mother speaks I look at her mouth which looks like a pretty mouth should. When an ugly person speaks, their lips move like a gash cut into dough covering a dark hole. I often stare at faces to see whether the mouth is pretty and looks like a mouth should, or whether it is ugly and looks like a crooked gash that opens and closes.

'John, it's time for tea,' says my mother.

I put my half-eaten banana under my pillow. I don't like to eat bananas in front of people.

'You can bring your banana with you if you'd like.'

My mother refers to my banana as though it were a pet.

'That's OK,' I say. 'I'll eat it later.'

'Suit yourself,' she says.

We sit at the kitchen table and eat cream of chicken soup. Granny's handbag is on the kitchen floor by the door and her coat is on the back of her chair. When she comes back from Dublin, she usually asks me to take her coat and bag to her room and she usually gives me a sweet when I come back with her slippers. Something is different today.

She drops her shoes to the floor and the smell of nylon and sweat climbs up the table and into my chicken soup. I watch her while she eats and her eating habits make me feel sick. My father is nearly as bad. Compared to my mother they are like wild dogs and the sounds they make fill the kitchen, like urinating fills a bathroom, and I want to block my ears. Their spoons clank against their bowls, their tongues slop in their mouths, and it is impossible to think of anything else.

When we have finished our soup, my grandmother goes to the dresser and comes back with six cream buns and a piece of wedding cake. The cake is covered in marzipan icing and smells awful, like fresh paint. I put two buns onto a plate and stand up from the table. I want to eat in my room. But my father puts his leg out in front of me so that I can't leave.

'Where do you think you're going?' he says, with anger that is too sudden, too ready; as though he has been saving it up from Sunday.

A pain, not quite sharp, but not dull either, darts up from my bladder and rushes to my throat. 'Nowhere,' I say, and sit back down.

'Well, then,' says my father to my grandmother, 'did you have a good time in Dublin?'

My grandmother's lipstick has smeared onto a bun and she has cream on her nose. Her mouth is full of sodden bread, jam and cream, but she doesn't bother to swallow the wet mess before she speaks.

'It was great. After the races I went to Evelyn's shop and I sat myself down by her fire for a while.'

Evelyn is my mother's older sister.

My father and grandmother talk for a while, and my mother and I watch them, waiting for something to happen. There is often a row when my father and grandmother are at the table together.

After drinking tea, my grandmother has a glass of sherry, and her shoulders drop under the pleasure of it. Her head lolls, her eyes close and, finally, her head falls forward. My father moves his chair, and the scraping wakes her. She looks at him, startled.

'What happened to your beard?' she asks, as though waking from a dream.

My mother and I laugh.

'I want to know what happened to my son's face,' she says. 'He's gone all soft and naked.'

She has hardly finished speaking when her eyes close and her head folds into her chest.

'Wake up!' my father shouts. 'The table is not a bed.'

She opens her eyes. 'It's my house and I'll sleep in the cupboard under the stairs if I want to.'

I wonder where Crito is and start calling for her. 'Puss, puss, puss. Heeeeeere Crito! Heeeeeere Crito!'

My father frowns at me, gets up, and leaves the kitchen without speaking.

Whenever my grandmother wins more than fifty pounds at the races, she takes me to Butlins holiday camp or to a circus if there's one near by. At Butlins last year there was an exhibition called *Amazing Wonders of the World*.

There were pictures of giants and midgets, of a man with no arms who played the piano with his feet, and of Siamese twins, who faced away from each other while they kissed their boyfriends.

My grandmother and I sat in the front row and watched a film of a man going over Niagara Falls in a barrel and a re-enactment of Harry Houdini escaping from a straitjacket and chains. Houdini's real name was Ehrich Weiss. He was born in 1874 and died in 1926.

My Aunty Evelyn has been to Niagara Falls. When she came home she said, 'I've got quite a tan on me.' But she was fatter than she was before she left, and nobody was looking at her tan. My mother says Aunty Evelyn is digging a grave with her teeth.

I look forward to seeing Aunty Evelyn because she tells me stories from that trip. She tells me about the town, with its big hill, called Clifton Hill, lined with museums and fun parlours;

houses of oddities, miracles, neon lights and astonishing amusements. She says that the city by Niagara Falls is our way of competing with nature. 'The natural freak of gigantic falls, and the human freak-show. It's all there at Niagara.'

It occurs to me that I could get to Niagara sooner if only my grandmother would help.

'Did you win?' I ask as I tap her on the arm. She wakes. 'Well? Did you win anything at the races?'

'Not this time,' she says. 'But winning isn't everything.'

'So you won no races?' I say.

'No,' she says. 'But I enjoyed myself.'

I feel dizzy, suddenly, as though I have lost my balance. 'Did you really not win any money?' I ask.

'Sure, didn't I tell you already?' she says. 'I didn't win a penny.'

I look down at the table.

'I'll make some more tea,' says my mother. 'Take Granny's coat and bag and put them in her room.'

I take my grandmother's coat and bag to her bedroom. Being inside her big bedroom is like being in another house, or in a chalet, like the one we stayed in at Butlin's. I put her bag on the bed and open it.

Her purse is bursting with wads of money. I look behind to the door and then I start counting the money by sorting the notes. Fifty, twenty, and five-pound notes in piles. Some of the notes are scrunched, a few are torn. I count once, and then count again, my heart pounding, shaking in my chest.

I'm going to be sick. I rush out to the bathroom, run the cold water tap, and I put my head over the toilet. It comes like last time, a rush of yellow liquid. I get most of the sick into the toilet and mop the rest up with toilet paper. My mouth tastes of bitter orange juice.

I go past the kitchen and look in. Granny is drinking tea and talking to my mother. I return to her bedroom and look at the money: seven hundred and forty-five pounds! I ask God to keep Granny in the kitchen so I won't be caught and my hands shake as I take some of the money for myself. I put it in my pocket, but I am not a thief. This is the proof I need that I have not imagined these riches and that I have not imagined her lies.

I go to my room and don't leave it again for the rest of the day. I can't let anybody see my shaking hands. I put my chest of drawers in front of my door and count the money again. I have taken ninety pounds. I sort the notes into small bundles. Three twenties, two tens and two fives. I will keep the money under my mattress and decide what to do with it later.

At nine o'clock, my mother comes to my bedroom to say good-night.

'How is Lord Muck?' she asks.

'Good.'

'What are you doing?'

'Thinking.'

'You do an awful lot of thinking. Be careful you don't turn into a hermit.'

I don't know why somebody spending their time thinking would surprise anybody. There are thousands of things to think about. When it comes to thinking, life is like a giant amusement park. When you walk into the park, you should want to go on all the rides.

I'd tell her this but she might think I'm being funny and laugh and I'm not in the mood for laughing.

'All right,' I say. 'I'll stop now. Can you stay with me for a while?'

She closes the door and sits on my bed.

'Can you rub my feet?' I ask.

'You'll have to get them out from under the covers.'

She massages my feet and I look at her.

'You seem sad,' she says.

'Because Da is a liar,' I say. 'That's why I was sick on the floor.'

'I beg your pardon?' She lets go of my feet.

'I said Da is a liar.'

'What do you mean your father is a liar?'

I want to tell her that Granny is also a liar, but then she will know that I looked in her purse and might suspect me.

'He's a liar and I have proof. I vomited because he lied to me. He lied about not feeling sad.'

'You vomited at the sight of the dead kittens.'

I sit up. 'No,' I say. 'I vomited because I knew he lied. If I tell you how, will you promise not to tell Da?'

'Go ahead and tell me.'

'Do you promise?'

'I promise. Tell me.'

'Swear you won't tell?'

'I swear it. Now tell me.'

'I've suspected Da was a liar before. Sometimes he promises to do things and I know he'll break his promise. Sometimes he says he'll be home for tea and I know he won't. I've suspected him for ages. I just needed proof. Now I have the proof because I vomited. I know that Da's a liar.'

'That's nonsense. You were sick because you were upset. Your father is not a liar.'

'It was more than being sick. I saw the expression on his face change when he told the lie and I heard the change in his voice and I saw his hands shake.'

She stands up and goes to the door without looking back at me.

'You're tired and upset,' she says. 'Go to sleep. I'll see you in the morning.'

'But . . .'

She has gone.

I look in the *Guinness Book of Records* to see whether there's anybody who has a gift for lie detection. There's nobody. I will write and tell them that I can detect lies. If they decide to test me and I pass the test, I might get in the book, not for breaking a record (like eating the most hard-boiled eggs, or having the longest moustache), but for doing an astonishing thing.

Perhaps, I should also write to Ripley's Believe It or Not! Museum. They might be interested in me. There's a photograph of Robert Leroy Ripley over my bedhead. He stands with his arm around the shoulder of a man called El Fusilado, 'The Executed One', who faced the firing squad and lived. El Fusilado's face is full of bullet holes, but he smiles, happy to be with Ripley. At the very least, I will make enough money from my gift to pay for a trip to Niagara Falls.

I listen out for my father and wonder if he will come to my room with my present when he gets home. I get my shoebox from under my bed and look at the postcards and brochures Aunty Evelyn sent to me from Niagara.

I know exactly how I want my trip to turn out. First of all, it will be Mammy and me, and I want us to sit together on a jumbo jet, and to see the Horseshoe Falls, the biggest falls, from the window of the aeroplane before we land at the airport at Niagara. And I want to take a photograph of the two of us in the cockpit with the pilot and the co-pilot.

I want us to get drenched from the spray of the falls and then to get dry — it will be summer — on our walk up Clifton Hill to the fun-fair, where there are rides and, most importantly of all, Ripley's Believe It or Not! Museum.

I check my watch at half nine and my father's still not home. I go to the living room and ask my grandmother where he is. She tells me he's staying overnight in Wexford. He had to see his old boss about a favour. I fall asleep with a brochure from Ripley's Museum under my pillow.

4

My friend Brendan comes to the cottage in the morning an hour earlier than he is due. He's always early, as though he wants to catch people doing something they shouldn't be. He comes to my bedroom window while I'm getting dressed and taps on the glass. 'Helloooooo,' he says, in his mock farmer's voice. 'I've sold nine cows this very day.'

'Hellooooo,' I shout back. 'Nine is better than eight, they say.'

'Front or back?' he asks.

'Through the chimney, for all I care.'

There's a front door and a back door and both are always open.

'Right, so,' he says.

He presses his mouth and nose flat against the window and licks the glass. Brendan is shorter than I am, but bigger and wider. Stronger, too. He has a habit of hunching over, his head and neck forward and low, so that he looks like he's trying to balance something on his back.

He comes to my room and we sit and talk on the floor for a little while. I don't sit on the bed with him. I only sit on the bed with my mother. I wonder should I show him the money, but decide I shouldn't. What if he wanted to spend some of it? What if he told one of his sisters?

We are on our way out to the field across from the cottage, when Granny stops us as we pass through the kitchen. 'Brendan!' she says. 'You must stop and talk a while.'

'OK, Mrs Egan,' he says.

* * *

My grandmother often dresses from top to bottom in one colour and today she is wearing a yellow shirt, a yellow skirt and yellow high-heeled shoes. Even her big eyes look yellow. She offers to make Brendan some boiled eggs and, as she boils the eggs and makes the toast, Brendan tells her that rowdy twin girls were over at his house playing with his sisters before he left, and that he couldn't wait to get away from them.

'Which twin girls?' asks my grandmother.

'Bernice Boyd and her sister Bernadette,' says Brendan. 'They brought a birthday card and a cake for my sister.'

'It would pay your sister to be careful with that card. Maybe give it a wipe with a damp cloth before she fondles it again.'

'You can't catch germs from a birthday card,' I say.

'The rabies,' says my grandmother, her voice loud, bits of spit falling out of her slackened mouth. 'You could end up with the rabies. That whole family is frothing at the mouth because of the rabies.'

I want to leave the room when my grandmother talks this way, but the eggs are ready.

'Here you are,' she says.

The eggs are not boiled long enough and are too runny to eat. The white is the worst part: a raw, clear liquid. The yolk doesn't look as awful as the raw egg white.

'You have these,' I say to her. 'I'm not so hungry.'

My grandmother uses a knife to break the cap off her egg and the egg white spills over the side of the shell and onto the plate. Instead of using a spoon or a piece of bread to wipe up the mess, she lifts the eggcup to her face and licks the egg from the side of the broken shell. And then she lifts the plate from the table, tilts it to her mouth, and licks some more until there is no egg left. She eats as though she thinks chewing will get in the way of her food, as though she wants all food to be slippery. If a fish came to the table, this is how it would eat.

*　　*　　*

34

I don't understand how such a neat and proper person can eat like this and make such a mess, always a sticky trail of food and dribble behind her. I get bad-tempered with her for being disgusting and a bad temper makes me short of breath. But she took us in when we had no money and tells us that this is our cottage; our home. And she sings fighting songs when she's in the bath and she plays Scrabble with me and she taught me how to play backgammon and poker and she doesn't let me win.

I grab hold of Brendan's jacket and drag him from the kitchen.

'We've got to go,' I say.

'Oh,' she says, 'if you really have to,' and there's nothing I can do to make her feel less sad about being left alone again.

We kick the football for hours and end up in the field about a mile away, half way between the cottage and our school. It's almost dark and getting hard to see the ball. I sit on my haunches to rest for a minute and Brendan sits on the ball.

'Do you know,' he says, 'when we start the sixth class, eight months from now, some of the girls will be wearing brassières.'

He bounces up and down on the football.

I stand and kick hard at the ball under him. 'I'll be in the *Guinness Book of Records* by then.'

'What?'

'I'm writing to them in a few days, before school starts.'

'Why would the *Guinness Book of Records* put you in?'

'I can't say yet, but I'll tell you once I get a letter back from them. It has to be a secret for a while.'

'Stop kicking the ball! Who am I going to tell?'

'It's just that the thing I'm going to get in for is kind of unusual.'

He gets up from the ball and pushes his chest out and I push mine out, too. It's a game we play when we're having a disagreement. I say 'so' and he says 'so' and we push each other around for a while.

'So?'

'So?'

'So?'

He falls back and I charge him.

'So?'

He charges at me. I lose my balance and fall. From the ground I say, 'So?'

And he laughs at me. 'It's five now. I have to be going.'

'How do you know it's five when you haven't even a watch on?' I ask.

'I saw yours a while ago and it was after three.'

I look at my watch and it is only a minute from five o'clock. 'It's not yet five,' I say.

'Bet you it is.'

I would usually start another fight here, for the fun of it, but I want to go back to my room.

'See you at horrible school on Monday.'

'See you,' says Brendan, as he picks up the ball. 'And don't forget to tell the cows on the way back that grass is bad for them.'

'Bye,' I say.

He begins to walk backwards and so do I. We look at each other too long; not sure whether to nod or smile and we end up making odd faces that embarrass the both of us. I turn away and walk home as fast as I can.

I go the usual way, down the long fir-tree lane way and then across the fields to Granny's cottage. In the last field there's a narrow path that I follow every day after school, where the earth is trodden flat and the grass doesn't grow. This is a path I've made and it bends three times in the middle like a snake.

At the edge of the field, to the north of our cottage and not far from the road, there's a doll stuck in a tree and I can't pass it without looking up.

She is wedged tight in the crook of two branches, about ten feet up, and out of reach; she has been there for years, ever since I started at the Gorey National School. Her dress is faded and some of the skin on her hands and arms is black, as though she has frostbite.

In winter I turn away from her as soon as I've checked that she's still there, but in summer, when it's not so dark in the afternoon, I feel sorry for her and want to pull her down. Some summer evenings, on the way home from school, I promise her that I will climb up the tree and take her down, but, as soon as I've had something to eat and drink, I forget her.

If not for Crito sitting on the kitchen table and purring, the cottage would be empty and silent. There are no lights on and the radio is switched off. Perhaps my grandmother is at bingo or the shops and my father is still in Wexford. Maybe my mother is at rehearsal for the summer pantomime. I sit down at the table and put Crito on my lap. I will think while I wait for somebody to come home.

My mother makes puppets but says she isn't good enough to be a puppeteer. 'I'll leave that to the experts,' she says. 'I'm no performer.'

But I know she is wrong. After last year's pantomime, when most people had left the theatre and the lights and heaters had been turned off, a little girl cried for the puppets to come back. The little girl's mammy lost her patience and said, 'I'm going now,' and left the little girl alone to howl, 'Where's The Wolf? Where's Chicken Licken?'

My mother showed the girl that the puppets are not real by making Chicken Licken speak like The Wolf and making The

Wolf speak like Chicken Licken. When the girl cried more, my mother knelt down and put her hands around the little girl's ribs. 'Be quiet now,' she said. 'The puppets have gone to sleep.'

The girl continued to cry until my mother kissed her hair. I walked towards them and my mother took her hands away from the little girl's chest. 'Leave us, John. Go and wait in the car,' she said. She gave me the keys, but I didn't go to the car. I went into the church hall's kitchen and watched through the window to make sure nothing else happened.

And that's how I know she is a better puppeteer than she says she is.

I make myself some toast with blackberry jam and go into the living room. And I see that my father has been home all this time. He is sitting in the silence, on the end of the settee nearest to the open fire, reading *Five Great Philosophers since Plato*. He's wearing slacks and a green jumper with a hole near his neck. There's dark stubble on his chin.

'Hello, Da,' I say.

'Hello, son,' he says.

'Do you have that present for me?' I ask.

'What present?'

'The one you promised.'

'Oh, yes. I couldn't get it yet. I'll get it tomorrow. It'll be an even bigger surprise.'

'But you said.'

'Amorphous perversity,' says my father 'That's what you have: the childhood belief that you can have, and should have, everything.'

I turn on the television and sit at the other end of the settee with my toast and, after ten minutes or so of watching *Doctor Who*, I feel cold. I get up to move the coals in the fire with the poker.

When I sit back down, he says, 'Hello, son,' as though he has forgotten that we have already started a conversation. 'Good day with Brendan?'

'Yes,' I say. 'All right.'

I take a few bites of toast but my tongue feels paralysed. 'Da? When you've got your degree in criminology, do you want to help catch criminals?'

He takes a deep breath and puts the book on his lap. I can tell that he wants to talk today. I pull my legs up onto the settee and move in close to him so that my knee touches his leg.

'Not especially,' he says. 'I want to understand them. You've heard the expression "prevention is better than cure"?'

'But you and Uncle Jack and Uncle Tony talk about criminals deserving everything they get. You said they should be strung up.'

My father senses that I have caught him out. He closes his eyes for a moment, then opens them, as though to start again.

'Sometimes it's almost impossible to know what somebody really thinks from what they say. People are very hard to know. What I really think is much more complicated. What I really think is that only a monster could hang a man. And the men who stop the death penalty in America will be amongst the greatest that ever lived.'

He looks at me to see if I can follow. I can. Better than he realises.

'And talk,' he continues, 'and words used in conversation, when people are trying to amuse each other and pass the time and swab the sore of boredom or loneliness . . . Well, these words are probably the worst way to judge somebody and the kind of talk you hear most of the time between your uncles and me, well, it's a kind of reflex, like when I tap your knee and your leg shoots up.'

Then, without another word, he returns to his book. I want to keep talking and he shouldn't stop this way.

'But do you mean that you'd not want to punish criminals. Even the really bad ones? What if one of them killed Mam?'

'They should be punished,' he says as he rubs his face, 'within reason. But maybe we should know why they commit their crimes in the first place.'

I move closer to him on the settee; I can feel the warmth from his body. 'But what if somebody knew that the criminal was lying? What if somebody was a lie detector?'

'That's a daft question.'

I get a sudden, unexpected and scalding pain, like rope-burn in my stomach. I move a piece of toast around on the plate and look at him again.

'But,' I say, 'I want to know what should happen when you know for certain that a criminal is lying.'

'Are you talking about polygraphs? Lie detection machines?' he asks.

'Yes.'

'But some people are very good liars.'

'What if there was a person who was like a human lie detector, who could tell when somebody was lying?'

He frowns. 'I don't think there's such a person.'

I sit up straighter and smile. It seems that my mother has kept her word and he knows nothing.

'What if there was?'

'Well, he'd have to prove it to me. But he'd probably be a crank, like one of the freaks in your books.'

I peel a crust off my toast and throw it into the fire and say no more. One by one I tear the rest of the crusts off and throw them into the fire.

'It's a bad habit to throw good bread away like that.'

I stand up. 'I'm not very hungry,' I say. 'I'm going to my room.'

But I don't. I go out the front door. Even though it's cold and

40

wet and dark, I sit on my jacket on the small lawn by the gravel driveway and pull the grass out in clumps. I watch the cars go by, and the cows in the field across the road; the cows that come to the fence in groups of two or more, as though they think some-body will free them.

I wave at these cows sometimes, and go over to them and give them the grass I have pulled from the lawn. I like pulling at the grass, I like the sound of the tearing, the tidy, ripping sound.

I hear my mother and grandmother arriving home, but I don't go out to them. I stay in my room and read.

It is late, but my mother hasn't come to my room to say good-night. I go to the bathroom and find her. She's wearing her nightie, hunched over the sink, brushing her teeth. I stand in the doorway and look at her. She stands straighter when she realises I'm watching her.

'Mmm?' she says, the toothpaste on her lips and chin, 'what do you want?'

'Nothing,' I say.

My mother finishes and, as she leaves the bathroom, she forgets to hand me my blue toothbrush.

'Can I've a word with you?' I ask.

'A word?' she says, as she smiles; some warmth at last.

'Yes,' I say. 'Right now.'

We go to my bedroom. I get in under the covers, and so does she. We lie on our backs, up close. Her arm is soft against mine, and before long we breathe together. Her long hair tickles my shoulder and her hand touches my thigh. I want to turn around to her, to have her face closer, but first I have to tell her.

'Granny lied too.'

She rests her head on her hand, and turns to face me.

'That's a very serious thing to say,' she says.

'Mammy, I know when people are lying. I feel sick and I know it.' She looks hard at me for a good while and I try not to blink.

'What lie did Granny tell?'

I explain about the money, but I don't say that I took any of it for myself. She sits up now, and doesn't touch me any more. I close my eyes and wait for her to speak.

'Did you take any money from Granny's purse?'

'No, Mammy. Of course not.'

I stop breathing. My heart thumps so hard I can feel it in my ears. Even though I'm nervous I must pay careful attention to how I feel. It will be important for me to know what lying feels like and to record exactly what it does to my body. I don't want to lie but if we talk about the money then we won't talk about my gift. If I tell one truth then more important truths won't come out.

'Are you sure?' she asks.

'Of course I'm sure.'

I can't look at her when I tell this lie and I frown to make myself look bothered and a bit cross.

'That's good to hear,' she says.

Good to hear. That's the same as saying that you know somebody is lying but you like to hear the lie because it makes you feel better than hearing the truth.

'Good,' I say.

'What happens when somebody tells a lie?' she asks.

'I feel sick and my ears and neck burn and I notice every single thing that's happening.'

She stares at the carpet for a while. 'I want you to promise you won't say a word to your da or to Granny about this lying business.'

Although she hasn't told a lie, I know she doesn't believe me and she's mostly worried I'll embarrass myself. She hasn't asked enough questions and, if she believed me, she would be more

42

curious. She's normally a person who asks questions, one after another, and I always answer her questions.

'OK,' I say. 'It'll be our secret.'

'Let's not call it a secret. Let's just . . . let's call it our sleeping dog.'

'What kind of dog?'

'A red-snorer with long hairy legs that twitch while he's sleeping.'

She lies down again. We smile but I want more: I want her to hug me. I lift my arm and put it over her shoulder. She puts her arm around my waist. This hasn't happened for quite a long time.

'Close your eyes,' she says. Once I have closed my eyes, she kisses me on the lips.

'Keep your eyes closed,' she says.

'OK,' I say.

She runs her hand along my side, and feels my hip, but she stops suddenly, pats me twice, takes her hand back to herself. And then she is up, too fast, out of my warm bed.

'Goodnight,' she says.

'But . . .'

'Goodnight.'

I sit up till late reading the library book, *The Truth about Lie Detection*, and with a new pen and a new exercise book I start writing about lies and the way people behave when they lie. I call the book The Gol of Seil and I write about my father's lie and about my grandmother's lie and then about my mother's strange reaction to the truth.

I wonder what will happen when people find out that I have this rare ability? Or when people realise they can't deceive me? I'll need to be careful. I'll need to be very careful.

5

I get up early and climb the narrow stairs to my parents' bedroom. My grandfather built this loft because he wanted a room away from the rest of the cottage where he could repair jewellery. It has two big windows and a low ceiling. Granny is the only one who doesn't have to stoop when she goes through door.

The door is open just enough for me to see inside. My mother is asleep on her side with her foot poking out from under the eiderdown.

My father is not in the bed. He is sleeping on a mattress on the floor under a brown blanket. He is awake, staring up at the ceiling, or perhaps he is asleep with his eyes open. I'm not sure which.

I stand on my toes and stare for too long and he sees me. He must see me, his eyes meet my eyes, but no other part of his face moves. He does not speak or look like he wants to speak. He stares at me, a long and empty stare, and I still do not know if he is awake or asleep.

'Why are you on the floor?' I want to ask, and I would have asked this question last week, but now, somehow, I have lost my nerve, the way I do at school, and I walk backwards, feeling along the wall with my hands until I am out of his sight.

The stairs are narrow and I go down sideways, holding tight to the rail.

I make more noise in the kitchen than usual, and hope that my grandmother will hear me from her bedroom at the other end of the cottage. Before long, she comes in.

'John!' she says. 'It's half six in the morning.'

'I was hungry.'

'You little devil. I thought there was a bandit in the house. Come over here.'

'Sorry,' I say, but I don't go to her.

'Well, I'm awake now. How about you bring me some tea and sit with me a while?'

I make toast and tea and bring it in to her bedroom.

'If you're cold,' she says, 'you can pop under the covers.'

'No,' I say. 'I'm not cold.'

I sit on the end of her bed and she eats her toast with her mouth wide open, the way she eats everything, as though she has the flu and cannot breathe through her nose.

'Isn't it funny,' I say, 'how when you have the flu you don't have a flue to breathe through.'

She pulls her chin in.

'Like a flue in a chimney . . .'

'Oh. I get it now. You'd need to be up nice and early to keep up with you.'

'But,' I say, 'it *is* early!'

She smiles but the smile fades quickly and her ugly mouth turns down again. 'You like living here with me, don't you?' she asks.

'Of course,' I say. 'It's much better than before. I can walk on the path I've made through the fields to school and I don't have to catch the bus.'

'That's grand,' she says.

We sit and eat our toast and do not speak.

46

I finish my toast and she finishes hers. 'Some more tea would be lovely now,' she says.

I fetch the tea and, when I bring it in, I leave the tray on her bed and remain standing.

'Never stand when you can sit,' she says.

I sit.

'Where's your cup?'

'I'm not having any.'

I sit and watch.

She slurps her tea and smiles at me. She sticks her tongue out to greet the cup before each sip and, after she sips the tea, she smiles at me.

There is only her slurping, and so much silence between us that, when a lorry passes, I am grateful for the noise and the distraction. I look out the window and watch the lorry as it makes its way slowly down the small road that runs alongside the cottage.

My grandmother drains her second cup and an embarrassing whiff of silage floats through the room.

'What did you see when you went upstairs before?' she asks.

'I didn't see anything.'

'Did you see your parents in the bed?'

The smell of rotted animal manure or fermented hay has made itself at home in my grandmother's bedroom and her question seems covered in dirt.

'Yes. I saw them sleeping.'

'Were they both sleeping? Sleeping together?'

There is mucus welling in my throat, around the back of my mouth. 'I saw Da sleeping on the floor,' I say.

'That's right,' she says. 'His back is giving him trouble again. Like last year when he slept in the living room for a week. But leave him be. He hates to have sympathy for it. Do you understand me? Don't talk to him about his back pain, or about his sleeping on the floor. Do you understand?'

47

'Yes,' I say.

She's lying. There is something happening between my mother and father and I should know what it is.

I go to my room and read the second book I have borrowed from the Wexford library about lie detection. From this book I learn that in ancient China people suspected of lying were asked to spit out a portion of rice. Dry rice indicated the dry mouth of a liar. I wonder if I might ever have an opportunity to use this trick. I make a note of this in The Gol of Seil, which I keep hidden under my mattress, along with the money I took from Granny's purse.

I now have three headings: Major Lies (Rojam Seil) and Minor Lies (Ronim Seil) and White Lies (Etihw Seil). But white lies backwards isn't a good word, so I've changed white lies to Etuh Seil.

I the Gol of Seil under my mattress, and as an extra precaution I also use code names for my family: Mother is Romtha, Father is Hafta, Grandmother is Mogra, Uncle Tony is Tolac, and Uncle Jack is Jatal. Although there are no entries for her yet, Aunty Evelyn is Lonev, and there's a page headed with her name, Lonev, waiting for the lies she will tell.

6

It is Sunday, a week since my father lied about the kittens, and I am reading a book about Sherlock Holmes investigating the Jack the Ripper murders.

My mother and father sit with me on the settee and I read parts of the book out loud to them. My father says, 'It's ridiculous and anachronistic to have Sherlock Holmes and Jack the Ripper in the same place.'

'How can it be anachronistic,' says my mother, 'when Sherlock Holmes is a fictional character and the other isn't? A fictional character can live in any time he wants. And besides, I think they were around at the same time.'

'What does anachronistic mean?' I ask.

'It means historically inconsistent,' says my father. 'It would be like Jesus Christ sipping Coca Cola before he went on the cross.'

My mother says, 'I'll get the dictionary. Let's see what the dictionary says.'

She leaves. My father stands to move the coals in the fireplace, then leaves, suddenly, without speaking. My mother doesn't return with the dictionary. I read the book alone

When it's over, I go to the kitchen. My father is at the kitchen table with my grandmother. I don't go in. Instead, I stand at the edge of the doorway where they can't see me.

49

My grandmother is reading a letter and, when she finishes, she looks up at my father. 'What do you want me to do about it?' she asks. 'I wasn't put on this earth solely for your benefit.'

My father speaks in a low voice. 'What about John? What about your grandchild?'

My grandmother presses her lips together before speaking.

'You might be the jew in this family,' she says. 'But you've no right to be giving out to me about money. And what kind of example are you for your son? A man should earn his keep.'

'All right, then. I'll get a job, if that's what will make you happy. To see me miserable.'

My grandmother holds on to the table. 'I'm in a fast-sinking boat,' she says. 'All day long I can feel it pitching and sagging and taking water. You have no idea what it is to face death. I want to live, but my living is almost done. If I want to spend what my husband left then that's my right. You will not tell me how to use up my last years.'

'You asked us to come here.'

'I invited you to stay until you could find some work and instead you descended on this home like locusts,' she says, so angry that she spits at him.

My father looks down at his clenched fists.

'When did I say you could stay here forever?' she continues. 'You haven't worked for three years. Oh yes, so you can do all those tests and puzzles. For what? And all that study, for what? You spend all your time proving you're clever, and no time putting it to good use!'

Before my father has time to answer, she heaves herself up from the table and walks towards the door. I try to sneak away, but she catches sight of me.

'Hello, John,' she says. 'I thought you were watching the television.'

'I got hungry,' I say.

'Well, so. Out of the way and let the dog see the rabbit.'

She grabs my arm and pulls me aside as though I am a piece of furniture in her path.

I go outside. My mother is getting in the car.

'Where are you off to?' she says.

'I don't know.'

'Well, I'm going to get some flour and sugar from Keating's and I'm feeling too lazy to walk.'

'Can I come? And then can we get fish 'n' chips in town?'

She frowns. 'We can't do that,' she says. 'We won't have enough time. I need to do some sewing for the puppets this afternoon.'

'I'll just come to the shop then.' I get in the car and we drive towards Keating's. My arms are hot and my heart is thumping.

'You don't want us to do things together any more,' I say. 'You've changed towards me.'

'I don't think I'm the one who's changed. I think something's come over you.'

'Nothing's come over me,' I say.

I want her to keep looking at me but I say, 'Stop looking at me.'

She smiles. 'What's wrong? Tell me. We have no secrets.'

'I heard Granny and Da arguing about money and about us living in her cottage.'

She sighs. 'Don't worry about that. That's not something for you to worry about.'

'But it sounds serious. She's going to throw us out.'

My heart thumps hard in my chest and I take a gulp of air to stop it, but it goes on thumping.

'Your granny has no intention of doing that. People say things they don't mean when they argue.'

'No,' I say. 'They say more of what they mean.'

51

I hadn't planned these words and I wonder if it's a lie to say something if the words come out before the thought.

'That's a big thing to say,' she says.

'It's true,' I say.

'Sometimes it is, sometimes it isn't. In this case, they don't mean what they say. There is no danger of us being thrown out. Your granny loves you far too much for that and they will make their truce soon enough.'

She's not lying, and I am calmer. My chest has stopped its hard beating and my palms are dry again. She drives slowly and sings.

'Do you ever get a thumping heart and sweaty palms?' I ask.

'Sometimes. When I'm nervous.'

'When do you get nervous?'

'When I'm afraid, I suppose, or feel somebody is watching me like a hawk.'

'I get nervous when I'm by myself sometimes. Does that ever happen to you?'

'Not usually,' she says.

'Because a person shouldn't scare their own self?' I say. 'Because it takes two people to make one person feel bad?'

'I suppose.'

We stop at the crossroads and wait for a slow lorry and a tractor to pass. I look out the window at a dog scratching itself against a fence post.

'That dog is going to cut himself,' I say.

'He'll be all right. He has a thick layer of fur.'

We are quiet for a minute and we watch the dog scratching until he stops and turns to look at us. I wind the window down.

'Woof,' I say.

'Woof, woof,' says my mother. And the dog looks baffled and walks away.

'Now,' she says. 'I can leave the puppets. Tell me what you'd really like to do. We can't stay at the crossroads all day. We can go wherever you like for the whole afternoon. As long as we're back for tea.'

'Will we still go to Niagara Falls?'

'Of course. We'll go when you've finished your Leaving.'

'I want us to go on my thirteenth birthday,' I say. 'When I'm older I might grow out of the idea of going.'

'That's not what we'd planned. That's less than two years from now. It's a very expensive trip.'

I wonder if ninety pounds would be enough for one ticket. I know that it is at least two weeks' salary for a man working in a factory.

'How much would it cost?'

'Much more than we have.'

'What if Granny would help to pay?'

'That's too much to ask.'

There's a car behind us, waiting for us to move.

'But what if she did? What if she gave us the money now before it's all gone?'

'I don't think . . .'

The driver behind us toots the horn.

'You haven't even asked her. What if you promise to ask her?'

'I could ask her,' she says, 'but you mustn't hound me and you mustn't hound her. Whatever she says will be final, and I'll tell you whether it is yes or no, and that'll be the end of the matter. All right?'

My mother waves the driver to pass and as he passes he shakes his head.

'Can you imagine?' I say. 'Can you imagine the waterfalls and the amusements and the funfairs and Ripley's and going on a 747?'

'Try not to get too excited,' she says, but she seems to be the one who is most happy and excited; her cheeks are flushed and her hands are fidgety on the steering wheel.

She turns left at the crossroad and drives faster again. And as we approach the big house – a mansion – near the road that turns off to Gorey town, she slows down and pulls into the driveway.

'Why are you stopping?' I ask.

'I have an idea,' she says. 'I've always wanted to look around the grounds. Why don't we see if we can?'

The big house is well known to everybody who lives in Gorey, and tourists come to look at it and the dark woods that surround it and the rose garden and lake out the back.

The people who own the mansion live in Dublin and come only once or twice a year; they pay groundstaff, gardeners, cleaners, maids and caretakers to keep it in good repair.

'I want to go inside,' I say. 'I want to go inside and see all the rooms.'

She looks at her watch. 'We'll see,' she says.

When my mother says, 'We'll see', it is my cue to think of something far-fetched to say in reply. It is a game of ours; a game only my mother and I play.

'And I don't want to be a person any more,' I say. 'I want to be a sleeping-in otter that can fly over mountains and eat ice-cream all day.'

'We'll see,' she says and we smile.

We park the car at the gates and walk down the path. The gardener stands near the main entrance, wearing a long green jacket and wellington boots. We walk towards him and he watches us coming and does not speak until we are standing a few feet away. 'These are private grounds,' he says.

'Yes, but my son would like to see inside,' says my mother. 'Could he have just a quick peek?'

The gardener wipes his face with the back of his hand. Otherwise he does not move. His blank expression makes him seem more asleep than awake. 'It's private property,' he says, again.

My mother wastes no time. 'My son is very ill,' she says. 'Just a brief look inside.'

She has lied but I have no reaction. It's the kind of lie many people would call a white lie. But it's still a lie and it's told to benefit one and deceive another. Perhaps white lies don't work in the same way because the person telling them doesn't feel as anxious or troubled. And yet a white lie could have consequences just as awful as a black lie.

'And we've no mud on our shoes,' I say. The gardener looks over his shoulder, towards the house, and wipes his face with the back of his other hand, which has a tattoo of a rose on it, and then he reaches for the keys in his pocket.

'It needs airing anyway,' he says.

On the way in, I cough a few times, pretending to be sick, and my mother blushes. Her face is redder than I have ever seen it. I look away until she is pale again and then I hold her hand as we walk through the rooms of the mansion. It's dark and cold inside and smells like Mr Sheen.

The gardener talks about the age of the furniture, and my mother, who is not usually a boring person, asks numbing questions in a strained voice.

'Are the chandeliers Waterford?' she asks.

When we are at the kitchen at the back of the mansion, and I know our tour is nearly over, I decide to break away. I turn and go back to the entrance hall. I look around once and then I run up the wide, bare stairs.

When my mother calls out for me I stand against the wall of the first-floor landing. 'John!' she shouts. 'John!' Then I hear her talking to the gardener and I expect him to come up after me. I mightn't have much time. I run up three more flights and when I reach the top floor, I am out of breath and nervous, but I go on. I open doors and look inside rooms until I come to one with toys in it. I go in and close the door behind me.

There is a rocking horse and boxes filled with games and two single beds covered with teddy bears and dolls and in front of the fireplace there is a row of milk bottles filled with sand.

There is a model village on a table beneath the open window, with a train station, post office and grocer's store. As I stand and look, a small gust of air comes through the window of the grocer's shop, a tiny puff feels just like Crito's breath on the back of my hand.

I am worried that somebody outside will see me through the tall windows. I take the model village from the table and carry it to the corner behind a bed, near the back wall. As I lower the model village to the floor, it buckles in the middle and two small trees come loose. I lower the village to the floor more carefully and put the trees back where I think they belong, then I sit cross-legged on the rug.

There are trains and shops and plastic people and shrubs and dogs. I take the train carriages off the tracks and lay them out in a row.

This is not a model of an Irish village, but a French one; there is a train destined for Pigalle. I play with the train for a while. It has a balcony at the back for passengers to stand on so that they can watch the scenery, and I wonder why our trains don't have balconies.

I would like to have one of the model trains for myself, but I have nowhere to hide a carriage. I take hold of the stationmaster instead, and put him in the pocket of my anorak. He has a moustache, wears a red cap with a visor, and he stands on a flat piece of green plastic, like the flat bits of plastic my soldiers stand on.

My mother is coming up the stairs, calling my name. I put the model village back on the table and walk down the stair to meet her.

She is alone.

'Why did you run away?'

I shrug.

'Come on,' she says. 'I don't want to get the gardener in trouble.'

As we walk down the stairs, I take her hand. 'Thank you,' I say.

'You're all right,' she says.

The gardener walks us to the gate.

'You shouldn't have disappeared like that,' he says. 'You could get me into a lot of trouble.'

'Sorry,' I say. 'I just wanted to run up and down the stairs. For the fun of it.'

'Right, so,' he says. 'But it's bad manners to run in a house that doesn't belong to you.'

'Sorry,' I say.

In the car, my mother turns to me. 'Well, what did you think?'

'It was great,' I say. 'I'm going to live in a mansion one day. Maybe I'll live in that one.'

'Maybe you will,' she says, but I don't think she believes me.

I am serious. As soon as I say the words I know that they will help what I say become true, so I say them again.

'I will live in a mansion,' I say. 'I know it. I'll be famous and I'll be rich. I won't be any ordinary person. I'll do something great. I know it.'

We pull into the driveway of Keating's grocery shop and my mother turns the engine off. I look out through the windscreen. 'I love you,' I say.

She takes my hand and what she says next surprises me. 'Words are not deeds, son. Your mother needs to be held sometimes.'

We hug for longer than usual and, when we stop, she is crying.

'That feels nice,' she says in a voice that sounds softer through her tears.

It takes her a long time to speak again but then she laughs and points at a car pulling into the driveway and I think she must be crying because she's happy.

'Look, that man's driving a cardiac,' she says.

I know because of her laughter that she has made the mistake on purpose, and it is my job to figure it out. This is another game we play.

'A Cadillac,' I say. 'Not a cardiac!'

'You're right,' she says.

When we get home, there's a chocolate cake that Granny has made, fresh out of the cooker, I take a big slice and go to my room to eat it. When I'm finished, I decide to find my grandmother and bring her a piece of cake with a cup of tea. I knock on her bedroom door, but she doesn't answer. I go in anyway.

She's asleep on the bed, on her back, with only underpants on. She has a bar heater pointed at her feet, and her clothes are in a pile on the floor. This is the first time I've seen a naked body and it's not like looking at a person at all.

Her hand is resting on her stomach, which is larger and rounder than I thought it would be. Her breasts hang down under her armpits like two bags of water, with blue and red veins, and dark brown taps stuck in the middle.

On her bedside table, there is a full cup of milky tea and a small white plate with two thick slices of brown bread with jam smeared on them.

I stare at her body for a while and then I shut the door and go back to the kitchen. My father is making a pot of tea.

'I went to the mansion today,' I say.

'Did you?' he says. 'Was it nice?'

'It was better than nice,' I say. 'It has hundreds of rooms.'

I want to show him the stationmaster, but I do not know how he will react to thievery.

'I saw a model village,' I say.

'Did you?' he says.

He walks past me to get to the fridge and puts his hand on my back. I am not sure if he is being affectionate or is trying to move me out of the way.

'The gardener let us in,' I say.

'Good for him,' says my father, as he gets a bottle of milk from the fridge.

'Yeah,' I say to his back. 'Good for him.'

'Anything else to report?'

'I saw a model village of a French town, with a train with a balcony going to Pigalle.'

'Stupid boy. There are no above-ground trains to Pigalle. Underground Metro trains, yes. Above-ground trains, no.'

My hands are in fists and my legs are shaking and all because of the hatred I have towards him now and, although he is holding the bottle of milk, and I have nothing in my hands, it is as though I am holding the bottle. I open my hands and can feel it: the coldness of the glass, the weight of it, and I feel my grip loosening on the bottle, and I feel the bottle slip through my fingers.

I hear the bottle smashing against the floor, and see the milk spreading over the slates and into the cracks between them, but when I look at my father, he is holding the bottle firmly.

He pours the milk into a white jug.

I look at him, as he stands by the range. I stare at his back and I gesture with my hands as though I am punching him in the head. He does not move. He must know what I am doing, but he does not turn to look at me. I stop the punching gestures.

His hands are steady; mine are shaking.

* * *

59

I go to my room and spend the night trying to find all of my plastic toy soldiers. I know that I've nearly two hundred of them and they are always turning up inside socks and under the settee. I don't play with them any more, but I want to know where they are.

I think my father scatters them, stomps on them, breaks their plastic stands off. When I ask if he has seen them, he tells me they are missing in action, or that they have gone AWOL. I used to think AWOL meant that my soldiers had gone over a wall.

When they are lost, lost at war, I imagine them buried alive in the trenches, and I sometimes lie awake at night and worry for them.

I want my soldiers not to be crushed beneath the settee or fall out of the window, in the same way that I want the doll in the tree to be comfortable when she sits between the branches; face forward, legs neat, arms relaxed.

I should keep the soldiers in their box where they'd be warmer and happier: boxes like bed-houses.

7

It is raining hard this morning and I run with wellingtons on my feet and my anorak pulled over my head. Granny offered to drive me but I want to go by myself and I don't want to be seen kissing her goodbye at the school gate. I cross four fields and two roads and I meet Brendan at the corner near our school and together we cross the road to begin our first day back in the fifth class.

'Hi there,' says Brendan in a fake American accent.

'Howdy,' I say in a Southern drawl.

'What a horrible boring day this will be.'

'I wonder what Miss Collins got for Christmas?' I ask.

'A cane made of foam or rubber, I hope,' says Brendan.

'But have you noticed that she doesn't use it as much as she used to?'

'On you, maybe. She's afraid of you 'cause you're twice her height.'

The bell rings and we go in. I open my schoolbag and put the current edition of the *Guinness Book* in my desk, along with my dictionary.

Our school is a small school run by the nuns; a convent school, with four classes of no more than twelve pupils each. Classes one and two and classes three and four are shared. But the pupils in the fifth and sixth classes have rooms to themselves.

I sit at the back and my desk is near one of two small windows along the left wall. I can see the playing field, the road, and the nuns as they pass by on their way to mass. Sister Ursula, who teaches first and second class, always looks in at us on her way to mass and she waves at us with her Bible. None of the others looks in.

During our first lesson, Brendan takes a pair of thick-rimmed bifocals out of his bag, puts them on and claims he is going blind. Miss Collins moves him from the middle of the room and sits him in the front row. I'm sure the glasses are plastic and that Brendan wants to sit up the front because it is close to the only heater in our cold, concrete-floor classroom. I don't know why he didn't tell me about this blindness lark. I'll give him the chance and the time to tell me and if he doesn't . . . well, I'll find out anyway.

It is break-time and still raining heavily. Brendan and I sit on the bench that runs along the corridor under the coat racks outside our classroom, and the coats hanging on the hooks above our heads drip rain from this morning's walk to school.

Brendan picks a scab off his knee and puts it in his pocket.

'What're you keeping that for?' I ask.

'To eat later.'

'You eat scabs?'

'If you don't eat your scabs,' says Brendan, 'you'll bleed to death the next time you get cut.'

I put my hand out and Brendan gives me the scab. I want to tell him about the scab I have on my head from scratching small holes in my scalp, but if I tell him he'll want to see it.

'Do you really have bad eyesight?' I ask.

'Why do you think I'm wearing these glasses?'

As Brendan speaks, wet biscuit crumbs fall onto his trouser legs and he picks them up with his wetted finger. I wonder what would happen if I played the part of detective with Brendan. What will happen if I interrogate him? Perhaps the tricks of detection will work even though I think I know the truth without having to inspect the glasses. Perhaps I will get proof of the lie from his hands and face and voice and from my physical symptoms.

'What exactly is wrong with your eyes, then?'

'I'm nearly blind!' he says. 'If I don't wear glasses I could get a brain tumour.'

'You weren't blind when I saw you last week.'

'It all happened the next day. Mam says I got a virus or something that causes blindness.'

He is lying, and I know it with the aid of only one physical symptom: my hot ears. And I know Brendan is lying because he looks away from me and up at the wall. One of the books says that a person usually looks up to the right or to the side to think, rarely to the left. Also, Brendan shrugs, and he speaks more slowly than he usually does.

The bell rings and we return to class.

I usually walk with him to his desk, then say a goodbye or tell a joke, something to keep us going until lunchtime, but I am short of breath and nervous. I've never felt nervous with Brendan before and it is the same kind of nervousness I've been feeling around my father since I caught him lying. This is not sickness: I know the difference.

8

School has been cancelled due to heavy snowfall. I am lying on the settee under a blanket. My mother is in her armchair next to the settee, reading a book. All day I've been wondering where my father is.

'Where's Da?' I ask, at last. 'Is he sick in bed?'

'No,' she says. 'He was out with his friend very late last night and decided to stay at the hotel.'

'Why?'

'Because of the state of the roads.'

My father is not a drinker. My uncles, Jack and Tony, say his disdain for drink is unnatural. My father tells them that when he took the pledge he meant it, and he sees no reason to do something he does not enjoy.

He goes to the pub once or twice a year. Whenever he drinks heavily he spends most of the next day sitting at the kitchen table, looking at the glass of Worcestershire sauce and raw egg he can't bring himself to drink.

'Mam?' I say. I move with my blanket to sit at her feet.

'What?' she says. 'Get off my feet.'

I move back to the settee. 'Can we toast marshmallows on the fire?'

'We don't have any.'

'What about toast then?' I ask.

'If you like,' she says.

She gets up without speaking, climbs up the stairs to her bedroom and does not come down again. I wait for a long time, watching television without concentrating.

I go up and knock on her bedroom door. 'Mam?'

No answer.

I knock again. 'Mam?'

'Come in,' she says.

She is under the eiderdown, with one arm hugging a pillow.

'What are you doing?' I ask.

'I'm having a rest,' she says.

'Why?'

'Because I need one.' She closes her eyes. 'Shut the door,' she says. 'There's a draught.'

I go over to the bed and lie down on top of the eiderdown and hug her from behind, with my arm over her stomach. 'What kind of draught was it?' I ask. 'A draught horse, or a draught from a game of draughts?'

'I don't feel like playing,' she says.

Perhaps she is sick.

'Can I get under?' I ask.

'Yes.'

When I get under the eiderdown, she rolls over and puts her arm around me, then she closes her eyes and falls quickly into sleep.

Her breath smells of eggs at first, and it is a hot, warm breath, and when I get used to it I do not mind it much. But after about ten minutes her breath begins to smell like the stale water in a blocked drain.

Her body is very warm. I get too hot, and take my arm off her and move to the other side of the bed. I look at her some more from over there, until, at last, I fall asleep.

* * *

She wakes me. It is dark now and, for a moment, I don't know where I am. 'What time is it?' I say.

'Time for some tea,' she says, as she turns on the bedside lamp. 'And your father's home. Better get up.'

I don't want to go downstairs. 'You're as cool as a cookie,' I say.

'Cool as a cucumber,' she says without smiling.

'Are you sure? Isn't it cookie?'

'I don't want to play, John,' she says. 'We can't be playing all the time.'

I rush from the room and ignore her when she calls out to me.

I meet my father coming up the narrow stairs. He sees me but says nothing. One of us has to move out of the way. He walks up the middle and I'm forced to turn sideways to let him pass. I press my back against the banister. His arm pushes against mine and his body feels as though it hates mine. He passes without saying hello, without looking at me, as though he is a blind man. I stand still and wait. When he is at the top of the landing, he stops and looks down at me. 'Is she up there?' he asks.

He should not call my mother 'she' and he should know she's up there because she just now called out my name.

'Yes,' I say, but he is not interested in my answer. He has asked me only to have something to say.

'Are you cross with me?' I ask.

'Can a man not just get up his own feckin' stairs?'

He doesn't look at me. I feel his anger even before I hear what he has to say. I take a deep breath. 'Mam's been sleeping,' I say.

'If I say now what I really want to say, I think I could regret it for the rest of my life.'

'What do you want to say?' I ask.

'Just move out of my way,' he says.

My stomach feels the way it does before I fall off a wall or from a tree: a rush of heat all the way to the bridge of my nose. When his back is turned, I speak in a soft voice. 'I don't need you,' I say, but he does not hear.

I watch television for a while and then I make some new notes in The Gol of Seil. I describe the lies people tell on the television (especially on the news). I have more trouble detecting these lies – because the signs are fainter – but I can still tell. I've noticed that when people are uncomfortable, as they usually are when they are deceiving somebody, they often reach for something, or touch something nearby: a cup, a book, or the collar of their shirt. In The Gol of Seil I call this reaching for comfort and reaching for distraction.

9

The snow has stopped and the roads are safe for cars. We are back at school. I am hoping that today will be the day I tell Brendan about my gift for lie detection. I plan to tell him on the way home, but just before the bell, Mr Donnelly, the headmaster, comes into the classroom and calls for me.

'John Egan, come here to the front.'

The room is filled with sniggering and whispering. If only they were laughing at Mr Donnelly's stupid, loud way of speaking and not at me.

'Now, stand up straight.'

'Yes, sir.'

'Please come with me now to my office.'

On the way to his office Mr Donnelly is silent but, once inside, he soon begins speaking in a loud rush. He sits behind his desk, and I sit in the chair nearest the window so I can look outside. I don't want to look at his big red face and his fingers so long and fat they can barely fit inside the holes to dial a phone number.

'Terrible bitter weather,' he says.

'Yes,' I say, as I look out the window.

I don't want to talk to him. I only want to know why he has called me in. He moves his chair in closer to his desk.

'How are you getting on?'

'Fine. Not a bother, sir.'

'How old are you now, John?'

'Twelve in July.'

'Is there anything you need?'

He opens his desk drawer and rummages through his supply of stationery.

'Do you have enough pens and pencils?'

'Plenty, sir.'

He sighs.

'Sit up straight.'

I look at the watch on his wrist.

'Don't sit on the edge of the seat like that. Now move back and sit up. That's much better now. That's right.'

I know what he really wants to talk about. He wants to talk about my body. He did the same thing last year. It was only a matter of time. I wish I had the strength to stop him. He is worthless, after all, an ugly man with red hair and a red beard. But I move in my chair just the way he tells me to.

'Listen to me, now, young man. You struggled with your Irish last term. Why is that? You're too bright to fall behind.'

I look at Mr Donnelly's red hair and I don't tell him the truth – that I use Irish lessons to read the *Guinness Book*. I tell him that I don't like Irish because it's hard to do well at something you don't like. I feel a bit light-headed and I hold on to the seat to stop myself from moving.

'So,' says Mr Donnelly. 'That's a bit of a chicken and egg. And which comes first we'll never know. So that doesn't really help explain the nature of the problem, but we might as well move along and you can tell me what subjects you *do* like.'

'I like history,' I say, wondering what causes red hair and whether it is because of Mr Donnelly that I am angry around people with red hair.

'*Why* do you like history?' asks Mr Donnelly, his arms folded across his chest.

I sit as far back and as straight up as I can in the wooden chair and I remember the day last summer, when I was watching a film at the cinema in Wexford. There was a red-haired boy sitting alone in front of me and I took my shoes off and put my feet up on the seat near his face.

When the boy turned around and asked me to get my feet down, I didn't respond or look at him, and I left one foot where it was, on the seat back, near the boy's face. When he turned again and told me that my feet stank and asked me to move them, I didn't answer and left my feet where they were.

'I like history,' I tell Mr Donnelly, making up my answer as I go along, 'because it's about knowing facts and stories, and you learn things that you can tell other people that they like hearing. Like that King Charles the First was beheaded.'

Mr Donnelly stares at me and shakes his head. 'It's like hearing a voice calling up from the bottom of a well,' he says.

'Yeah,' I say, 'it is.'

But I realise I have made a mistake: Mr Donnelly is talking about me. He means that the sound of my voice is deep for a young boy's and that it is like somebody calling up a deep hole.

'You're very tall, John,' Mr Donnelly goes on. 'You're the height of the senior boys. If you were performing like you are growing we might be able to consider putting you up a class so you would not stand out like a sore thumb. You're doing well in most classes, very well in some, but quite poorly in Irish. So you're not really ready to go up, except in height, if you get my drift.'

I don't want to talk about my height. 'I already fit in, sir, and Brendan is in class with me. I don't want to go up.'

'Well, that's not an option, as I've just finished saying. Not unless you can get your act together with the Irish.'

'OK, sir.'

I get out of my seat.

'Sit down, John. I've some questions I need to ask you. Sit down there like a good boy and concentrate on our purpose today.'

I sit down and he watches me as I take my seat so closely it is as though he has the right to me and can do what he likes with me.

'Now,' he continues, looking at my whole body one more time, looking me up and down, all the way down and all the way up again, 'do you feel well? How is your body holding up?'

I open my mouth but all I can feel is thickness in my throat.

'Don't be shy, now.'

I shrug, feel beaten. I am nothing. Even an animal can move if it wants to get out of the way of something.

'Have you had any strange or unwanted activity below the waist?'

I shake my head, too fast. I must look like a fool. But I should not care what I look like to him.

'Do you have any questions about what your body has been doing?'

'No!' I say. My voice is shaking.

'Have you been to the doctor recently?'

'Yes.'

'What height does the doctor say you will become?'

I am dizzy with embarrassment. 'I have to go to the toilet, sir. Can I come back after I've been to the toilet?'

'When you come back, I'll give you a brand new eraser, and a few new exercise books. Nothing like new stationery for a fresh start in your lessons. Would you like that?'

I don't answer. I open the door and run down the corridor to the boys' toilet and I wonder what's wrong with a man like Mr Donnelly. He likes to abuse me with his badgering but he can't stand to have me hate him. And so, at the end of a session of beating me with his opinions he almost always offers a parting gift or kind word, something free and nice for me; always just short of an apology for his ugly manners.

I don't go back to his office.

At home, I go to the kitchen and find my mother there, with a book on her lap and Crito by her feet.

'Mammy, Mr Donnelly made me come to his office and he talked to me about my height and all.'

She nods and moves her chair out from the table. 'Sorry, John. I meant to tell you.'

'Meant to tell me what?'

I stand next to her and fold my arms across my chest.

'I asked him to have a word with you. He rang to ask me how you were getting on and one thing led to another.'

'Why would you do that? I don't even need help and it's none of his business!'

Without meaning to, without knowing, without planning to, I have moved forward and my legs are pressed hard against my mother's chair and I am looming over her. She looks up into my face and I can see my reflection in her eyes.

'There's no need to suffocate me,' she says, her voice weak and small.

I move away and stand by my usual chair and feel its wooden back under my hands. I'm shaking and my teeth scrape together.

'Sorry,' I say. 'But I don't know why you made me talk to him. He offended me and treated me like a circus freak and looked me up and down.'

She smiles. 'He does the same to me and sometimes he even licks his chops. I was wrong. I shouldn't have suggested it. I'm sorry.'

'But why did you think he should talk to me? Do you think something is wrong with me?'

'At the time, it seemed a harmless enough idea. I wondered if you might like a good heart-to-heart with a grown man about the things you're going through. Early adolescence can be a difficult time.'

'Isn't that what Da's for?'

'Yes, he's here for that, too. But I worry you won't talk to your da even if you need to'

'I will if I want to.'

I go to my room and half an hour later she comes and asks whether I'm in the mood for a puppet show before tea and she gets her finger puppets and puts on a small show. Afterwards, she dances and she sings and moves around my room as though she is alone, nobody watching. But I'm watching and the way she moves reminds me of something I saw in a film once: a beautiful lady alone at night in a swimming pool with blue lights in the water.

A week later, on the way home from school, I stop on my path, about two hundred feet before the doll in the tree. There's a cow, asleep or dying, lying across my path. I kneel down and look at her. She is still breathing and her eyes are closed.

I hear hooves stomping further out in the field and there is a cow, alone, running. It runs as fast as I've ever seen a cow run, and then it stops near the boundary fence. I look down at the dying cow and then I hear the hooves again; the same cow is sprinting back to the place it took off from and, when it stops, it looks at me.

I don't know what I should do with the sick cow whose breathing is shallow and pained. I stand and walk around her, to get a better view of her whole body, to see if there are any wounds or if she is pregnant. I prod her stomach with my boot. The sprinting cow is no longer watching me and I feel freer;

I can do what I think is best. But I don't know what that should be.

I kneel again and look at her. If she is dying and if she's in pain, then the vet will probably put her to sleep. I don't want to leave her here on my path to die. I take my anorak off and put it over her face. She doesn't react. I will need to sit on her to put her to sleep. But I can't do that. I move my anorak across her face to make sure the lining, which is made of wool, is not touching her eyes, in case it sticks to her.

I sit facing the sprinting cow but it has decided to eat grass instead of looking at me. I sit for a while and the dying cow does nothing. I say, 'It'll be all right soon. You'll be asleep soon.' I don't know what to say, but not talking to her seems rude.

I'll go now. I'm very cold and the icy wind is pushing its way up under my jumper. I'm hungry, too. Later the farmer will find her and he can take her out of my path and bury her, if she dies. I take my coat from her face and say, 'Goodbye.'

I leave for school early the next morning and walk quickly in case the cow is lying across my path, but when I get there she is gone, and there is no sign of her. I should have counted the herd last night so that I could know if any were missing. I look towards the boundary fence at the cows huddled together but none of them looks back. It is as though nothing at all has happened. But something has happened. I have a pain in my stomach, down low, and it's a feeling almost like an emotion but I don't know which kind, which one.

During class, I sit forward in my seat and lean on my desk, my chin on my hand. My bladder is full and I've been hanging on since before breakfast, and now it is nearly midday. I want to see how long I can hold on, how much I can make my body follow my orders. I like the sensation, the stinging and the pressure. I hang on until five minutes before the bell and then I realise I've waited too long. I jog my leg up and down as fast as I can but my piss is about to come out even though I've told it not to, even though I've tried to make it wait.

I put my hand up, but something goes wrong. My bladder opens without me telling it to. It feels good, briefly, to let go, and I tell myself that letting out this trickle of urine is deliberate, that I can stop the rest.

But I can't stem the flow. Hot urine floods my trousers and spreads around my backside. The backs of my legs are saturated too, and I am sitting in a warm puddle.

I want to put my hand up and ask to be excused for the toilet, but it is compulsory to ask in Irish. I wait until I have the words clear.

'*An bhfuil cead agam dul amach, más é do thoil é?*'

'Can't you wait?' says Miss Collins, who faces the blackboard and keeps her back to the class and doesn't even know who is asking.

'No, miss,' I say. 'I need to go to the toilet now.' She pretends not to hear me because this time I've used English instead of Irish.

I must keep the urine a secret, but I don't know how, since it runs down my legs and into my socks and shoes. 'Please, miss,' I say. 'May I be excused?'

Miss Collins turns from the blackboard. 'John, can you not wait till lunch?'

I stand, and the urine sloshes underfoot and the smell rises up to meet me.

'No, miss. I need to go now.'

The slope of the floor carries a small trickle of urine towards the front of the room.

Miss Collins doesn't notice the piss heading towards the blackboard, nor the stench, but Jimmy the red-headed boy with the desk in front of mine notices.

'Oh, miss!' he cries. 'John's wet himself.'

76

Everybody turns to see what I have done.

I have my hand in the air, as though waving at a bus that has already sped past. Miss Collins walks towards me with her mouth open, showing her underbite and the stained and crooked teeth of an old dog.

'Oh dear,' she says. 'You'll need to see Sister Bernadette about getting something to clean yourself up.'

Sister Bernadette will take me to the district nurse's room, which is in the convent next door. I don't want to go there.

I run from the classroom, down the corridor, past the coat rack, past the other classrooms and out the front door and I keep running until I get to the laneway and the darkness and privacy and stillness of the fir trees, and then my skin begins to sting from my wet trousers rubbing together and chafing my legs.

I want to get into my pyjamas and I want to get into bed and destroy time. I want to sleep, then wake to the smell of tea and sausages, to find that what has happened has been erased.

I don't think I can ever go back to school.

I sneak through the back door and tiptoe to my room. I take my wet trousers off and change into clean, dry ones. I go to the bathroom, run a sink full of hot water, and scrub my trousers clean.

My mother is coming down the stairs. 'Hello?' she calls.

'Hello,' I say.

She comes into the bathroom. 'What are you doing home?'

I felt sick, I tell her, and Miss Collins has sent me home.

She asks me why the school didn't call. 'I would have come and got you.'

When I lie, I feel heavier and when I try to move it is as though my legs are filled with hot water. The lie moves through every part of my body, like sickness.

They rang twice, I say, but there was no answer. I use fewer words, just in case they get stuck in my throat, besides, my voice is tighter, almost squeaky. She asks me why I'm washing my clothes and I tell her I vomited on them.

'Again?' she says. 'More lying?'

'I wasn't lying.'

'I didn't say you were. You jumped to that conclusion all by yourself.'

She smiles now and I wonder if I have been caught out.

'Oh,' I say.

She holds my hand up and feels my palm. I'm not sweating, if that's what she's checking for. Most people sweat when they lie. But I don't.

'Smiling stops the gag reflex,' she says. 'Did you know that?'

'Da already told me that.'

'Well, he's right. And you'd better get straight into bed if you're sick.'

I sit on the bed and wait for her to come to see me for a chat, but she doesn't. I hope she'll go to the kitchen and make me a toasted ham sandwich or get me some biscuits and a cup of cocoa, but she doesn't.

I listen to her go up the stairs to her bedroom, and then I hear my father.

They are talking in loud voices. Something falls on the floor, and then they are silent.

I lie under the covers for a while, and think of a funny thing to tell my mother. I wish that she'd come to me.

Please come, please come, please come.

She does not come.

I lie in bed but can't read or sleep.

I talk to myself for an hour or so. I talk to myself in two voices, as though two people are having a conversation.

I talk about what has happened. I ask myself questions in one voice, and answer them in another, different voice. I talk about what I will do tomorrow.

I would rather die than let my father find out. I would rather die than go back to school.

I go into the bathroom and scrub my legs with a nailbrush and then I hang my trousers on the clotheshorse in the living room in front of the fire, and wish somebody would come and talk to me.

It is half two and nobody has visited me. I stop saying, please come.

10

In the morning I tell my mother that I'm too sick to go to school, but the phone rings during breakfast and I know I've been found out. She comes to my bedroom to tell me that it was Miss Collins.

'She says I need to come in today. The district nurse is at the school and Miss Collins and Mr Donnelly would both like you to see her.'

'Why?'

'I've been told what happened yesterday.'

'Oh.'

'You go to school now, and I'll meet you outside the nurse's office at eleven o'clock.'

'Why?'

'That's where I've been told to take you.'

'I won't go to school.'

'You must.'

'Please don't tell Da.'

'No, I won't. But I can't promise he won't find out for himself.'

I get dressed and go to the kitchen for some breakfast, but when I look at my half-eaten boiled egg, hatched and jagged in its eggcup, I can't be bothered sticking another piece of toast into its yolk.

I get up from the table and walk to school but I don't go to class. I wait around by the back of the shed and pace up and down and try to keep warm.

At five to eleven I go to the front door of the convent and ring the bell. Sister Ursula lets me in and then returns to her position behind the glass and grille. It's dark and warm inside and two old women are told to sit in the corner and wait for the priest. I stand by the front door and they look at me as though I have stolen their place in the queue.

My mother comes in and we go through to the nurse's office.

'Don't worry,' says my mother. 'It'll be over in a minute.'

Sister Bernadette is waiting outside the nurse's door. When she see us, she runs her hands along her rosary beads as though to get the dust off them, then she knocks and puts her head through the gap.

'Nurse, I have John Egan and his mother here to see you.'

'Tell them to come in,' says the nurse, and Sister Bernadette leaves.

In the small, square room, which smells of laundry powder, there is a desk, a filing cabinet, and a gurney covered in a white sheet. I look at the gurney while my mother talks to the nurse. I try to work out how I might climb on, if I'm asked to.

I like the idea of lying on the white sheet and having my temperature taken. The retractable legs of the gurney are like the blades of my Swiss army knife, which can slide easily and neatly in and out of their home. I think about faking an illness; clutching my stomach and groaning, so that the nurse might ask me to lie down and cover me with the soft blue blanket that is folded at the gurney's end.

'I'm very surprised,' says my mother. 'He's never done anything like this.'

The nurse looks at me as though I wet my pants on purpose. I want to tell her that I was conducting an experiment; that the wetting wasn't the accident of a baby.

'Is your boy enuretic?' asks the nurse. 'Is he a bed-wetter, Mrs Egan?'

'No,' says my mother.

I've been in the nurse's room only once. When I first came to this school, a few days after our move from Wexford, I had nose-bleeds every day for a week. I was eight years old, and the nurse sat me down and told me to put my head back while she pinched the bridge of my nose to stop the bleeding.

Because I swallowed some blood, I felt sick, and when I told her she gave me a brown kidney dish to vomit into. I tried but nothing came out. After my failed attempts to vomit, she said, 'Be careful not to cry wolf too often, little boy.'

Now, as then, she smiles weakly and rocks her head from side to side, as though she has just stood out of the bath and is trying to drain the water from her ears.

I want to leave. I want to go home. 'My bladder burst,' I say. 'It won't happen again.'

'I don't understand,' says my mother.

The nurse suggests possible causes – nervousness, anxiety, worry about trouble at home – and my mother denies each one. I begin to feel ashamed.

The nurse blames the fact that I'm an only child. She asks my mother if perhaps I am lonely.

'He is not lonely,' says my mother. 'He has the company of his parents and his grandmother who love him very much.'

'And my cat,' I say.

The nurse ignores me and holds out a piece of paper for my

mother to take. My mother looks at the piece of paper but doesn't take it.

'You should read this,' says the nurse. 'And maybe John should take the day off today. He can start again on Monday.'

But then it occurs to me: taking the day off school is a terrible idea. It would give my classmates more time to think up torments. I should go back in and behave as though nothing has happened, as though I don't care. Even better, I will make it not exist. I will act. It won't have happened.

'I want to go to class today,' I say.

The nurse tucks her chin into the folds of fat in her neck. I look past her and out the window. Joseph the Tinker is walking his piebald horse across the field. I want to wave, but he probably wouldn't see me.

'It's up to you, Mrs Egan. He's your boy.'

The break-time bell rings and my mother reaches out for my hand but I don't let her hold it.

'Are you sure you want to go back today?'

'Yes. I'm sure.'

We stand to leave and the nurse follows us out. 'Mrs Egan,' says the nurse, holding the same piece of paper, 'you've forgotten this.'

My mother shakes her head. 'We won't need it,' she says, 'Sister . . . I'm sorry. I've forgotten your name.'

My mother has met the nurse before but she forgets names deliberately. It's her way of making unpleasant people feel inferior.

The nurse looks at me as though it is my fault. 'My name's Sister Carmel,' she says.

My mother takes my hand and we walk down the corridor to classroom 5G.

I look up at her when we are outside the door. My classmates are standing behind their desks: it must be a spelling test, and I would like to win it. 'Why am I an only child?' I ask.

'You ask me that every time somebody else talks about it.'

'I want to know again.'

'You're an only child because I wanted you to be the only one. Is that all right with you?'

I wait for her to say more, but she turns and walks down the corridor without saying goodbye, without kissing me.

As soon as I sit at my desk, the whispering and laughing begins. Mandy, the girl on my right, sings, 'Wee, wee, wee, all the way home' and the boy on my left joins in. I look at Mandy until she stops, and the boy stops soon after. Jimmy, the redhead, puts a ruler against the crotch of his pants and makes a pissing sound. I look away. Miss Collins doesn't call on me during lessons and Brendan doesn't turn in his desk to make funny faces or pass signals.

When my classmates tease me and whisper things against me, I use a new trick. When Miss Collins speaks, I repeat what she has said three times in my mind. When she says 'The Tuskar Rock is a dangerous low-lying rock six nautical miles north east of Carnsore Point on the south east of Ireland and the lighthouse was lit for the first time on the fourth of June 1815', I say the same thing in my head three times and promise I will never forget it.

I know I haven't the brain of a scholar and that, if I did, a good memory would come naturally. But I can make myself clever. There's no reason whatsoever why not. So I practise. When I read a sentence in a book, I read every sentence three times, close my eyes after each one, and repeat the sentence in my mind. This trick is not only good for my brain, it helps me to ignore the whispering and teasing, and it helps me not to think bad thoughts. The more I do it, the more I begin to see that it will help me with other things too. If I am going to do important things, and become a great person, then having a good memory is sure to come in handy.

I check in the *Guinness Book* and see that, on the 14th October, 1967, a man recited 6666 verses of the Koran from memory, in six hours. This man, Mehmed Ali Halici, has an eidetic memory and he can remember everything he has read.

By the time the lunch bell rings, I have spent several hours without feeling nervous, and I have discovered a new way to think. I get my lunch and meet Brendan at his desk. 'Let's go,' I say.

'I want to stay inside,' he says.

'All right,' I say. 'We'll stay in.'

He looks at his desk. 'I want to stay in by myself, I mean.'

'Come on. Let's go to the shed,' I say.

On cold days – and this is a cold enough day – Brendan and I usually sit by the stove in the caretaker's shed and read all the annuals and my favourite Beano comics. The caretaker likes Brendan and me, and we talk to him and he is happy for us to be in his shed, and he comes and goes, and works around us.

'It's too cold for the shed,' says Brendan.

'So?' I say. 'We can sit by the stove and then it won't be cold.'

'I'm sick of sitting in the caretaker's shed,' says Brendan. 'It stinks.'

'It doesn't stink,' I say.

'It does.'

'So?'

'So, I just don't want to go in today,' he says. 'I want to stay inside the classroom today.'

'Fine.' My anger makes me nervous and I don't know what I'll do, so I leave Brendan without looking at him.

During class, I wait for him to look around at me, but he

doesn't. I stare at the back of his head sometimes, but mostly I read and memorise things, or look out the window to stop my anger from hurting my teeth.

On the way home, I recite the things I have memorised during the day and, when I can't remember, I stop walking and close my eyes until I do. When I reach the tree with the doll stuck in it, I stop and look up at her.

Her hair has gone. I thought she had blonde hair. This was the one thing about her that hadn't changed or decayed. But she has no hair. There is only black scalp. Maybe the person who put her in the tree has come to take her hair. Maybe it fell out gradually and I didn't notice. I feel angry with people and I run home.

When I get to the last field before the cottage, I stop and look across at the lighted window in the kitchen. I can see the dark outline of my mother, father and grandmother. They stand by the table, my father nearest the range, their dark shapes moving slightly, and my father's hand goes up, then down, and then my mother's hand takes hold of her long hair and she lifts it away from her shoulder. I want to know what they are saying, I want to know what is happening, but even if I dart across the road and through the gate and down the gravel path and get through the front door as fast as I can, I'll never know what they have said. This part of what has happened will always be missing. And they will stop talking and change the subject as soon as they see me.

But I am happy to see the light on, to know they are there and it is warm and there's a place for me at the table.

'You're late,' says my father. 'It's after five.'

'I walked the long way,' I say.

He goes to the cooker and takes out a plate. 'Here. Eat these,' he says. 'They're jumbo fish fingers.'

I sit at the table and my mother sits too. Granny stays by the stove, stirring a pot of custard.

'How was school?' asks my mother, and I notice that her eyes are bloodshot and her hair is messy. 'Good,' I say.

'Do you want me to fry an egg to go with your fish fingers?' she asks.

'No,' I say. 'Why is your hair all messy?'

My father stands up from the table so abruptly that his chair falls backwards. Nobody speaks. We wait to see what he will do. He leaves the kitchen and when he comes back he stands behind my mother and brushes her hair.

'There'll be hair in the baked beans,' she laughs.

I watch my father brush my mother's hair and can see that the knots are catching and she must be hurting.

I say, 'With the hair in the beans we can say, "Whose bean hair?"'

She reaches under the table and strokes my knee. 'Want some more food?'

'No,' I say as I push the beans around the jumbo fish fingers.

'Eat your fingers,' says my father.

After tea, my father brings out a large box of Cadbury Roses and we sit together on the settee in front of the television and take them one by one out of the foil and paper wrapping and eat them. He has agreed to let me stay up late to watch an Alfred Hitchcock film, *Strangers on a Train*.

'If you can spot Alfred's appearance, I'll give you a quid,' he says.

'All right,' I say. 'Consider yourself one pound poorer.'

'Want to know one of the reasons chocolate is addictive?' he asks.

'Yes.'

'Because it melts at blood temperature.'

'Maybe before the film you and Mammy could teach me how to do cryptic crosswords.'

'We need a good afternoon to do that. Remind me on Saturday.'

'Did you remember my present?' I ask.

'What present?'

'The one you promised.'

'These chocolates are your present and I'll get an even bigger one for you later.'

The book from the Wexford library, *The Truth About Lie Detection*, is the best book so far and I have copied thirty-five pages of it into The Gol of Seil.

I will memorise as much of this book as I can. Already I can recite several passages, such as this one, which I say out loud on the way to school.

'Many people mistakenly believe that if somebody lies they will not make eye contact and will rub under their nose. Neither lack of eye contact nor nose rubbing is a sure sign of lying. It is vital to look for a cluster of signals. It is also important to compare the way a person is behaving with the way they usually behave.

When a person is lying he needs to concentrate on keeping his story straight and will often slow his speech or become more hesitant. Some people try to control their facial expressions, but most people are not able to keep their feelings from showing, because some of the muscles of the face involved in expressions are not under conscious control, especially when people feel strong emotions.'

The author of *The Truth About Lie Detection* also says that these strong emotions are called primary emotions and that they show, for a fraction of a second only, as micro expressions.

I also know from reading this book that only a small group of people are exceptional at spotting lies and these people are sometimes called wizards. Such a person can pick up behavioural signals that most people miss, most of the time.

I copy four more pages from *The Truth About Lie Detection* into my book and then I write a letter to the *Guinness Book of Records*:

> Dear Guinness Book of Records,
> My name is John Egan and I have a rare gift. I think you will be interested in this gift of mine and you should let me prove it to you.
> I can tell when somebody is lying with nearly 100% accuracy.
> I hope you will write back to me soon and let me do a demonstration for you.
> Yours Sincerely,
> John Egan.

When I've finished the letter, I daydream about being on television. I am being interviewed by Gay Byrne who hosts *The Late, Late Show*. In the daydream I am already famous and I am touring the world to talk about my gift. I tell him about the work I have been doing for the FBI, helping to catch spies in Russia. Gay Byrne shakes his head as he says, 'Astonishing. Really very astonishing. Can we test your gift on a few members of the audience? May we conduct a live test? An experiment?'

I sit forward in my leather swivel chair and say, 'Yes, of course.'

Gay Byrne calls for four volunteers and he asks each of them to tell me something. The first says, 'My name is Bernadette and I have three daughters and a son and I live in Galway.'

I rub the side of my face before I answer. 'That's a lie,' I say. 'But not all of it. You were telling the truth until you said you live in Galway.' In the daydream I don't feel sick, not even a little bit queasy, when I detect the lie.

Gay Byrne and the volunteer look at each other, delighted and amazed. 'That's right,' says the woman. 'I do have three daughters and a son but I don't live in Galway. I live in Doolin.'

When I'm finished with the daydream I read about The Great Train Robbery. On the 8th of August, 1963, between 3.10 am and 3.45 am, a General Post Office mail-train from Glasgow was ambushed by a gang of thieves who escaped with 120 postbags containing more than forty-two million pounds. One of the thieves has not yet been caught and his name is Ronald Biggs.

I wonder what it felt like to steal so much money. If I felt as though my heart was trying to escape through my ears when I stole ninety pounds from my grandmother's purse, then Ronald Biggs must have felt like his arms and legs would fall off with all the thumping of frightened blood. Even when I look under my mattress, to see if the money I stole is still there, my hands shake for as much as an hour afterwards. And how did Ronald Biggs know what to do with the money when I cannot even decide what to do with my scrawny little pile of notes?

And then my father shouts my name and I know it's time for the Hitchcock film.

11

For two days my classmates have teased me. Some have made a special effort to ambush me on my way into class. Yesterday, the redhead threw water at my feet while I sat at my desk, and whenever Miss Collins turns her back to the class the girl next to me says, 'Wee, wee, wee, all the way home.' And, with one exception, Brendan has not spoken to me since it happened.

It is half three. I sit at my desk and wait for everybody to leave before I go out to the corridor. Brendan is walking along by the coat rack. I don't need to ask him why he is walking up and down the corridor like this. I know that he can't find his anorak. He can't find it because at lunchtime I took it off the hook and have it stuffed in the bottom of my schoolbag.

I ask him why he is still here.

'I can't find my anorak.'

'I'll help you look,' I say.

I try to sound calm, but my hands are sweating in my pockets. We look for his anorak and, when we can't find it, I suggest that we should walk home together. I give him my anorak to wear, and he doesn't ask why I don't need mine, or why I have worn two jumpers today.

At last we are alone together and I can tell him the story about why I wet my pants. I lie to him in order to keep him as my friend and I don't feel sick. I tell him it was a record-breaking attempt.

'That's a pretty stupid record,' he says.

'I nearly broke it. I held on for twenty-six hours.'

'You held on for twenty-six hours!'

'Twenty-five hours and fifty minutes.'

'You should tell everybody that.'

'Maybe,' I say, 'but they probably won't believe me. The record is thirty hours. So I nearly broke it.'

He looks away.

'Do you want me to come over on Sunday and play football or something?' I ask.

Brendan coughs, like my father does when he's not sure what to do. 'I don't know yet. I might have to go to a christening.'

'OK,' I say.

It's Friday morning and, after breakfast, I wait until there is nobody in the kitchen so that I can call Brendan to tell him I want to carry out a special experiment.

'Like the piss experiment?'

'Completely different. Can you stay at my house tonight?'

'I don't think I'll be allowed,' he says.

'It's important.'

'Maybe. I have to go now. My porridge is going cold.'

'I'll give you five quid,' I say.

'Liar.'

'I'll bring the money today and show you.'

'How'd you get five quid?'

'I saved it.'

'Liar. That would take a hundred years.'

'My granny won some at the races and gave me a bit. But you can't tell anyone and if you do I'll get the money back off you.'

'OK.'

'And bring your sleeping bag.'

'Why?'

'Because.'

I have told my mother that I am staying at Brendan's house tonight and that I'm going there straight after school. She won't check on me; she has no reason to.

It is half three. I tell Brendan to come to the shed. 'Why? Aren't we going to your house?'

'Just follow me. You'll see.'

We go to the shed. The caretaker is cleaning a desk with steel wool. 'Hello,' he says. 'Any of this graffiti yours?'

'Nope' I say. 'We need to have the keys to the shed for one night.'

The caretaker looks at the floor then slowly back up at me. 'And if you're caught you'll say you stole the keys from the office?'

'Definitely,' I say.

'And you'll be using my shed to get up to no good?'

I look at the floor, then slowly back up, the way the caretaker did. Confident people seem able to handle silence and are good at pausing.

I've been thinking about how I should behave and I think I should have a confident way about me in time for my first meeting with the *Guinness Book* people. I'll work first on my hands, then on my voice, and on my walk last of all.

'Something like that,' I say. 'It's a long story.'

'Clean the toilets. When you come back the shed will be ready.'

The caretaker hands me the keys. I take note of the way he doesn't have to use many words to tell you what he wants.

* * *

As we walk to the toilets, Brendan grabs my arm. 'What's going on? I thought we were going to your house?'

'We need the shed for the night for my experiment. But I can't tell you what it is yet.'

'You have to tell me. I'm not staying unless you tell me.'

I open the door to the toilets. 'All right. It's a lie detection test. I'm going to prove that I'm a human lie detector.'

'That's stupid.'

'How do you know it's stupid? I haven't shown you yet. It's like I'm a polygraph, only I don't need a machine.'

'What's a polygraph?'

'It's a machine that's hooked up to criminals to see if they are lying, but I'm probably a better lie detector than any machine.'

'What are you talking about?'

'The polygraph measures breathing and blood pressure and how much the suspect sweats. But some people don't feel guilty when they lie and the needle of the polygraph doesn't move. These people are super-liars. And some innocent suspects get so nervous that the polygraph thinks they're guilty. But when I detect lies I see in a split-second what a machine can't see, and I detect loads of signals and things called micro-expressions. And I feel sick and my ears burn, but not as much as in the beginning.'

His eyes are wide and his mouth is open. 'What are you talking about?'

'I have a gift for lie detection.'

'You're making it up.'

'I'm not.'

'You are.'

'I'm not.'

'So how did you learn how to do it? Who taught you?'

'I didn't learn. I found out that I could just do it. It's just some-thing I can do. But I've read all the books now and they help me know what's going on. The books tell me what my brain is doing when I spot a lie.'

'Can't we do the experiment at your house?'

I tell myself to use fewer words. 'No privacy there,' I say.

I turn away from him and use the mop and bucket to splash already dirty water on the floor. Brendan leans against the wall and watches me clean and does not offer to help. He has the upper hand now; but I'll get it back soon enough.

'How do you know when somebody's lying then?' he asks.

'In the beginning I used to feel sick and vomit, but now I get hot ears and I can just tell by what happens to a person's face and hands.'

'That's stupid.'

'No, it's not. Wait and see.'

'Give me the money and then I'll do it.'

I give him the five quid and he holds it up to the light, as though to check whether it's counterfeit.

I laugh then because he laughs, even though I am having to pay him to do something he should want to do because he's my friend.

On the way back to the shed we stop by the classroom and collect our sleeping bags, and the food I took this morning from the pantry at home: two pieces of chocolate cake, a chunk of ham and a loaf of bread. I have brought a spare blanket and pillows too.

It's a foggy night and, as we walk to the shed, it covers our coats and makes them wet. When we get inside the shed, we lay our sleeping bags on the floor. I'm cold and have no idea how to light the stove. 'We're going to freeze to death,' I say just for something to say.

'Don't be a molly,' says Brendan. 'I'll get some wood and get the fire going.'

'Good,' I say.

The stove is lit and piled high with wood. The room is a little warmer now, and we are comfortable as we eat cake inside our sleeping bags. But I'm worried that if we don't begin the experiment soon we might not start at all.

'The caretaker's left us a note,' says Brendan.

Dear Boys,
  I hope you have a good night. There are some new comics on the bookshelf!
  The Caretaker

Brendan looks for the new comics and my stomach drops; he is more interested in comics than my experiment.

'But we don't need any comics,' I say. 'We haven't even started.'

'Just looking,' he says.

We flick through the caretaker's books, and among the comics Brendan finds a sex magazine. It is not possible that Brendan knew it was there, but he says, 'I had a feeling he'd put something weird here for us. I just knew it.'

Brendan climbs back into his sleeping bag and turns the pages of the magazine. He keeps saying 'Cor blimey' and 'Wow!' and 'Look at the size of them!' and he sounds stupid and fake. 'Come and look at this!' he shouts.

I pull my sleeping bag in closer to his and sit beside him to look at the pictures. Some have three or four people in them. They don't make sense. I feel seasick. There's pressure and spinning in my gut. I hope Brendan doesn't look at me, but he's too busy swearing and making noises with his throat. I won't make any noise. All I feel is a heavy pressure on my bowels, a feeling like needing to shit.

Without any warning, Brendan pushes me hard in the arm, and shouts, 'You don't have to sit so close! You're giving me the creeps.'

Before I have time to answer, he is out of his sleeping bag and putting the magazine back on the shelf. He stands for a while, looking down at me, shifting his weight from one foot to the other. 'I'm going out to piss and then I'm going home,' he says.

He doesn't look at me, and I don't look at him. He goes outside and I wait for ten minutes for him to come back. When he returns he says, 'I'm going now.'

'What about the experiment?' I ask.

He shrugs. 'We'll just tell our mams we decided not to sleep over,' he says.

I stand and we pack our things without speaking. I want us to speak. I want to know what Brendan thinks of the pictures. 'But what about the experiment?' I ask.

'What about it?' says Brendan.

'Fine,' I say. 'Do what you want.'

I want more to happen tonight, but I don't know what. The idea of him leaving makes me angry. I want something more to happen in the caretaker's shed, tonight, between Brendan and me. I want something between us, in the dark, during the night. I don't want us to part, not now, and not so suddenly.

'Let's stay and do the experiment,' I say.

'Just forget it,' says Brendan. 'It was a stupid idea anyway.'

'Well you must be stupid, because you wanted to do it, too.'

'So?'

And we stand and shout 'so?' at each other. Brendan is pretending to be angry but I know he is lonely and feels strange just as I do.

'Let's turn off the lights and sleep and not even talk,' I say quietly, with what is left of my voice. 'We'll go home as soon as it's morning.'

Brendan doesn't answer.

'Please,' I say. 'Just to sleep.'

Brendan switches off the light and we get into our sleeping

99

bags. When Brendan has settled down, when he has stopped moving, I move my sleeping bag closer to his so the bags are touching.

'G'night,' he says.

'G'night, Brendan,' I say.

I turn over into my usual sleeping position, my temple resting on my hand, but I can't sleep. I turn over on the hard floor and feel the cold of the concrete under my arms and legs. I can't stop thinking about how I want to touch Brendan, or be touched by him, and I want to see his body. I've never had thoughts like this before, have never felt anything like this. It's not about liking Brendan; not in that way. I look over at him in his sleeping bag and want to wake him. No. I will only think about it.

I will only imagine waking him. I imagine this: I wake him and ask him to sleep by me and he says yes and we lie naked together and I see his body and he sees mine. But this is wrong; this is a sin. I sit up and shake my head. I open my eyes and the pictures go away. I lie awake for a long time, confused. The more time passes, the more I feel like a prisoner, trapped awake. I turn and turn again and more time passes, and more, slow time.

My head, as though filled with helium, has nothing in it to carry me down to rest, to dark, down to sleep. It is pitch-black and yet there is no darkness in my mind. There is a blinding bright day when it should be night. Thoughts I know are very bad won't stop coming. They are very bad sins. This is why my mother doesn't want me to lie down with her.

I want the thoughts to stop and yet I want to see what happens to the thoughts, to the stories about my body and Brendan's body and all the other stories I am making up in my imagination.

I smack my hand into my head until it hurts. I punch myself in the chest and on the arm and then I smack myself in the face.

I will never think like this again.

I get up and turn on the lamp and sit in a chair under the window with my sleeping bag wrapped around me. I look at Brendan, who sleeps on his side, his mouth open and his tongue resting on his bottom teeth. I like that I can look at him like this and he cannot do anything to stop me. I stare at his nostrils twitching and for a moment I hope that he will wake and talk to me, keep me company, but if he wakes he might want to go home and, if he goes, I won't be able to look at him.

I stop looking when I get bored and read a comic book, but nothing is funny. I kick my sleeping bag. *You are not a sleeping bag. You are a waking bag.*

After an hour or more of sitting up by the lamp, beneath the cold dark window, I decide to try for sleep again. I climb back down into my sleeping bag, at the foot of the chair.

It is colder now, much colder than before, and I can feel the concrete like ice beneath the bag. My arms and legs feel bruised.

And it is this way until the birds start to sing, and when they start to sing I become drowsy, at last, and I sleep, briefly, then wake.

The caretaker is standing in the doorway. 'Get up,' he says as though we are two strangers, 'I need to use the shed.'

12

It is Saturday morning, the first day of the Easter school holiday, and my father comes into the kitchen while I'm having breakfast. 'Hello,' I say.

'Morning,' he says.

He's wearing a white shirt and blue jacket and stinks of after-shave. His beard is gone again and I hope he doesn't let it grow back. He takes my plate from the table then comes over to where I am standing, near the cooker, and holds it out under my nose. 'Don't you eat your crusts now?' he asks in a whisper, as though he doesn't want eavesdroppers to hear.

'I don't like them,' I say.

'Don't be so feckin' daft,' he says. 'The crusts are bread just like the rest of the bread.'

He speaks in an angry rush and the plate tilts in his hands. The crusts are at the edge, ready to fall off.

'No they're not,' I say. 'Crusts are chewier and harder.'

He hands the plate to me and speaks in a normal, slower voice. 'Eat your crusts,' he says. 'Bread doesn't grow on trees, and wasting food is a sin.'

'They hurt my teeth,' I say. I take the plate and put it on the table but he pushes it into my hands.

'Eat them, you big eejit, or I'll ram them down your throat.'

I eat the crusts while he watches. He stands by the cooker with his arms folded. I look up at him when I've finished. He smiles without showing his teeth, a tired, cold smile.

'You see,' he says. 'They won't kill you.'

My mother comes in to get her handbag: she is getting ready to go to the grocery shop in Gorey town, where she now works three mornings a week. She wears her pink coat over a yellow apron.

'Why don't you come with me?' she says. 'You can spend the morning in the shop and afterwards you can have a bag of sweets to take home.'

'I'd rather stay here,' I say. I want to read my new book about lying.

'Go with her,' says my father. 'You've hardly left the house lately.'

When we are near the junction, and we should take the right-hand turn, my mother goes left and she says, 'We need to see Dr Ryan. Just for a minute.'

'Why?'

'You need a check-up.'

'What for?'

'You're getting very big.'

'Is that why you don't touch me any more?'

'I do touch you.'

'Not as much.'

She puts her hands over her face and rubs her forehead with her fingers. 'You're not a little boy now.'

'So? You're tall and Da's tall. I'm just like you.'

'You're only eleven and you're nearly six feet tall and your voice is getting deeper.'

'I'm twelve in July,' I say.

'Why don't we just call into Dr Ryan's and see what he has to say?'

'Unless you are going to get me an operation to stop me growing, I'm not seeing any doctors.'

'There's no need for an operation.'

'Then I don't need to see the doctor. I'm not sick.'

'I didn't say that you were sick.'

I hit the dashboard with my open hand. I don't understand why I didn't detect the lie when she first told it at home. Why didn't I know she was lying when she told me she was taking me to spend the day in the shop with her?

'If anybody's sick it's you,' I say.

She looks at me, to see what I'm going to do. I put my hands under my legs and she looks back at the road. But I can tell she is nervous: she touches her face and swallows too much.

'What does that mean?' she asks, at last.

'You told me I was going to the shop with you. You lied. You tricked me into coming with you.'

'We're still going to the shop, so I wasn't lying. We're just seeing Dr Ryan first.'

'If you make me see Dr Ryan now I'll never trust you again.'

I say this in a voice I've never used before, a voice that's just a little way away from a punch or a kick. My hands are balled up when I say it, and I feel strong. I mean what I say.

'I don't see why you're so upset about this,' she says, about to cry.

'It's very important to be honest,' I say, almost whispering now and short of breath. 'You're a mother. Mothers shouldn't lie. I don't want you to ever lie.'

She says nothing.

'Other people can lie if they want,' I say. 'But not you.'

She frowns at me but seems not to be on the brink of tears now. I wonder why she has stopped herself from crying and whether I could still make her cry if I wanted to. 'Besides,' I say. 'It's a sin to lie.'

She looks at me, calm, as though I have said nothing at all and she turns the car around. We go back to the junction and she makes the turn that takes us to Gorey town. We are going to the shop after all.

'Are you quite finished now?' she asks, with the voice she uses on my uncles.

'Yes.'

I sit in a chair behind the counter next to my mother, listening as she talks to customers about crops, sicknesses and babies.

A woman comes in and says, 'Helen, we all thought you'd join the Legion of Mary this year!' and my mother says, 'How I'd love to, if I only had the time.'

When the woman leaves, my mother tells me that the Legion of Mary is a useless waste of time: a pack of housewives with nothing better to do than complain and gossip and defame their husbands.

I will eat soon and the shelves are packed with tins and boxes of food, and there are dozens of different kinds of sweets under the glass counter.

And then something happens to make my mood brighter still.

Just before it's time to close up, a salesman comes in wearing a black suit. My mother tells him she has no need for any more biscuits.

'Are you sure now? Do you not want to discuss it with the manager?' he says.

'I am the manager,' says my mother. 'And I'm sure.'

He looks at the shelves, makes some notes on his clipboard and says, 'I think you have a short supply of biscuits here. There are some good ones new on the market.'

My mother lifts the hatch and comes out from behind the

counter. She stands close to the salesman. 'I appreciate the time you've taken,' she says, 'but I don't need any more biscuits.'

'All right, so,' says the salesman.

My mother puts her hand on his back. Her hand is covered in flour and on his dark suit she leaves the imprint of a perfect white hand, smaller than hers, like the hand of a toddler.

She watches the salesman leave the shop, then she opens the door and stands on the pavement to look at him as he disappears down the crowded street. 'Bye now!' she says.

The door closes and the little bell rings. I leap to my feet. 'You left your handprint on his back,' I say.

'I know,' says my mother. 'And I'll never forget the pleasure it gave me.'

I give her a hug, as if we are celebrating some great news. She laughs and squeezes me tight. When she lets go, she kisses me on the cheek and smiles.

She sings as we drive home, and when we turn at the junction she asks me if I would like to come for a walk on Courtown beach and I say yes. This means another half an hour in the car with her on the way there and another hour on the way home.

I eat my sweets as we walk down by the shore. In summer the sand is yellow and the water is blue. Today the sand is not so yellow but bright still, and the water is not so blue but the waves still crash and make white foam and there's the smell I like of salt and seaweed, and behind us the dunes are covered in green shrubs and the shrubs look woolly.

Then it rains, it rains hard, but she keeps walking as though she doesn't notice.

'Mam! The rain!' I say, excited by the change in the air, its thinness and the strange smell of metal.

'Never mind the rain,' she says.

She holds her face up to the rain and catches the drops in her mouth. I do the same and we laugh as she takes my hand and we walk in the rain with our heads up, while other people rush to the shelter of their cars. It isn't cold, and once I am completely wet, the rain feels as warm as a blanket.

We arrive home drenched and my shoes and socks squelch as I walk up the drive. My father is sitting at the kitchen table eating soup and my mother goes to the end of the table and stands next to him.

'Look at your wife,' she says. 'Drenched from head to foot.'

My father smiles without showing his teeth. 'Like a drowned rat,' he says.

'How many rats do you know that collect shells?' my mother asks, as she empties the shells from her coat pocket onto the kitchen table.

My father smiles again and holds one of the shells to his ear. 'Hello?' he says. 'Michael Egan speaking. No, the old bat's not here. She's at bingo.'

My mother laughs and seems happy. She tells him the story of the salesman in the dark suit with the flour handprint on his back.

They laugh so much that my mother has to lean against the sink and wipe the tears from her red eyes.

They laugh so much, and for so long, that the joke must have gone beyond what I understand, and I wish I knew what it was. If I ask them what has made them laugh so much, my father would probably lie so that he could keep me from knowing too much about him, too much about what it's like to be him. My mother would probably tell me most of the reason for the laughing, and leave out the complicated parts. She would lie, I think, to make the talk easier and more pleasant, to stop the talk becoming too serious.

'It's not that funny,' I say. 'Why are you laughing so much?'

At last my mother stops laughing enough to speak. 'We're laughing this much because a long time ago, before you were born, I did a very similar thing to your Uncle Tony before we all went out to a wedding.'

My father shakes his head, his eyes still full of water from laughing. 'And he deserved it.'

'Why?' I ask.

They look at each other before my mother answers. 'Because he was rude to me and I took offence. You can ask what he said to me till you're blue in the face, but I won't tell you.'

I don't need to know. What's important is that they've been honest; the both of them, honest.

'I'm going to watch TV now,' I say and I leave the kitchen with two jam and shortbread biscuits.

An hour later, I go back to the kitchen. It is getting dark and we have just turned on all the lights when my grandmother comes home.

She takes her coat off and drapes it over the back of the chair nearest the range. It's a new fur coat, brown, with black cuffs. My father looks at her, shakes his head, and leaves. She sits down and eats her soup using pieces of bread to soak it up and she keeps her head so close to the bowl that her hair is splashed with soup.

I can't stand to watch.

'I have a toothache,' I say, and I leave. This lie causes no reaction, perhaps because I am walking when I say it. I'll make a note of this in The Gol of Seil.

13

It is Easter Sunday and after mass we all go into the living room. I sit by my grandmother's feet and laugh when she falls asleep and begins to snore. My mother holds my hand and smiles at me as I open my presents and Easter eggs. I am anxious, as I always am on holidays because of my father's habit of promising gifts, and forgetting them. No matter what he gives me, it never makes up for the promised gifts never delivered. I keep my father's Easter card till last; it has one pound Sellotaped inside. 'Thanks, Da,' I say.

I smile at my mother. 'Could we have some of that chocolate cake now?' I ask.

'Of course, I'll finish putting the icing on.'

She leaves and, since Granny is sleeping, I am as good as alone in the room with my father.

I take the card in my hand and turn it over a few times. I make sure my father is watching me. This card, like all the others I can remember, is worn and faded, and has the same picture of a boy playing with his puppy, and the inscription: *For a Wonderful Son, This Holy Easter*. My Birthday and Christmas Cards are almost identical: *For a Wonderful Son, This Birthday* or *This Holy Communion* or *This Christmas*. There is dirty dust around the clean square where the price sticker would have been.

It occurs to me that all my cards are from the same batch; perhaps from a box of a hundred or more, purchased wholesale when I was born. He might as well give me the same card each year, ask for it back, and re-use it.

I look at him, sitting in his armchair, legs crossed, his short dressing gown loosely tied with the cord that dangles between his hairless knees. I stand directly in front of him so that he must look up at me.

'When I was six,' I say, in my surest voice, 'you must have bought a box of a million identical cards with the same stupid picture on them!'

He looks at me blankly; a complete lack of interest. But I stand my ground and don't speak to fill the silence. 'Show me that card,' he says.

He grabs the card, then shoves it back in my hand. 'There's nothing wrong with this card,' he says. 'It's brand new.'

I throw the card into the fire.

He watches the card burn in the orange and pink flames but does not speak. His hands and face are stiff: he is nervous. I wonder whether my mother has told him about my gift. I'll soon find out.

'You are cold-blooded and selfish,' I say. 'And I'm eleven now. Not two.'

He gets up and we are almost standing chest to chest, but I will not move.

'How dare you!' he says, without moving aside. 'I bought that card yesterday afternoon. That's a brand new card.'

'Did you? Did you buy this card yesterday?'

'What do you mean, *did you?*'

'It looks like all the others you've given me, and it's faded and old-looking. Well, Da?'

He walks towards the door, reaches out for the handle, and misses it. 'I'm not hanging around for this rubbish.'

'But did you, Da? Did you really buy the card yesterday?'

His hand finds the door handle. 'Of course I did.'

'When did you leave the house? What shop did you go to?'

'How many times do you want me to repeat myself? I bought that card in Gorey yesterday.'

There it is: he can't have gone to Gorey yesterday unless he took Granny's car. But I don't need to interrogate him about this. He is lying. My ears are hot and my stomach churns.

'But which shop?' I ask. 'And how did you get there? By magic carpet?'

'You suspicious little bastard,' he says. 'Go to your room!'

My grandmother wakes up and seems to know there has been trouble. I stare at my father and refuse to go. I know he would hit me if I was not so big. But I don't know how to finish what I've started.

I go to my bedroom.

I leave my door open, to listen out. I expect to hear my father telling my mother what has happened, but instead there is a brief silence followed by singing: my mother and father and grandmother singing along to one of my father's favourite records, and probably eating my piece of cake. Nobody comes to get me and I talk to myself and read The Gol of Seil to stop myself from feeling lonely. I lie on my bed for a few minutes but know I must go back or lose this Easter Sunday for good.

I go back into the living room and sit on the rug in front of the fireplace. I look at my father. He sits cross-legged in his armchair with a cup of tea in one hand and a slice of cake in the other.

'Those African Watutsi can jump very high,' I say. 'Why don't they compete in the high jump at the limpics?'

He does not look at me. 'It's Olympics,' he says to my mother, with a fat grin. 'O-limpic. Not limpics. Limpics are for spastics.'

My mistake was a deliberate one, but he laughs and turns the joke against me.

'*Limp*-ics! Get it!'

He stamps his foot and they all laugh and I laugh with them because it is one of the worst things to be in a room full of people and not laughing when everybody else is.

14

'Good morning, class,' says Miss Collins. 'I'd like you all to meet a new pupil.'

The new girl stands straight, with her feet together and her hands by her side. 'Hello, everybody. My name is Kate Breslin. I am an only child, and I've just moved here from Dublin.'

She has long brown hair – down to her waist – and green eyes and a straight posture. 'My father has taken over a deceased estate in Gorey,' she says. 'We are four miles from the school.'

She sounds as though she's reading. I wonder what a deceased estate is, and I want to put my hand up and ask, but I lose my nerve and open the lid of my desk to hide.

'We lived near the Shelbourne Hotel,' she says. 'Where all the famous people stay.'

Miss Collins gives Kate the spare desk in the front row, next to Brendan's, and appoints him, and Mandy, as Kate's minders. I watch them carefully. During the first lesson, Kate leans across and says something to Brendan. He smiles when he answers and pushes his hair back with his hand.

In the second and third lessons, Kate leans across and speaks to Brendan again. I wish I could hear. At the beginning of break-time I go to Brendan's desk and they both look at me, then at each other. Brendan gives the impression that he has known Kate for a long time.

I leave the classroom and go around to the window where I see Brendan run his hand through his hair and give one of his exercise books to Kate. 'Oh, thank you,' she says as she touches him on the arm. I want to be touched on the arm like this. I like the way it looks. And even though Brendan is being touched and not me, I can feel it in my stomach. I keep watching.

On the way home from school I throw a rock at the doll in the tree, but it misses her and hits the branch instead. I bury the rock in the ground near the trunk. When I get home, my mother and father are sitting at the kitchen table with a pile of letters and bills in front of them.

My father gathers them up when I sit down. 'Good day at school?' he asks.

'All right,' I say. 'A new girl started today.'

I tell him about Kate Breslin. He is surprised that a new girl has started in the middle of the school year.

'It's because of a diseased estate,' I say. 'They moved into one.'

My father laughs in the loud and horrible way he sometimes does when my uncles are with him or when somebody has made a fool of himself on the television. My mother lowers her eyes to the table.

'A deceased estate,' he says, still laughing at me. 'Not a diseased estate.'

'I know,' I say. 'That's what I said.'

'No you didn't,' he says. 'You said a diseased estate.'

'No I didn't,' I say.

Crito jumps onto the kitchen table and, instead of pushing her off, my father pats her on the head. 'Crito? You heard. Didn't John say a diseased estate?'

'Michael,' says my mother, 'he just had a slip of the tongue. Let it rest! Leave him be.'

The three of us sit in silence. There's no tea on the range, no food on the table, and nothing to do. My mother takes the papers from the pile and looks through them. My father pushes Crito off the table so hard that she wails.

I watch my mother, hoping she'll tell me what those letters and bills and papers are. I want my father to leave so we can talk. Then it occurs to me: they are both waiting for me to leave. They are willing me to leave.

I won't.

I look at my mother and keep looking at her as she rifles through the papers.

'Stop staring at me,' she says.

'I'm only looking,' I say. 'There's nothing wrong with looking.'

'You're staring. I want you to stop.'

'You never tell me not to stare when we're by ourselves.'

My father puts his book down, suddenly interested. 'Go to your room and leave us in peace,' he says. 'We've things to talk about.'

My mother is running hot and cold, just like him. Just like my father, she has become two different people. Now there are four of them. Four different people instead of two.

I go straight to my room and get under the blankets. I listen to them eat and talk and laugh. I lie on my side, all my weight on my arm. I turn to my other side. I want to sleep to stop the thinking. My blood is pumping so fast and so hard it makes my whole body shudder. My blood pummels me, pumping through my arm; there's too much of it, like a dam that wants to burst, and it won't let me sleep.

At half eight my mother comes to me. 'John,' she says. 'Come and eat something. You can't go to sleep without food.'

'I can,' I say. 'What difference does it make?'

'You're too old to sulk. Come out to the kitchen and make yourself a sandwich.'

She closes the door and a minute later my father comes. He doesn't knock. 'I've made you a blackcurrant jam sandwich. Here.'

He puts the sandwich on the bed, near my feet. I want to kick the plate onto the floor, but I can see there's thick butter on the fresh bread and I'm very hungry.

'Thanks,' I say. I want to say more, but I'd prefer him to start. I want him to say something first, so that it is his idea to talk to me. I look at the sandwich and wait.

'John? Is anything the matter?'

'No, not really. But there's something the matter with you and Mammy. You seem different.'

'Different from what?'

'Different from yourselves.'

'In what way?'

'I don't know. You seem strange around me.'

'Maybe you're strange.' He laughs but when I don't join in, he pulls at his fringe and keeps pulling at it until it covers the right side of his forehead and right eye.

'Sorry, son. I just don't know what you mean. The only thing I can think of is that we're worried about you. We want you to be all right.'

'Are you sure? Are you sure there's nothing wrong?'

'No, the only thing wrong with us is the worry about you. Worried a bit about how you're getting on.'

'I'm getting on fine. I'm better than anybody realises.'

'That's good to know. Shall we stop worrying so?'

'Yes. Stop worrying.'

'Will you eat the sandwich I made specially?'

'Probably not.'

'Will I give it to Crito then?'

'No. Leave it. I'll give it to her myself. Later.'

'Shall I send her in to you then? Will I tell her she's wanted in the master's bedroom?'

He is smiling now and I can't help it. I smile back and once I start I notice that I feel happy. Happiness makes my body warm, my stomach and all the way down. He laughs and I laugh too.

'Wait here. I'll fetch the jam-eating contraption.'

I want to act out my happiness, get to my feet, jump up and down on the spot and clap my hands. I want to get up off the bed and run and go after him and not be ashamed and keep him with me longer, just now, just the way he is now, just us, and with him smiling at me the way he did.

I wait for him. But he doesn't come back straight away. I won't go out to the hall and I won't go to the living room. I take my watch off and wait for the second hand to get to twelve and then I start the countdown to sixty seconds. If he doesn't come in one minute, I'll never wait for him again. The second hand reaches the nine and he comes back, with Crito wrapped in a blanket, her black-and-white face sticking out.

'Special delivery for Master Egan,' he says. 'A four-legged friend in need of jam.'

No, my brain says to me, *the only thing wrong with us is the worry about you.*

'Thanks, Da.' And he goes and I keep Crito in her blanket while I eat the blackcurrant sandwich.

At school the next day, I am alone during the break, sitting in the empty classroom reading a book about Harry Houdini and eating chocolate cake, biscuits and a ham sandwich. I like reading about Houdini's underwater escapes from locked containers while handcuffed and shackled with irons. But I'm disappointed to learn that his escapes were 'protracted and agonised' and that the fastest straitjacket escape he performed was 138 seconds. I know from the *Guinness Book* that this is a long way from the world record broken last year by Jack Gently. On 26th July, 1971, in front of an audience of 600 witnesses, Gently escaped from a standard straitjacket in forty-five seconds.

A few minutes before the end-of-break bell, the mongoloid boy comes in. His name is Osmond and he spends one day a week here and the other days at the special school in Enniscorthy. Every Tuesday he spends break and lunchtime alone, walking around the playing field, talking, and singing off-key. I've never been up close to his droopy face and I've never spoken to him.

He stands in the doorway with his mouth open and shifts his weight from one leg to the other, smiling at me, humming, waiting for me to speak. I look away but he comes closer and, when I look up, he is standing by my desk, an inch from my arm. He doesn't speak, but smiles at me, rocking from one foot to the other. I don't want him near me.

'Nice book,' he says.

He smells of vomit. I don't want to talk to him. If I'm seen talking to him, it will be as though I am his friend, that I'm the same as him: the two of us lonely. 'Nice book,' he says. 'Nice pictures.'

His spit falls out when he speaks and there's a glob of it shining on my jumper sleeve. I close the book to stop him looking at Harry Houdini. But he is staring at my food.

'Nice biscuits. Nice cake. Nice sandwich.'

Could he be hungry? I check my watch: only five minutes until the bell for the end of break.

'Are you hungry? Do you want some cake? You can take it to your class? Take it to room 3G? Wouldn't that be good?'

He holds out his fat hand and I put the last of my chocolate cake in his palm. He pushes the cake into his mouth, like a tractor shovelling dirt, and then he closes his mouth, moves his closed lips from side to side and, finally, swallows. He has dissolved the cake in his mouth without chewing. I like that I can stare at him; he lets me stare and doesn't mind.

'Nice brown cake,' he says. His voice is not too spastic, but too loud and it sounds strangled, as though somebody is sitting on his neck.

'Ssssh,' I say. 'Please be quiet.' My leg is jumping up and down and I put my hand on my knee to stop it.

'Nice biscuit.'

'Here,' I say.

He eats the biscuit by the same method – no chewing – and then he says, 'Nice book.'

'You can't eat the book,' I say.

I've made him laugh and he jumps up and down. 'Cookie monster! Cookie monster!'

He's not so stupid. He can say what he wants to and he only wants somebody to say things to. That's all. But I put my finger against my lip to tell him to be quiet. He looks hurt and walks away. I look at my watch: one more minute before the bell.

'Look,' I say. I open the book to the page with the photograph of Harry Houdini in a glass cage, his body covered in thick chains. 'Harry Houdini,' I say, quietly. 'He could do magic.'

'Magic! Magic makes rabbits.'

'Can you whisper?'

'Yes,' he whispers. 'Magic makes rabbits.'

'Yes,' I say.

'Magic makes hats and ace of diamonds and no rabbits and rabbits.'

'Yes,' I say. I didn't know he had so many words. If he had a normal face I'd probably want to talk to him. I keep whispering and hope he will too. 'Do you know what an escape is?'

'Escape.'

'Yes. Get out of trouble. Escape from boxes and glass cages.'

He points at Houdini. 'He escapes from glass jar!'

His voice is loud again, but I don't mind. He's right. He understands. I smile at him. Even though his face is droopy, he looks better than I thought he did and he looks better when you are closer to him, paying attention. I thought they all looked like identical twins, but now I see that isn't true. Osmond has his own nose, his own lips, his own eyes, and his own expressions.

The bell rings and, when it finishes ringing, and we can hear the sounds of people coming down the hall, he says, 'Nice book.' His voice is even louder than when he first came to me, as though he thinks the bell is still ringing and he needs to shout to be heard.

'Sssssh,' I say.

'Nice book, nice cake, nice biscuit, nice big boy. Nice John.' He reaches out to touch my eyes.

'No!' I say. 'Don't touch! Go away.'

I don't want him to know my name. No, that's not right. I do. But I don't want him to say it. He stops smiling and steps away, backwards. There are tears in his eyes.

'I go,' he says.

'Bye, so,' I say.

'I go. I escape backwards. I go out of way of John.'

'All right,' I say, and then, even though I haven't planned it, and even though I think I shouldn't, I smile again and I say, 'See you next week.'

He smiles back. 'Giant biscuit escape backwards from cookie jar.'

I laugh and, when Brendan walks to his desk with Kate, they look at me, and they see that I am laughing and seem to wonder what they have missed. I stare at them until they look away and, when they smirk at each other, I don't think I care.

15

When I go to breakfast, nobody is there. My mother has left a note.

Dear John
I've gone to the church hall today to help build a set for the school
pageant and your Da has gone into town on the early bus. We'll both
see you tonight for tea. Your lunch is on the dresser. Have a good day
at school.
Love, Mammy

I decide not to go to school. When they get home I'll tell them I wasn't feeling well. I eat some porridge and fried eggs on toast in the living room in front of the fire while watching TV and then I eat some chocolate and two bananas. Crito sits on my lap and together we watch some of a Carry On film set at the seaside and then, at half eleven, I go to my grandmother's bedroom.

'Hello,' I say.

She's sitting in a recliner by the fireplace, facing the door, and she has her feet up on the empty armchair across from her. She's not reading or sewing or knitting; just plain sitting. There's a song-book by her feet so maybe she has been learning new songs to sing for us from the bath.

'Hello, John. Why aren't you at school?'

'I'm sick,' I say.

'You don't look sick.'

'I am.'

'Then you should be in bed.'

'I don't feel as sick when I'm standing up or sitting.'

Lying like this makes my heart feel squeezed, as though there's a belt tied around my chest.

'All the same, if you're really sick you should be in bed.'

'I will,' I say. 'I just wanted to talk to you.'

'Why don't you get the thermometer from the toilet cabinet and we'll see if you have a temperature?'

'In a minute. I want to have an important talk first.'

'Well then, come in and close the door behind you.'

It's cold, but she has no fire burning. 'Let me take off my glasses,' she says, 'so I can hear better.'

I want to sit in the armchair she has her feet on because I'd rather not sit on her sagging mattress which is stuffed full of horsehair and stinks of wet animal. I stand by the armchair until she moves her feet. I sit.

'What's new and exciting?' she asks.

'Nothing really,' I say.

'Well, aren't you lovely company? I thought you wanted to chat.'

I clear my throat. 'Has anybody said anything to do with me and lies?'

'Have you been caught telling fibs?'

'No. But has anybody been talking about detecting lies?'

'No. Should they have?'

'No. It's just that I'm reading lots of books about lie detection and I just wondered if anybody had mentioned that.'

'No.'

'Can I ask you something else?'

'Yes.'

'Has Mam spoken to you about getting money for our trip to Niagara?'

'No.'

'Do you know how much it would cost to go to Canada?'

'What are you after?' she asks.

'Well, she's always said she'll take me to Niagara after my Leaving is finished, but I want to go sooner. She says we can't afford it now and I was wondering whether you could help.'

She laughs. 'She's the cat's mother.'

'Sorry. I meant Mammy. All I want to know is whether you could help us with the money.'

'That's blunt.'

'Maybe you could come too.'

'Where do you think my money comes from?' she asks.

She laughs again and I look down at the red swirls in the carpet, but they make me dizzy. I look back up. 'You got a whole lot of money when Grandad died, didn't you? From all the jewellery you sold, and from the shop and things like that.'

'And how long do you think that money will last?' She moves forward in her recliner.

'A long time,' I say.

'Maybe it would be better to wait until you've finished your schooling, and . . .'

Suddenly she stops talking. She looks past me, over my shoulder, towards the door behind me, as though I am not there.

'Granny?'

'Yes.'

'I was really hoping . . .'

'And I was really hoping you wouldn't turn out like your father. Do you know he thinks he has a right to my money? Yes. He thinks if I didn't spend any on myself, he'd have a nice living allowance.'

Her voice is loud now and she doesn't look at me, she looks at my elbow.

'But bearing children doesn't make a woman a martyr. And those that sacrifice too much for their children are often sorry.'

It is as though I'm not in the room.

'Next year I think I'll go on a cruise around the world. Maybe I'll go twice. Until my head spins!'

'But why does Da have to work when he's studying for an exam at Trinity?'

She looks at me as though I have hit her. 'He's had three years of study. If he was serious, he'd have done that exam by now. If I believed your father was going to study for his degree, I'd not nag him to work, but I don't believe him.'

Now she almost shouts. 'And I've got exactly nine days of patience left. Yes, that's all. Nine days of patience left and then the light goes out!'

'That's not fair,' I say.

She points behind me and laughs. 'You're not always as quick as you like to think you are, young John Egan.'

I look behind me at the door, and I see what she has been staring at. In the two-inch gap under the door, there is a pair of black shoes. Somebody is standing outside; somebody has been standing outside all the while.

I thought Da had gone into town on the bus, and I didn't hear him come back in. I get out of the armchair and rush towards the door, but my grandmother stands and grabs hold of my shirt.

'Leave it, John. There's no point going after an eavesdropper. There's no good whatsoever in going after him.'

But I can't help it. I open the door and look. He has gone.

'Sit,' she says. 'There's more I need to say.' I sit down and she reaches across to take my hand. It's a long way for her to stretch but I don't lean forward to make it easier.

'Will we have to leave now?' I ask. 'Will you throw us out?'

'Of course not. I'd never ask you to leave here.'

'Do you swear?'

'I'd swear on the Holy Bible only it's over there on the dressing table,' she says. 'Maybe if I shout, the Bible will hear me.'

She jokes, but there is nothing funny in what she says and I will not laugh. Besides, she is lying.

Her voice is high-pitched, she doesn't blink and doesn't wave her hands the way she usually does. Her hands are dead in her lap.

'All right,' I say. 'That's good.'

'And as for Niagara,' she says, 'if your mother has promised she'll take you there when you've finished your Leaving, I'm certain she'll do it. Your mother doesn't break promises.'

Maybe Mammy forgot, but I now know she hasn't asked Granny about Niagara like she said she would.

'I'm going to watch TV now,' I say.

But I don't watch television. I look everywhere for my father. I go outside and wait for him by the front gate. It is very cold and the cows in the paddock across the road have steam blowing from their nostrils. I rub my hands together and jog up and down on the spot. Some of the cows look at me. Usually I wave at them or say hello, or stare back. Animals are good at staring and they don't mind it.

After nearly an hour of waiting outside by the gate I go into the kitchen. I eat a jam sandwich and then I go to the living room and watch television by the fire until half five. At half six I hear my mother coming through the front door. I go out to the hallway to greet her. I watch her carefully as she removes her coat. She stands for a moment, looking around.

'Let's have a cup of tea,' she says.

I go with her into the kitchen and watch while she puts the kettle on the range and rinses two cups. When the tea is made she shuts the door. She opens a packet of Digestives and puts six of them on a plate. I don't want to tell her I didn't go to school.

'Is that all we're having for tea?'

'I had a big dinner at twelve o'clock at the church hall. But I'll make you some soup if you want.'

'Where's Da?' I ask. 'Did you see him on the way home?'

'He's probably gone to visit your Uncle Jack while he's in Gorey.'

'Why is Uncle Jack in Gorey? Where is he staying? In a hotel? What is he talking to Da about?'

'Your uncle's here from Dublin on business.'

'What kind of business?'

'Boring business.'

'What kind?'

'Mind-your-business kind of business.'

I don't laugh. I stand up and walk around the table. I walk around it twice. I don't really know that I'm doing it until she says, 'Sit down!'

I sit and scratch my head. 'You've been like a crazy ghost,' she says. 'What's the matter?'

I've been waiting for her to ask me but, now that she has, it's not the way I wanted her to ask. 'Why am I like a ghost?' I ask.

She puts her hand on my hand. She looks tired. There are bags under her eyes, almost black, and she has grey hairs. I don't know how long they've been there, but her hair is messy today and the grey sticks out.

'I'm sorry, John. I only mean that you creep around. You keep appearing in places.'

'What places?'

'You come to my room and don't respect my privacy, or your father's.'

'That's not true.'

She ruffles my hair and pretends to laugh. I pull away. She has no choice but to speak to me in a different way. 'Oh, but you do, John. When I lie down to take a nap, suddenly you appear. I'm

128

thinking of getting one of those Do Not Disturb signs from a hotel.'

She is trying to make me laugh, to cover up for the bad things she has said.

'All right,' I say, 'I'll leave you alone.' I stand up.

'John, darling. Please sit down. I don't want you to leave me alone, I just want you to tell me what's wrong. Will you tell me?' She tugs on my arm until I sit down again.

'Everything is different,' I say. 'You're different and Da's different and Granny's different and even Brendan is different.'

'Well, I don't know about Brendan, but people who love each other sometimes have disagreements.'

'That's not it,' I say. 'Everybody is strange with me. Nobody treats me the same as they used to.'

She takes her hand away from mine and puts both hands around her cup. 'You're growing up, John. Sometimes things change when you grow up and it takes a while to get used to them.'

'Like what?'

'Like people don't baby you any more. They don't mollycoddle you. Be flattered by that. When people see you can stand on your own two feet, then they'll not let you lean on them. If you can stand straight and tall, then that's what people will expect of you. The tougher and stronger you are, the less they'll look after you.'

Her words are strange and her head jerks up and down as though she's trying to get a fly off her face. It's not the kind of lie my father tells; it's a white lie, a lie about how she feels; a lie to make me feel better. But it's a lie.

I'm standing now, and my voice is loud and spitting. 'You think I'm weird. If I were smaller everything would be different. The way it used to be.'

She swallows and looks away, afraid of me. 'No, John, that's not it at all.'

I move towards the door.

'John, darling. Stay a minute. Let's finish our tea and biscuits and then you can come and help me wash my hair.'

I stand near the door.

'You're very dear to me, John. Very dear to me.'

I ignore her and go to my room. A few minutes later she comes to me. She has a towel in her hand. 'Come. Help me wash my hair. It's in a desperate state. Don't you love to help me wash my hair?'

She pulls her long brown hair over the top of her head so that it covers her face and she sticks her arms out in front like a ghoul and walks around my room bumping into things.

I get up and we go to the bathroom. I help her wash her long brown hair in the sink. I like how, when she dunks her head, her hair fills the sink and floats to the top and reaches out like seaweed.

I tell her about Brendan and Kate.

She stands and wraps the towel around her head and puts her hands on my shoulders.

'If your friend is not tugging at your arm or calling you back, then he isn't a friend. A friend must need you as well as love you. Wait and see whether he comes to you and tugs at your arm.'

'Like you did before,' I said.

'Did I?' she says.

'Yes. Twice.'

'Well then, I practise what I preach.'

I will write about this in The Gol of Seil. I will write that a person can change during a conversation, tell the truth, then tell lies; change from mean to kind, suddenly, without any warning at all.

16

At the end of school the next day, Kate bumps into me when I'm taking my coat off the rack in the corridor outside our classroom. 'Whoops,' she says. 'So sorry.'

'That's all right,' I say.

'I've heard all about you,' she says. 'Brendan's told me.'

I try to put my coat on, but it falls from my numb fingers.

'The smell of urine makes me feel sick,' she says. 'It puts me off drinking my milk. I'm already squeamish about milk and your smell just puts me off my milk even more.'

I'm hurt and I'm curious. I've never heard the word squeamish before, and it swims in my head.

'Do you know what surreptitious means?' I ask.

'No, but I bet you don't either,' she says.

'I do,' I say. 'It means in secret. The day I wet my pants, I was breaking a world record for not going to the toilet. I was doing it surreptitiously.'

I have an itch in the back of my throat, the kind of itch that threatens to turn into an uncontrollable cough. This is probably because I have lied. It will be good to learn to lie without my body doing anything bad to me.

'You?' she laughs. 'How hilarious.'

'Don't worry about it,' I say.

I walk away.

But I can barely manage it. My legs, like my fingers, feel numb.

The sound of my shoes on the floor is odd, one shoe making a louder noise than the other. My steps are out of rhythm; the stride on my right side is longer than the stride on my left.

I hold my breath and wonder if I might fall over. I want to lean against something. I have lost the knack of walking. I hold my breath until I'm out of the school grounds, until I reach the first tree at the start of the laneway. My heart is hurting. I walk quickly, then stop.

It's a bright, clear day and the birds seem to know it. I look around and pay attention to the trees. I pay attention to the clouds between the trees. I turn three full circles like a discus thrower and throw a stone as hard as I can at the sky.

It's a good, strong throw.

I wait for the sound of the stone, but it doesn't come back down – at least, I don't hear it land – and I stand in the laneway, puzzled about where it might have gone. And still the stone doesn't land, and I smile at the sky.

By the time I arrive home, I'm not as sad as I expect to be. I go to the living room; there's nobody there. I go to the kitchen; there's nobody there either. Granny isn't in her room but she has a fat, white candle lit on her dresser. She must be saying a novena. That was what she meant about having nine days of patience left. The novena will take nine days. But what is she praying for? For my father, praying that he'll get a job? I will tell him when he comes home. I sit at the kitchen table and wait.

When my mother comes home, she goes straight upstairs to her bedroom. It's night-time and when I see my father standing in the kitchen doorway, I realise that I've been sitting in complete darkness.

He comes to me and puts his hand on my head. 'I'll make you some sausages for tea,' he says.

'Where have you been?' I ask.

'Working,' he says as he turns on the lamps.

'Where? What work?'

'Let me make these sausages and then we can watch the idiot box together and we can talk. All right?'

'Granny is saying a novena so you'll get a job. It must have worked already.'

He throws his head back and opens his mouth and keeps it open and his head thrown back. This is his way of laughing without making any sound.

'Why are you laughing like that?' I ask.

'Is laughing a crime now?'

'No.'

'Just as well, because I'm in the mood for it.'

He tousles my hair and smiles at me.

'Where's Mam?' I ask.

'Upstairs. Bedroom. Leave her in peace.'

'I want to talk to her,' I say. 'I have to tell her something important.'

'Is something the matter?'

'There's nothing the matter with me. But isn't there something wrong with you and Granny?'

He pulls hard at his fringe, tugs the thick hair, using his fingers to pull it down, straight and flat over his right eye. 'We've had a few discussions and we've disagreed over a few things, but we've made our peace. Anyway, it's not anything for you to worry about.'

'I'm going upstairs,' I say.

'I said to leave her.'

'I have to talk to her about something.'

'John, can you not just leave your mam in peace? You'll see her soon enough.'

We are silent while he makes the sausages and then he leaves the kitchen with his plate and goes to the living room. I follow. He sits on the settee and I sit down with him. We each have a plate of sausages; four sausages each.

'If you've anything to get off your chest, you can always tell me,' he says.

I pick up a sausage and put it back down again. 'Brendan's not talking to me,' I say.

'Why not?'

'I don't know.'

He eats a whole sausage without chewing, swallows it in three mouthfuls. The chunks of sausage are so big I can see them going down his throat.

'Have you asked him why?'

'No,' I say, looking at my plate.

'Well if you don't ask him you won't find out, will you?'

I don't want to talk about the day I wet my pants. 'He's made friends with the new girl.'

'Oh. Well then, I think you should make friends with her.'

'But I don't think he wants me to be his friend any more.'

My father has already finished his sausages. 'Are you going to eat yours?' he asks.

'Yes,' I say.

'I think you should talk to Brendan.' He scratches his chin. 'I think you should talk to your friend and not go running to your mother.'

I make a sausage stand upright and use it to push another one over on its side.

'Do you agree?'

'I agree,' I say.

I don't know what he's talking about. I'm sick of the way he changes in the middle of a conversation. He can do what he likes from now on. I know what I want to do.

'Time for the news,' he says. 'Shall we watch it together?'

* * *

We watch the news together, in silence. There's a policeman on the news and he says: 'The suspect allegedly tore at the victim's night skirt and asked her to undress but the female did not comply with this alleged request and the evildoer's intentions were quite clear.'

Without looking at me, my father says, 'I love the way the guards talk. They're always trying to sound intelligent and end up sounding brain-damaged.'

'I s'pose,' I say.

'You *suppose*, not you s'pose.'

Crito jumps onto my father's lap and my father pushes her off. 'I've had just about enough of that cat's dander,' he says.

'What's dander?' I ask.

'The stuff that gets up my nose. I hate stuff that gets up my nose.'

He laughs then, like a madman, and gets up to take a cigarette out of the box kept on the mantelpiece. He sucks at the cigarette as though it is a burning sweet, as though he has to get to the end of it as quickly as possible to receive his reward. He rarely talks while he smokes. He prefers to squint and look at the fire. Let him. I leave.

My mother still hasn't come downstairs and it's nearly nine o'clock. I go to the kitchen and fry another six sausages and I bring them up to her with some bread and a bottle of tomato sauce.

She's sitting up in bed, wearing a cardigan over her pink shop coat.

'Room service!' I say. I put the plate on her bed and she laughs.

'Six sausages! You sausage!'

'Do you want them?'

'No, you have them. I'm too tired to eat.'

'Are you going to sleep now?' I ask.

'Yes.'

'Where's Da been?'

'When?'

'Yesterday and today.'

'Working. He's got himself some odd jobs.'

'Does that mean everything is normal again with Granny?'

'It will be soon,' she says. She closes her eyes.

'Will you turn off the light on your way out.'

I didn't know that I was on my way out.

She turns over and doesn't look at me. The room smells of farts.

I feel embarrassed for her.

17

My father doesn't come downstairs for breakfast. I ask my mother where he is and she wipes her hand along the side of my face. 'He went on the early bus to Wexford to talk to his old boss.'

'Again?'

'He's still trying to sort out a few things,' she says.

'But it's three years since he stopped working,' I say.

My granny lowers a rasher into her mouth the way a zookeeper lowers a piece of steak into the mouth of a lion. 'He's doing the things a man does,' she says. 'He's getting his nose out of the books and he's getting off his bony backside.'

My mother stands up and goes to the window. She's counting to ten to control her temper the way she taught me; I can see the fingers of her left hand tapping out the numbers on her thigh. She's wearing pink lipstick, a long pink woollen skirt, a white blouse and her hair is out. She looks beautiful and she knows I'm staring and does nothing to stop me. When she's finished counting she comes back to the table and smiles at me.

'Another lovely day,' she says. 'Fine and fresh and crisp.'

'Who wants a game of backgammon?' asks Granny. 'John?'

'There's not enough time.'

'You've got ten minutes. How about a few quick hands of black-jack then?'

'OK.'

My mother starts whistling and Granny gets the cards from the dresser and deals.

On the way to school I think about last night's dream in which Ripley found out about my gift for lie detection. I was living with him in his big house in America and it was as though I was his son.

I could see every one of his small, crooked teeth. I said, 'Even though you have small and crooked and buck teeth you are still famous,' and he smiled and put his arm around me and we walked together down his driveway towards his convertible sports car.

Because I can't do an American accent very well, not even in dreams, Ripley had to mumble when he spoke to me, and because he was mumbling I couldn't exactly understand what he was saying, but I felt sure he was telling me that I'd be famous one day soon.

There was only one bad part in the dream. The roof of Ripley's car was made of cardboard and, as we drove along the highway together, the cardboard buckled and warped and seemed to want to break off.

When I told Ripley I was worried about the roof, he turned to look at me and his teeth were suddenly straight and big. He didn't look like himself any more. I woke up then, and blamed the last part, the bad part of my dream, on the noises in the hallway outside my room; the noises of my father and Granny arguing.

At twenty past nine, Mr Donnelly comes into our classroom. For a few minutes he tidies things on Miss Collins' desk, takes things out of her top stationery drawer and puts them back in. Then he speaks.

'Miss Collins is sick and while she's getting better you'll have a new teacher who will be starting today — as soon as he can get here. The new teacher is a nice man from Dublin. His name is Mr Roche and he will be your substitute until Miss Collins is made better and back on her feet.'

Now he stuffs his hands in his pockets.

I stop listening and look out the window.

Mr Donnelly tells us to play outside. 'And pray for Miss Collins until your new teacher arrives.'

It is another clear day and the sun is out. I walk down by the edge of the playing field and run a stick along the fence. I don't look back at the school building or to see what Brendan and Kate are doing.

I see Joseph with his horse on the other side of the fence near the road. He's with another man. I go up to the gate to say hello.

Joseph's friend says, 'Would you like a ride on my horse? His name is Zorro.'

I don't know Joseph's friend's name, but he is friendly and shorter and fatter than Joseph. 'All right,' I say. 'Yes, please.'

I go out through the fence and Joseph's friend helps me on. This horse is sick, and covered in sores, but it is too late to say I don't want to ride. When I climb on, I can feel his ribs against my calves.

I'm riding along by the edge of the road, with Joseph and Joseph's friend chatting and joking, and I feel like the world belongs to me. I don't feel nervous and I don't mind that Brendan and Kate are playing together without me. I don't care that I am like Osmond, playing on my own. At least when I talk to myself I do it quietly without waving my hands about and nobody can see my lips moving.

I get hungry after a while. 'I better go back now,' I say. 'I better eat my lunch.'

I get down from Zorro and look at him. I want to stare into

his eyes the way I do with Joseph's horse, Neddy. But Zorro doesn't want to stare and he turns his face away. I suddenly feel nervous again, and I wonder if it's because I can only see one of Zorro's eyes and I don't know what the other eye is doing.

'Thanks Joseph,' I say. 'Bye now.'

'Bye now young John,' says Joseph's friend. 'What's your name?' I ask him.

'Joseph. Same as him.'

'So long,' I say. 'I'll say hello to Granny for you.'

'Yes. Bye now.'

'Be good, so.'

I sit on the bench under Mr Donnelly's office window feeling happy and begin to eat my jam sandwich. I should have given the Josephs some biscuits and I look up to see if they are still out by the gate.

I see Kate. She is coming towards me, pulling Brendan's jacket. 'Come on, Brendan,' she says. 'Let's get his sandwich.'

Kate looks around after she shouts at me. She wants to be watched. Brendan looks down at his feet, and leans in close to Kate, as though for warmth, or in case he falls. And he puts his hand over his nose, the way he does when he's embarrassed.

Kate stands over me. 'Have you wet your pants today?'

I put a crust into my mouth and try to chew, but it feels as big and dry as a sock. I push it between my bottom lip and my teeth but the piece of crust gets stuck there.

'Pants-wetter! I'm talking to you!' she says.

My penis tingles as though somebody has touched it. I squeeze my thighs together.

'Get his sandwich off him,' she says as she grabs Brendan by the jacket. 'Kick him in the kneecap. Get both his kneecaps.'

Brendan kicks my knee and I let him. I could fight back, but

140

I won't. I will act as though they don't exist. I will watch Brendan as though he were a picture on the television.

After he has kicked me, he staggers and needs to step back to get his balance. And because I don't react he seems confused. He looks down at his shoe.

I stare at him, and he kicks me again, in the other knee, harder this time. Maybe to show he doesn't need orders from his master. He's quite strong, so the kick is hard. I look at him. I look at them both as though I don't care what they do. My face is blank. I put my hands on my knees and the heat from my palms helps the pain. But I show nothing. I'll say nothing; like the caretaker.

'Get it now!' Kate says. 'Get the sandwich!'

Brendan takes the rest of my jam sandwich and without meaning to says, 'Thanks.' He looks confused, as though he wants to change his mind.

I stand up and walk away.

I go back to the classroom and sit and read my geography book. But after a few minutes, when I turn the page, I see that there's sticky blood on the end of my finger. I've been scratching my scalp so much that there is a small hole in the crown of my head. I scratch it at night when I can't get to sleep and I dig at the hole, sometimes without noticing, until it bleeds. It doesn't hurt as much as it should. The hole doesn't exactly belong to me.

After lunch, Mr Donnelly orders us back inside. He stands in front of our classroom, but he doesn't speak. He holds the blackboard duster in his hand and it looks as small as a biscuit. He puts the duster down and, when he tries to stuff his hands into his pockets, only the tips of his red fingers fit and the rest of them poke out, squashed, full of blood and shiny. They are red fingers, just like my father's, but fatter.

Kate stands up and yells, 'If the new teacher is so late, he should get the cane!'

The cane is leaning up against the left-hand corner of the blackboard and Mr Donnelly looks at it for a moment before turning to face the window.

I look out the window too, at the playing field, the school gate, and the narrow, tree-lined country road.

It is nearly two o'clock when a man gets out of a taxi at the gate and walks across the field towards us.

He is young – younger than my father – and, although not tall, he looks strong, with black hair to his shoulders. I have never before seen a man with long hair, or a man getting out of a taxi at our school gate.

He looks made of hard materials, steel and iron, not easily broken. Most of the men in our town seem like they are made of sponge cake or leftover turnip, like my uncles, Jack and Tony, who are overweight around the stomach and chin. Their blotchy skin is like turkey stuffing.

Most of the men in our town not only look the same, they act the same too; even my father becomes more like my uncles when he's with them. But at least my father is more handsome than they are.

The man comes closer and I am full of hope: I have always wanted a smart man for a teacher, a man with mettle and brains, and as I watch him disappear from view I can hardly stop myself smiling.

Mr Donnelly seems confused and wipes the teacher's desk back and forth with the blackboard duster, as though erasing a mistake.

A minute of silence, and then the man walks through the door and to the front of our classroom. Mr Donnelly puts the duster down and stands next to him.

They speak for a minute or two and then leave the room together. Mr Donnelly ducks his head and shoulders under the doorway and they are gone.

Sister Ursula comes to keep watch. She stands by the blackboard and tells us to read. 'As quiet as mice,' she says.

Thirty minutes later, the man returns alone and Sister Ursula leaves without speaking.

'You'll call me Mr Roche, not sir,' he says.

We snicker and fidget and stare.

He walks along by the blackboard.

'You live in a beautiful town. I bet if you were quiet enough you could hear the boats rub against the pier and the fish burp and the seagulls snore.'

We laugh because Courtown's sandy beach and Courtown Bay are four miles from Gorey and we cannot hear the seagulls or the boats. This is a lie, a story, told for fun and I like it; I like him.

I watch as Mr Roche moves between our desks, and I can smell him. Perhaps he stood in manure in his walk across the field; it's the same smell as the farmers who have breakfast at Kylemore's in town. It doesn't suit his fancy clothes and posh voice to have this smell on his shoes and I wonder when he'll notice and clean them.

'Now, I'm going to have a short quiet chat with every one of you,' he says and he crouches down at each desk in turn, asking questions in a whisper.

I wait anxiously for my turn, thinking that he'll soon discover me and know that I'm different. I'll tell him about my gift.

At Brendan's desk, Mr Roche crouches down and this time he does not whisper. We can all hear him say, 'Are you easily influenced, Brendan?'

Brendan shrugs, then Mr Roche puts his mouth against Brendan's ear.

'OK, I will,' Brendan says and then he drops his head and keeps it down, as though looking for an important message written on his desk.

Mr Roche reaches Kate's desk, but he doesn't kneel down to whisper in her ear. Instead, he sits on the empty desk behind hers, taps her on the shoulder and says, 'And who might you be?'

Kate turns to look at him. 'I'm Kate Breslin,' she says. 'I'm an only child from Dublin and my family has taken over a deceased estate.'

'Well, Kate, I believe you're the clever one. That must make you feel quite special?'

And then I know it: Mr Donnelly took Mr Roche away to talk about each of us. Now I am sure Mr Roche will realise who I am.

'Not really,' says Kate, her voice trembling.

'Clever or not,' Mr Roche says, 'I hope your coffin is airtight.'

He laughs and the whole class laughs with him, because what he has said makes no sense. Even Brendan turns round to show me his laughing teeth.

Mr Roche walks to the front, sits on the edge of the teacher's desk and smiles directly at me. Although he didn't come to my desk, I'm sure he knows. I'm sure he will help me.

As soon as I get home, I make a toasted ham sandwich and then I lie on my bed and spend two hours writing another letter to the *Guinness Book of Records*. I'm confident I'll get a reply this time.

Dear Guinness Book of Records,
My name is John Egan and I have written to you once before.

I am the boy with the gift of lie detection. I have now read all of the books on the subject available on the East Coast of Ireland and I have tested my talent a few more times since my first letter.

I am even surer that my gift is rare and unusual to say the least.

Please write back to me this time and I will arrange a demonstration for you either in Dublin or in London or wherever it suits you best. I will prove that I can detect lies with 100% accuracy.

John Egan

Age 11

Gorey, Ireland

My mother comes into my room at teatime without knocking. 'Why don't you knock?' I say. 'Don't I have any privacy?'

She laughs and sits on my bed. 'Aren't you a cheeky one? Maybe I did knock and your ears are too full of earwigs to hear.'

She rubs my leg as she speaks.

'I hate talking about housework, but it's high time you did some of your chores. Could you please do them without being reminded? You haven't done the hoovering for a week and you haven't dusted the mantelpiece either.'

'Sorry.'

'All right. You can eat, then. We're having chops for tea and I've made some rhubarb and custard for dessert,' she says.

And suddenly, even though I haven't seen my father in two days, I am happy.

18

It's Friday and I walk to school quickly and get there early so that I can watch Mr Roche prepare his classes at the teacher's table. I watch him all morning. I like him very much and I especially like his voice.

But then, during second lesson, I realise that I have been holding on too long and I must go to the toilet. I can't have another accident. I stand and put my hand up and ask to be excused.

Mr Roche comes straight over to me, takes my hand, and leads me into the corridor. I'm embarrassed to be led like this in front of my class, but he looks at me as we walk, and he smiles at me, as though leaving the classroom like this is normal, as though I am his friend.

In the corridor, he asks me to sit under the coat rack and I sit with my head under somebody's duffel coat, holding on to my urine.

'Keep it in,' he says. 'Just a minute longer.'

I manage to hold on. Then he takes me to the bathroom.

He waits for me and I wait for him to leave. But he stays by the door, looking all the while as I stand with my hand on my zipper.

'I won't bite,' he says. 'Go ahead.'

I turn away from him and open my fly. I urinate. So little comes out I worry that I'll soon need to go again.

When I have finished I turn to look at him.

'Good lad,' he says.

I walk over to him and he pats me on the back.

'You're a good lad,' he says. 'You have a very nice way about you.'

I smile and he smiles back, and I feel all right, even when we return to class, and everybody is talking and laughing. But they're not laughing at me. Kate is standing up next to the teacher's desk, impersonating Mr Roche by speaking in a posh voice.

Mr Roche tells her to return to her desk and, as she walks away from him, he slaps her across the back of the head. 'You cannot sell your phlegm and then ask for it back again,' he says.

Nobody understands, but everybody laughs, because Kate is stunned and, for the first time since she came to our school she is silent. For the rest of the day Kate doesn't move unless Mr Roche tells her to and even Brendan does not talk to her.

After school, when everybody has left the classroom, I go to Mr Roche's desk. He looks up at me and smiles. He has straight, white teeth and deep laugh-lines around his mouth.

'Mr Roche?' I say. 'I was wondering if you could help find me some books about lie detection from America?'

I am hoping that he'll ask me why I'm interested in the subject, but instead he grabs my hand.

'You've reminded me of something that's been bothering me.'

'What?' I ask.

He stands up and walks to the window. 'It makes my blood boil that this school has no library. Every school should have a library.'

'Yes, sir,' I say. 'Yes, Mr Roche.'

'No storybooks,' he says, 'means no reading stories.'

'Yes, sir,' I say.

'No reading stories means no imagination. We all start life with

148

an imagination, of course, but without stories to feed it the imagination, like a starved dog, dies.'

He stares out at the playing field. 'And when a person doesn't read and when a person has no imagination they are sure to end up with no inventiveness of mind and spend a life with nothing but hackneyed, worn-out things to say. A life of slogans, jargon and clichés.'

I nod.

'A weak man repeats what he hears and makes himself dumb.'

'I agree, sir.'

He walks away and then walks straight back to me to say, 'And science and invention stem from the imagination.'

I've been searching for something to say, and now I've found it. 'Einstein thought that, too,' I say. I read this in the book my father left on the coffee table last week.

He looks up at me, excited. 'You're right, John Egan. You're no fool. Full points for you.'

'Thank you, Mr Roche.'

He comes to me and puts his hand on my arm. 'And no imagination means the only life you can live is the one you've been given. And God knows, looking around here, I'd say some of you haven't been given much of a life.'

I wonder if I should say something, but he walks to the blackboard without speaking.

I stare at his black hair and the way it slides smoothly over the shoulders of his jacket. He must be made at least partly of silk.

'I'm sending you home at half two tomorrow,' he says. 'And on Monday morning there'll be a surprise waiting.'

Does he mean a surprise for me, or for all?

'Go home now,' he says. 'Your mammy is probably waiting.'

*   *   *

My father paces up and down in front of the fire while waiting for his tea. The way he walks is not at all like Mr Roche's walk. He takes small jerky steps, while Mr Roche's stride is longer, calmer. My father's head is jumpy on his neck and shoulders.

'Why are you walking up and down?' I ask.

'I've got restless legs,' he says. 'When I sit for too long they get ants in them.'

'Why?'

'I don't know why. Maybe they're the ants that fell out of my pants. They come at night too when I'm trying to get to sleep.'

He must be in a good mood to talk this way, playful like Mammy, the way he sometimes talks when he's with her.

'Do they keep you awake?'

'Yes, and I have to kick my legs to shake them off.'

'Is that why you sleep on the floor?' I ask.

He stops pacing and stands in front of the television. I expect him to be angry, but he smiles.

'I've slept on the floor once or twice but just so the ants don't bother your mam.'

'Is that why?'

'Jesus, Mary and Joseph and all the feckin' apostles! Not the third degree again. Yes, son. I sleep on the floor to stop from bothering your poor mam so she can get a good night's rest for work the next day. No other reason! Are you satisfied?'

I was worried that he would be silent, that he might stop telling me things because of my gift. But here he is talking and telling another lie. It took him longer than usual, but here it is. I am certain again. He is lying.

His voice is higher and tighter and his hands and arms are life-less. My ears are hot, but that's the only physical symptom I have. Lie detection is becoming easier.

'Maybe you should kill one of the ants,' I say 'and then the rest would go to its funeral.'

He sits down next to me and looks at the television. *Doctor Who* has finished and the news is starting.

'Good idea,' he says. 'You're full of good ideas.'

'I didn't make that up,' I say. 'I heard it in a joke once.'

I tell my father the joke even though he's watching the television. 'A horrible witch captures an Irishman, an Englishman and a Scotsman and she makes them sleep in a bed of flesh-eating creatures. The Irishman has to sleep on a bed of fanged army ants. In the morning, the witch goes to the room where all three men have slept, expecting to find them dead, but the Irishman has survived. "Why have you survived?" asks the witch. "Because," says the Irishman, "I killed one of the flesh-eating army ants and the rest of them went to his funeral."'

My father smiles, but he doesn't laugh.

I don't care any more. I don't care what he does or doesn't do. I don't need him to like me. I don't need him at all.

I spend the weekend in my room, reading the *Guinness Book*, writing in The Gol of Seil and doing homework so that on Monday I can impress Mr Roche again. I'm getting used to not playing with Brendan.

19

Just as Mr Roche promised, there is a surprise on Monday morning. Our desks have been pushed closer together so that there is barely room between them and, at the back of the classroom, two red velvet curtains are strung up on white poles. The curtains are tied open with black rope. They are like the red velvet curtains that open and close in front of the screen at the cinema. And, about a foot and a half behind the curtains, there is a small wooden desk, with a box of books on it and, behind the desk, a chair.

'All right,' says Mr Roche. 'Take your seats and keep your eyes forward. When you are all quiet and still, I'll tell you about the curtains and the desk at the back of the classroom.'

We get into our seats and wait.

Mr Roche goes to the back of the room. 'Now, turn around,' he says.

He sits behind the desk, behind the curtains, and takes a dozen books out of the box. The books are Reader's Digests, every one of them. He takes a nametag from his pocket and pins it to his jacket pocket: *Chief Librarian*.

He smiles. 'Welcome to my imaginary library.'

Then he stands and removes the ties from the curtains so that they close in front of him. From behind the curtain he tells us what to do. He shouts like a man on stage. We all look around at each other.

'You must line up quietly and single file, and when you are at the front of the line, ring the bell attached to the curtain on the right-hand side. Then open the curtains and step into the imaginary library.'

'There's nowhere to step into,' says Jimmy, the brother of Osmond.

'You'll have to pretend,' says Mr Roche. 'And once the curtains close behind you and you are alone and standing before the table, I will ask you what book you'd like to borrow.'

The idea is that, although the books are Reader's Digests, we must pretend that the library is a real library and we should request the books we'd most like to read. Mr Roche will keep a record of all the books we request over the next few weeks and eventually persuade the school to install a proper, bigger library.

'At half two every day you will line up here. And when you ask for a book, I'll give you a project based on that book. And because the book is imaginary, so too will the contents of your project be.'

At twenty past two, I have a premonition; Mr Roche will call my name, and this is exactly what he does.

'John Egan,' he says, 'you're a keen reader. Why don't you get us started? Why don't you be the first boy to visit the imaginary library?'

I stand up. 'Yes, sir.'

'Good. Go to the curtains and wait. Everybody else form a queue behind John Egan.'

Mr Roche goes to the desk behind the curtain. I ring the bell, open the curtains, then let them close behind me. It's red and snug behind the curtains and it's nice to be hidden. 'I'll have a book about Vikings,' I say.

He reaches into the box and pulls out an old Reader's Digest.

'Ah,' he says, 'we have a volume of the encyclopaedia dedicated to that very subject. Take it home, and let us hear your report in the morning.'

On my way home I can think of nothing else. I make a sandwich and go to my room and think about Mr Roche and his great idea. I rehearse what I will tell him about my gift and fantasise about what he will say. After tea I sit on my bed – not stopping even to watch television – and write an imaginary account of the life of Vikings. I cheat only once by looking in one of my father's history books.

I walk quickly to school and wait all day for my chance to talk about Vikings.

At half one, Mr Roche asks me to stand in front of the classroom. And I begin my version of the lifestyle of the Vikings. I stand with my hands by my side and I squeeze my toes in my shoes to stop myself from moving and then I begin.

'The Vikings liked to sing as they rowed their big Viking boats and there were prizes given each week to the Viking who thought of the funniest song. When Vikings went to a new port they always stole a female child (she had to have long hair down to her waist) and they took her back to the boat and made her lie down in a hammock while they cut off her plaits. Then they threw her into the water and watched her sink. After that, the Vikings ate some cake and drank some whiskey and then they went into the nearest village and took all the gold and emeralds and rubies and diamonds. And sometimes they took cats and kept them on board for company.'

I'm not nervous. I've never before been calm talking in front of my class. I usually feel nervous. Sometimes I even feel nervous when somebody else is nervous, like the time I was at a school concert and the girl who was turning the pianist's sheet music was shaking so much the pages fell from the stand.

When I'm finished, Mr Roche walks towards me and puts his hand on my shoulder. There is silence as he says, 'That was splendid, John. First class.'

I sit down, and he gives the class a long history lesson about Vikings. We learn some of the names of the swords of the Vikings, including 'baby-killer', 'brain-biter' and 'man-splitter'. I write these things down and keep the piece of paper in my pocket.

I will call my Swiss army knife 'father-biter' from now on.

From the moment I walk in the door at home I know that the mood has changed; it is as though my good fortune at school has spread. The house is warm and there's a smell of roast chicken and my mother, father and grandmother are together in the kitchen, talking. My mother is cooking onions and rashers in a frying pan; the radio is on and the range is full of wood. My father sneaks up behind her on tiptoes, and pretends to take a rasher from the pan.

'Mmm,' he says as he wipes his hand on his trousers.

'Don't do that!' says my mother, but she is laughing, not cross.

My father's fringe is long and messy over his eye and he looks happy. His lips are red and so too are his cheeks. He takes a rasher from the frying pan and hands it to me. 'Here, son. This one's for you.' I go forward and take the hot rasher and I lower it into my mouth.

'Nothing finer than stolen meat, wouldn't you agree?'

'Yeah, I would,' I say and laugh with him.

My mother lunges at him and they race around the table. 'Catch him, Mam!' I say.

My grandmother finishes frying the rashers and laughs as she watches my father crawl under the table. My mother crawls under the table too, even though she's wearing her good pink dress and high-heeled shoes.

I want to join in, so I go to the table and crouch down. 'Chase me,' I say. 'Give me a go.'

'Another time,' says my father. 'I think we've had enough running around for one day.'

They crawl out from under the table and my father pushes my mother's backside and keeps pushing her until she is on the other side of the kitchen, nearly at the door.

'Oh, you rascal,' she says and they run around the table again.

I want to join them. 'Why are you dressed up?' I ask my mother when she finally sits down at the table, panting and flushed.

'We're going to a dance tonight, and your granny is going to be our chauffeur.'

Granny smiles.

'Am I staying here?'

'Yes, but no need to worry. We won't be very late. And you can eat all the custard.'

I leave them and go to the living room. They come to say goodbye and I hardly look at them. I watch television until after ten, then I sit on my bed with Crito on my lap and wait for them to come home. It is late, past eleven o'clock. When a car drives by the cottage, Crito jumps up and goes to my bedroom window, then comes back when nobody walks up the gravel driveway.

I hold her tight so she won't jump off again, and I squeeze and stroke her stomach and talk to her.

'Whatever you do, don't have any more kittens,' I say.

She tries to jump off when another car goes by, and so I hold her tight.

'Don't,' I say. 'Stay here.'

She struggles and I take hold of the middle of her tail and, as she struggles to get away, I feel the strange rubbery bone under her skin and fur, and I pull it too hard. She pulls but I don't want to let go.

She hisses at me. I feel bad. I let go but I don't go after her. Instead, I stare up at the ceiling and daydream about going to Niagara Falls. I meet two tall men from the *Guinness Book* at the airport in New York and they offer to carry my suitcase. They tell me we're going to stay on the fourteenth floor of a big hotel near the Empire State Building and in the morning we'll go to Niagara in a first-class carriage on a train that has a restaurant, a balcony and its own band. In Niagara, near the Horseshoe Falls, there'll be a television camera crew waiting to film my first meeting with Robert Ripley. I fall asleep before the daydream ends but even this little bit does the job of stopping me from wondering when they'll be home.

20

It is half two and time once again for us to form a queue behind the curtain of the imaginary library.

Brendan is first. He rings the bell, closes the curtain behind him and goes to Mr Roche. 'I'd like a book about how to make umbrellas because me ma keeps losing ours.'

'A book about the making of umbrellas. Ah, here we are,' says Mr Roche and he makes a label for the front of the Reader's Digest, as he always does, and this one says: *The Making of Umbrellas.*

When Brendan has taken his book, Kate pushes her way to the head of the queue, rings the bell and goes behind the red curtain.

'What about a book about stopping your brother from wetting the bed?' she says.

'I'll have to go to the archives for that one,' says Mr Roche. He comes out from behind the curtain and goes into the broom cupboard and emerges with another Reader's Digest. He makes a special show of clearing the dust from it and humming to himself.

But does he not realise that Kate has asked for that book so that she can tease me? Does he not see what she will do?

'Here's just what the doctor ordered: *Ten Steps to the End of Bed-Wetting,*' he says as he hands the book to Kate.

'Thank you,' she says. 'This will be very helpful.'

Perhaps Mr Roche suspects her and wants to give her some time to reconsider. Perhaps he has forgotten that he is here to protect

159

me. When he has returned to his place behind the curtain, Kate takes the book and puts it in my desk. 'Here,' she says, as she closes the lid of my desk. 'Read this and stop pissing your pants!'

Kate sits at her desk with her arms folded across her chest and I can hardly breathe as I try to find something to say. But I don't need to speak: Mr Roche comes out from behind the curtain and, as though he was able to see Kate through the curtain, he walks straight over to her desk.

'Where did you put that book I just now gave you?' he asks.

'In my desk.'

Mr Roche looks in Kate's desk and, when he sees that the book isn't there, he checks mine. He sees the book in my desk. He walks to Kate and takes hold of her hair and she struggles, until the pink ribbon tied to the end of her long brown plait comes loose and falls to the floor, and he stops.

'Ow,' she says.

He is so angry that he doesn't bother to speak. Instead, he pulls her out of her seat. Kate frees herself and runs to the window. Mr Roche stands by her desk. 'Kate Breslin, get back over here. Everybody else sit back down at your desks!'

He is on his toes with anger now; his neck is fat with it and pulsing. Kate takes the edge of the curtain in her hand and Mr Roche goes to her.

'You lied to me,' he shouts. 'You lied to me.'

'No I didn't.'

'You did. Why did you do that? Why are you so cruel?'

'What?' she says. 'What did I do?'

We watch from our desks as Mr Roche goes to the blackboard and stands with his arms folded across his chest. His arms rise up and down with his heavy breathing. 'Let's return to our spelling,' he says.

As Mr Roche lowers himself into his chair, Kate turns to Brendan and whispers something that makes him laugh. Mr Roche gets to his feet and leaves the classroom without speaking. We hear him rummaging in the cupboard in the corridor and, when he returns, he is carrying a coal bucket filled with water. He clears a space on the floor near the front of the classroom, a foot from his desk, and puts the bucket down.

'Kate Breslin, get down there on your knees and drink like a dog.'

'What?'

'Get down here on your hands and knees and drink from this bucket.'

'No,' she says. 'I won't.'

'Do it now, or I will do it for you.'

'You must be mad,' she says. 'I won't do it.'

Mr Roche rushes to her desk, clutches her hair, drags her by the scalp, pushes her to the floor and holds her head over the bucket of black, sooty water.

'Do you know what your evil does to the world? Do you understand nothing about cause and effect? Do you think evil springs from nothing?'

She is silent. He pushes her face into the water. 'Drink,' he says.

She drinks and, when he is satisfied, he pulls her head out of the bucket by the roots of her hair. He pulls so hard it seems his grip will soon separate the scalp from her skull. Water trickles down her neck and blackens her shirt at the back, like blood.

I think it is over when she begins to cry, but he kneels down and holds her bottom in one hand and, with the other, presses on the back of her neck, pushing her down again, her face in the water.

Kate moans and, at last, he stops.

'OK,' he says. 'Now stand up at the back of the classroom.'

She moves to the back wall and he gives her his jumper so she can mop herself up. She holds the jumper to cover her face.

'It's the likes of you who make the men that rape,' he says. 'At every school in the country, the killers and madmen are made by bullies like you.'

Kate sobs.

'Please don't do any more,' she says. 'I'm really sorry. I need to go to the toilet.'

But Mr Roche hasn't finished.

'You're not going anywhere.'

'Please, sir, let me go home. I'm sorry.'

He folds his arms and stares at her.

We all sit and wait. It's three o'clock and the home bell has rung. We should be leaving. But nobody stirs, and it is quiet enough to hear stomachs churning. Nobody speaks when the teachers and the other children pass by our classroom to get their coats. Mr Roche stands by the door and smiles and waves at them.

Mr Donnelly walks by at ten past three, and Mr Roche tells him we are taking a test and won't go home until the last pupil has finished. Mr Donnelly looks in, sees that nobody is writing, opens his mouth, but doesn't speak. He looks at his watch, then leaves.

Nobody is able to move. We are turned to face the back of the room and we watch Kate, who watches Mr Roche. Then it happens: at fifteen minutes past three, Kate wets herself.

It is as though I am the one doing the wetting. The urine that runs down her legs and forms a pool on the floor belongs to me. I can feel the urine on my own legs and the wet heat of piss in my own socks. When Mr Roche goes to her and puts his hand on her shoulder, it is I who feels the comfort of his touch.

'Clean yourself up,' he says. 'The rest of you go home.'

I stand by my desk and wait until everybody has left the class-room. He comes to me and takes my hand. 'You'd better go home now, too,' he says. 'I'll see you tomorrow.'

I smile weakly.

'You've no reason not to hold your head up high, John Egan,' he says. 'Hold it high for me and show me what you look like when you are proud.'

And, even though Kate is crying and watching, I hold my chin up.

'Not that high,' he says. 'Like this.'

And he puts his hands on my face and puts it where he wants it.

'Like this. You are strong and you should look strong.'

And when he lifts my chin up he stares at me and I get a surprising and nice feeling in my stomach.

'Thank you,' I say. 'Thank you, Mr Roche.'

'Go now,' he says. 'I'll look after Kate.'

When I get home the cottage is quiet and there are no lights on. I think, at first, that nobody is home, but when I go to the living room I find the door won't open. Somebody has pushed a chair under the handle. My heart thumps too hard and hurts my chest. I can hear low voices behind the door. I push, but it will not open. I call out, 'Who's there?'

My mother answers. 'We're having a bit of a talk, John. We'll be out in a minute.'

'Can't I come in?' I ask.

'Just hold your horses,' says my father, and I turn away and go to my room.

My nose tingles the way it does when I trip over and fall, the same tingling that happens on the way down to the ground. I need to go to the toilet but when I get there no urine comes out.

I go to my room, close the door and reach under my mattress to make sure The Gol of Seil is still there. It is. And I check the money I took from Granny's purse. It is still there.

I have put a hair in the first page of The Gol of Seil so that I'll know if anybody has moved it, and I have put the money carefully under the mattress between two pieces of cardboard with a line marked with a black biro on the bottom piece of cardboard where the first note should be. Nothing has been moved. Still, I worry.

At half six, my mother comes in.

'I'm sorry the door was locked, John. Your granny wanted to talk about some very private things.'

'That's all right,' I say.

'There's nothing to worry about, John.'

'I'm grand,' I say. 'I'm not worried.'

'We're having stew for tea. Will you come and help me with the carrots?'

'OK.'

I don't need to know what the talk was about.

21

Kate is not at school the next day, and Mr Roche behaves as though nothing has happened. He makes us laugh with stories of Dublin, and he explains how fractions work.

I look carefully and closely at him all day. I pay attention to everything he does, the way he speaks, the words he uses, what he does with his hands and how he holds the chalk and a pen. He looks at me, too.

He doesn't smile or wink at me, but that's because he should be careful: nobody should know that what he did yesterday was done for me. It would be wrong to make it obvious.

I'm happy on the way home and I follow the path I have made. But, after a while, walking doesn't seem right for the mood I'm in and I pretend I'm running the marathon for Ireland in the Olympic games.

When I get to the doll stuck up the tree, I think, for the first time, that she looks comfortable, as though the branch is an arm holding itself up for her so that she can have a better view of the world.

But my happy mood does not last.

When I arrive home, my mother and father are waiting by the car. The engine is running and there are six suitcases on the gravel driveway. One of the suitcases — the small, blue, cardboard one — is mine.

I wonder if we might be taking a surprise holiday in a caravan park, the kind of holiday my father so often promises.

My grandmother's car is at the side of the house, instead of in the front drive, and this change in the usual order of things tells me that something has happened to her, and that something other than a surprise holiday is about to happen to me.

'We're going to Dublin for a few days,' says my father.

I need him to say a bit more before I can know if he's lying. I wasn't paying enough attention. Maybe he has passed his exam.

'Why?' I ask.

He comes forward with his arms outstretched, with the intention of putting his hands on my shoulders. I move away from him and he puts his hands on his hips, as though this is where he has always meant his hands to be.

'Why are we going so suddenly?' I ask.

'I'll tell you in the car.'

My stomach drops. What about my money and The Gol of Seil?

I stand up close to him and look him in the eyes. 'But Da, is Crito coming? Can I go and get her? She's probably on my bed. I'll go and get her.'

I start walking but he grabs my arm. 'Stop worrying about that stupid cat and get in the car,' he says.

'You're hurting me. Let go.'

He lets go and I step away from him. I move back, back towards the door, towards Crito and my money.

My mother comes forward, her arms outstretched. 'I'm sorry, darling. But we need to go before it gets dark. And you can't stay.'

'What about my *Guinness* books?'

'We've packed five of them. That's all you'll need. Please get in the car.'

'Which five?'

'Get in the car,' says my father.

We travel a few miles in silence and then my father asks my mother to light a cigarette for him. She takes a few puffs before she hands it to him. He holds the cigarette between his thumb and index finger and sucks on the filter until it is flattened and wet.

'But are we staying with Aunty Evelyn and Uncle Gerald?' I ask.

My mother turns in her seat to look at me and as she turns she reaches out and puts her hand on my knee. 'Yes, for a few days.'

'Why?' I ask.

My father slows the car and speaks in a low voice. There is a lorry behind us and I can barely hear him. 'I'm going to tell you why but you must promise not to hound me for more information.'

'I promise.'

'There's been a bit of trouble with your grandmother and she's asked us to leave.'

'Just for a while,' says my mother.

'What kind of trouble?' I ask.

My father swerves the car and almost takes us into a ditch. The lorry blows its horn as it passes, and the driver looks at us.

'I'll only say this once,' says my father. 'Right?'

He throws his cigarette out the window without extinguishing it.

'Yes,' I say.

'Right then,' he says, 'I've had a bit of a falling out with my mother and until things are patched up, we'll be living in Dublin. You won't ask what the falling out is over, and I won't tell you.'

'Is it because of money?'

My father pulls over to the side of the road and begins to shout; a kind of screaming, so loud it's hard to hear what he's saying. He is screaming at me, I think, but he looks at my mother. And then he leans his head against the steering wheel and he cries. At least, it sounds like crying, but I can't see his face.

'Why can't I just live?' he says. 'That's all I want. Why can't I be allowed to live?'

And he says this, and words like this, over and over — sometimes loud, sometimes quiet — while my mother tries to calm him by putting her hand on his arm.

'Will I drive?' she asks.

'No,' he says, his voice hoarse and tired. 'I'll drive.'

And we drive without another word.

We drive slowly through rain on dark country roads. When we stop in towns at traffic lights I look into the other cars and notice that, even when the person I am staring at can't see me, they often sense that I am staring and they look around. Each time somebody looks at me, I turn away, embarrassed. I would like to be able to keep on looking and to smile at these people, but this is difficult to do. I wonder what it is that makes the other person know they are being watched. Perhaps it has something to do with my gift.

After an hour of driving I start to feel cold in the back of the car. 'I'm cold,' I say.

'OK,' says my mother. 'We'll stop and get the picnic blanket out of the trunk.'

'Not yet,' says my father.

It is pitch dark when we stop for our tea in a hotel just beyond the Wicklow mountains. My father chooses a table near the back corner. I can't look at him. I concentrate on looking around.

The hotel smells of beer and chips. The tables are covered in white cloths, and the heavy cutlery is neatly lined up. The glasses are turned over and the salt-and-pepper shakers are full. The lamps make it feel as though it is the middle of the night. There is a packet of Tayto crisps in the middle of the floor, but nobody picks it up. Eventually, an old man kicks the packet, and the crisps fall out and become sharp crumbs on the carpet.

There's a noisy little girl playing with the front door. She runs in and out, and when she leaves the door open the people at the end of the bar complain about the draught. Each time the door is left open, the little girl's brother gets up and closes it. Nobody asks him to; he just does it, and he leaves his meal to go cold on the table.

I pay attention to all the details: what the little girl is wearing, and the colour of her hair; what the people say when they shout out for her to close the door and what the people do with their hands when they are shouting at her. I decide that for the rest of our journey I will test myself to see how much of the hotel I can remember.

After we've eaten, my father talks to the barman about Dublin, and my mother points to a map on the wall to show me where we have travelled from.

'I know where we've come from,' I say, 'and I know where Dublin is.'

'Of course you do,' she says. 'I wasn't sure if you'd remember. It's a long time since you've been.'

My mother gets the rug out of the trunk and, before we drive away, I try my best to curl up in the back seat, but I don't fit, and my knees hit my father's seat. I sit up instead with my back against the passenger door.

My mother puts the rug over me and tucks it in around my arms. My father looks at me in the rear-mirror, bites his lip, and starts the engine.

'We need to go,' he says.

My mother gets in the passenger seat and does not speak to him again.

I can't sleep. I wonder what will happen to me now, where I will go to school and whether I'll ever see Mr Roche or Brendan or Crito again. I wonder whether the stolen money will be found. 'Then what?' I ask my mother. 'Will Granny come and visit us?'

'No questions, John. Not yet.'

'But what will happen? What about school?'

'We'll see,' she says.

I stop asking questions and fall asleep in the back seat of the car. I don't wake again until we arrive in Dublin and reach the gates of Phoenix Park.

My father says, 'There's a lion in the zoo in that park.'

'And tigers and an elephant,' says my mother.

I'd like to go to the zoo. I want to see a tiger. I read once about a Siberian tiger that escaped from his cage and ran amok in a city until he was shot in the hind leg with a tranquilliser. I want to look at the cages in the Dublin zoo and see what would be involved in getting out. I think Houdini once escaped from a monkey cage in a zoo. I hope they have packed the edition that has that story in it.

Aunty Evelyn greets us at the door of her three-storey terrace house, which is above the basement bookshop that she manages. She is wearing a big black coat over her nightdress and Uncle Gerald stands behind her and says nothing. He rarely speaks and it is easy to forget he is there. He once came to visit us in Gorey with Aunty Evelyn and the next day I asked my mother, 'Why doesn't Uncle Gerald ever come to visit?'

My mother laughed. 'He was here yesterday,' she said. 'You told him that awful knock-knock joke. Knock Knock. Who's there? I diddup? I diddup who?'

I laughed. 'Oh, yeah. And he said, "You're a dirty boy."'

'Yes, he did.'

'But I'm not, am I?'

'Clean as a whistle,' she said.

In the long, narrow street where Aunty Evelyn lives there are no lights on in any of the houses and three men coming out of the hotel two doors down from the bookshop are singing.

I remember the street and Aunty Evelyn's house from the time we came to stay when I was seven. But I don't remember her house being painted dark red, like dried blood.

Aunty Evelyn takes hold of my hand. 'Cheer up. You look like somebody just stole your brand new bicycle,' she says.

'Maybe they did,' I say.

She pulls my hand. 'Come and I'll show you to your bed.'

On the way up the stairs she suddenly stops and looks over her shoulder at me. 'You'll share with your cousin Liam,' she says. 'He's not in much of a talking mood at the moment, but he won't bite.'

Liam is fifteen and, even though he's my first cousin, I don't know him very well.

'I don't care.'

We get to the third floor, the top floor, and turn left into a small, dark bedroom. Liam is lying on his back on his bed, with his hand down his loose tracksuit pants. His room smells like sour milk and his hair is dull yellow, like wet hay.

'Howya,' he says, without moving.

He doesn't remove his hand from his pants and it rests there, doing nothing; keeping warm perhaps. The heating is off, and the house is icy cold.

'Right, so,' says Aunty Evelyn. 'I'll leave you two alone now. But don't make too much noise. You'll wake the twins.'

I put my case down next to Liam's bed and since he doesn't look at me, and doesn't seem to want me in his room, I go back down the stairs to the bathroom on the first floor. There are spots of urine on the toilet seat and on the floor, and the bathroom smells like Crito's box when her blanket hasn't been changed for a long time. I stand over the toilet and stare into the water. There's one pence in the bottom and a bronze stain around it. I take two pence from my pocket and, as I throw it in, I say, 'Get me home to Gorey. Get me back there within one week. Please.'

I find my mother. She is in the only bedroom on the first floor, the same floor as the bathroom, living room and kitchen.

She is unpacking her case on the floor next to a single bed, which is covered in a yellow eiderdown. The only other thing in the small room is a small desk and a typewriter.

'Hello,' I say. 'Where will Da sleep?'

She looks up at me and smiles. 'I'm busy this minute, John. Go back up and unpack your case.'

I go to Liam's room and unpack. He doesn't talk to me. He sits up in bed eating a packet of crisps. I have the five most recent editions of the *Guinness Book* and most of my clothes. When I've put my books and my clothes on top of Liam's chest of drawers, I sit on the bed next to him and still he doesn't speak.

Half an hour later my father comes in. 'Come down to the kitchen for a chat.'

'I don't want to,' I say.

'You will,' he says.

I follow him down the stairs to the first floor.

* * *

My mother makes a pot of tea and Aunty Evelyn wipes the place-mats on the kitchen table with a smelly dishrag. The table is dirty and covered with schoolbooks, fish-and-chip wrappings, and milk bottles. I sit down and clear a space in front of me, knocking a pencil to the floor. I don't pick it up.

'You're going to need to be patient,' says my mother as she uses her hands to gather crumbs from the table.

'Patient about what?' I ask.

'There'll be lots of changes, and some of them will take time,' she says, as she drains the last of the milk from a bottle.

'What changes?' I ask.

My father leans forward and reaches out for my hands. His hands are sweaty. 'Such as where we'll live,' he says.

'But can't we go back? You said we were only staying for a while.'

'We might be Dubliners from now on,' says my mother.

'Won't that be good?' says Aunty Evelyn.

I am angry and don't know what to say or how to say it. What about the money and The Gol of Seil under the mattress?

'What about Crito?'

'OK,' says my father. 'That's enough for now. Go up to bed and we'll have porridge for breakfast tomorrow.'

'What's so good about porridge all of a sudden?' I say.

My father stands up. 'Porridge has always been good,' he says.

Uncle Gerald is smiling at me but all I can see is Granny hitting Crito over the head with a shovel and saying, 'You have too much dander.'

I go up to the third floor and sleep, head to toe, in the single bed, with Liam. He snores and gyrates in his sleep, as though he's having a fit. I move to the edge of the bed but fall back to the deep sag in the middle of the old mattress and find myself up against Liam's legs.

22

I wake early, before the streetlights have been turned off, and I think that Liam is also awake. I hear him say, 'To the bearer,' and 'One million pounds.'

'What?' I say.

'To the bearer. One million pounds,' he says again, as clear as though he were awake.

He is sleeping on his back, with his mouth wide open. I want to put something in it, like the lightbulb that hangs from its broken socket above my head.

I get out of bed at half eight and go into the kitchen in my pyjamas. Nobody is there, but the lights are on. I don't want to be alone.

I go down the stairs that lead to the bookshop in the basement. The staircase is dark. There are rats scratching behind the walls and they sound like the ones we had behind the walls in our old flat in Wexford. Sometimes, when we had been sitting in silence in the living room, one of the rats would come out onto the carpet in the middle of the room and look around, as quiet as a pillow, as though it were sightseeing. Then it would see or smell one of us and run back to the hole it had come from.

The rats always came out alone, never as a family, and there was one especially big brown rat with a long black tail. I decided he was the boss rat. After I saw him a few times I expected to see him all of the time. If I walked into the living room and saw something brown or black on the floor, I thought it was the rat, and I'd feel jumpy. Sometimes if I saw something black and brown anywhere near the floor, or out of the corner of my eye in my bedroom, I'd think it was that rat. My father said I had a rare case of rat psychosis. 'You saw one rat in the middle of the floor,' he said, 'and now you think everything smaller than a shoe is a rat.'

A few weeks after my father said this the rats stopped scratching behind our living room wall.

I stand for a while and listen to the scratching and then kick the wall once before I open the back door that leads to the book-shop.

'Morning,' says Aunty Evelyn, who is standing on a short stepladder reaching up to some bookshelves.

My twin cousins, Celia and Kay, sit on the floor and look up at me. They are seven years old, but small for their age and, like their father, hardly ever speak. Instead of speaking, the twins look at people; fix their eyes and stare. No matter where you move to, their eyes are on you. But they don't seem to see anything. They aren't really watching, I don't think, not properly watching. Their eyes move as though pulled by magnets, as though they have no choice.

'Morning,' I say as I sit down behind the counter. Aunty Evelyn climbs down from the ladder and sits next to me. She takes hold of my hands.

'Where are they?' I ask.

'Who? Mammy and Daddy?'

'Yes.'

'They'll be back soon.'

'Where are they?'

'They were in the greasy spoon a few doors down a while ago, but I'm sure they've gone somewhere else by now.'

'But where?'

'Ask them yourself when they get back. And move over out of the way. You're taking up a lot of room.'

Kay and Celia, sitting shoulder to shoulder on the bare floor, look up at me.

'How old would you say I am?' asks Aunty Evelyn.

'I don't know,' I say. 'About the same age as my mam.'

'No! I'm eight years older, but I don't look as old as I am, do I? I use this cream. See here! It works. So, how old do you think I look? Not as old as I am, right?'

'I suppose not.'

She stands. 'Go up now, John, and get some breakfast.'

'I'm not hungry.'

'You are hungry,' she says.

'Aunty Evelyn?'

'Yes.'

'Can you tell me one more story about Niagara Falls before I go upstairs?'

'I'm busy now,' she says.

It is ten past nine.

She tidies books on the shelves and serves the only customer who comes in. He is old, has one false eye, white, like a marble, and uses a walking stick. He buys a crossword puzzle book for 5p. When he leaves, she sits down again.

'All right,' she says. 'Let me see. OK, there was a woman in one of the museums. It was night-time and the foyer was very dark ...' She puts a pile of books down on the counter and wipes her dusty hands on her apron.

'Why was it dark?'

'Because this was a museum of ghouls and ghosts and old medieval torture contraptions. Anyway, this woman had long

177

painted fingernails, very long and painted orange, and the fingernails were painted with glow-in-the-dark polish. Can you imagine?'

I want more. 'Can you tell me something else?'

She picks the biggest book off the counter and holds it to her chest. 'If you're not happy with the story I've told, there won't be any more. Go on, get away with you. Up the stairs please and let me get on with my work.'

I go up to the kitchen. Liam is at the table, eating cereal. In between mouthfuls, he picks his nose, and then eats what he fetches from his nostrils.

'It's after ten,' I say.

'What's it to you, goody-two-shoes?'

'Nothing,' I say.

He holds the bowl of cereal up to his face and slurps the milk; the noise makes me think of my grandmother and I wonder what she's doing, what Crito is doing, and whether Brendan is still playing with Kate. And Mr Roche. I wonder has he asked about me.

'For your information,' says Liam with a mouth full of mush, 'our school has two sessions, the morning and the afternoon.'

'Why?'

''Cause there's too much kids.'

He has a Dublin accent and mumbles most of the time. I fiddle with the bowl of sugar, but I can't eat. I'd like not to fight with Liam and so I keep talking, try to be friendly.

'What time does the afternoon session start?'

'Twelve,' he says.

'What're you going to do till then?'

'Kick the football over the road with me friends,' he says. 'I dunno.'

I am just about to ask him if I can join in when my mother and father arrive home.

178

My father is wearing a suit and tie.

I stand up. 'Hello,' I say.

'All right?' asks my mother.

'All right,' I say.

My father looks at me and frowns. 'Not getting out of your pyjamas today?'

'Why should I?'

'You're not sick, are you?'

'No, but . . .'

'Go and get dressed, please. Then come back and help your mother.'

When I come back, my father is gone again and my mother is at the sink, peeling potatoes. Aunty Evelyn comes up the stairs with some rashers from the grocery shop next door. 'Sit,' she says to my mother. 'I'll start the dinner nice and early. It'll be ready by twelve.'

My mother sits next to me.

'Where's Da gone?' I ask.

'To see a man about a dog,' she says.

'Why won't you tell me what's happening?'

'When your father gets home.'

'We have to go back to Gorey,' I say. 'You have to help with the summer pantomime. You haven't finished making the puppets.'

'We'll see,' she says and, because I hate the expression unless it's used as part of our game, I hate her for using it.

We sit in silence.

Aunty Evelyn moves quickly while she cooks, and seems nervous. She's not normally a nervous person. She knocks a cup from the dresser and then a vase from the sideboard and catches both before they hit the floor; she moves very quickly for a woman with a body like Alfred Hitchcock's.

'Reflexes!' she shouts.

'Oh dear,' says my mother, laughing in an odd way and putting her hands over her face.

While we eat, the conversation is about weather, weddings and christenings. I don't speak. I get bored and go into the living room and watch TV. It is raining hard outside and the room is dark. But watching the television in the middle of day isn't as much fun as it should be. I try to force myself to enjoy it but I think of Mr Roche and how I'd like to see him and how I was looking forward to sitting his first test and passing with flying colours.

I scratch at the scab on my head and stop when it bleeds.

It is nearly four o'clock when my father comes home. He smells of aftershave.

'Your mother and I have to go out again. We've a few things to do,' he says. 'Keep yourself busy for a few more hours.'

'But I'm bored. Can't I come?'

'Not this time,' says my mother. 'Read a book, or watch the television.'

My father throws a Mars bar at me but I don't have time to catch it. It lands on the carpet about a foot away from me. I stare at it and he stares at it too. I'm not going to pick it up. 'But where are you going?' I ask.

'To see a man about a dog,' says my father.

My mother winks at me.

'A different man about a different dog,' she says, but I don't want to join in with her joking.

* * *

When they leave I go back down to the bookshop to be with Aunty Evelyn. I sit on a chair behind the counter with her. She seems happy to have me with her and she offers me a bag of peanuts. The peanuts make me think of the zoo. I wonder if she might take me. Liam says it's about fifteen minutes by bus. I wonder if anybody has ever helped an animal escape.

'Could you take me to the zoo?' I ask.

'Not now,' she says, without even thinking about it. 'Maybe you'd like to go next door for a while.'

'Why?'

'I need to do something in private, that's why.'

I walk down to the greasy spoon and go inside. The walls are covered in striped paper, red and yellow, and the radio is turned up loud. It is crowded with old men and old ladies and a few young women near the front with prams. Nearly everybody is facing the front, as though they are on a train. The tables are covered in plastic yellow cloths and every table has a bottle of HP and Worcestershire sauce. The smell of chips and sausages is a good smell and I feel hungry. I want to look at the red plastic menu book on the table near the door, but then I'd have to buy something even if I changed my mind.

The woman at the till looks at me and, even though she doesn't speak or ask me anything, I say, 'I'm just looking for my parents.'

'Have you lost them, love?'

'No. Thanks anyway. I'm going now.'

I don't understand why I feel nervous.

I go into the grocery shop next door and as I walk in the bell rings.

Maureen, the old woman who works behind the counter, remembers me from the last time I visited. She comes rushing over. 'John!' she cries. 'How you've grown! To the size of a man. Quite amazing.'

She grabs hold of my right arm. 'And the manly muscles on you, too!'

I pull my arm away.

'Come sit with me and help me put the stickers on.'

I sit with her and put stickers on tiny cubes of beef and chicken stock. Maureen takes the cubes out of the bigger packets and sells them individually, even though on the box it says, 'Not for Individual Sale'.

'So, what brings you all the way to Dublin, John?'

'We just came because we wanted to come.'

'Oh yes.' She peels a sticker from the back of her wrinkled hand and puts it on a cube of stock. 'Were you tired of the country air?'

'Yes. Sick of it. Sick of the cows and the mud.'

For four days, my mother and father are out during the day, and don't come back until it's dark. I am left alone. Liam goes to school in the afternoon and I watch television or read the *Guinness Book of Records*.

I read and make notes about Jean François Gravelet, alias Blondin the Great, who crossed Niagara Falls on a three-inch rope in 1855. When Liam is at school I clear a space and make a three-inch strip with packing tape stretching from one wall to the other. I walk along it with my arms held out and I try to imagine being 160 feet in the air without a safety harness.

I can't get my feet to stay inside the three-inch boundary. I don't see how it can be done. But when I look more closely at the photo of Blondin, I notice for the first time that his feet are not straight; to walk the tightrope he has to flatten his slippered feet and keep them side-on to the rope. The more I think about it, the more puzzled I am. I will ask Aunty Evelyn to get me a book about Blondin and the other tightrope walkers.

At night, my mother and father go downstairs to the basement to talk and to make phone calls. My mother tells me that my father is looking for work, and they are both looking for a place for us to live.

When I ask why we can't live in the cottage with Granny, she says, 'Maybe later. We'll be living in Dublin for a while.' And when I ask if I can ring Granny on the phone in the kitchen, she says, 'Yes, but maybe later. Just leave it be for a few more days.'

It's our seventh night in Dublin. I'm in Liam's bedroom, trying to see if there's a way I can play Cluedo by myself. My father comes in and sits down on the end of the sagging bed.

'Howya?' he says in a mock Dublin accent.

'All right,' I say as I put my Swiss-army knife down on the board where he can see it.

'I was wondering if we could ring Granny? Maybe we could do it now?'

He takes a deep breath. 'Not just now, John. But soon. I promise we'll do it soon.'

I look at the Cluedo board and at the pictures of the rope and candlestick. I want to know if Crito is all right and I want to know whether The Gol of Seil is safe and my money, too. I want to know whether the *Guinness Book* has written.

'Don't be so sad,' he says. 'Why not treat this as a holiday? An adventure?'

I stare at him until he looks away. I stare at him as though his face is a playing card or a photograph, or a piece of graffiti on the wall; something not real or human.

He stands up. 'Don't look at me like I just kicked you in the head,' he says. 'Everything's going to be fine.'

'But when are we going home?'

'We are home,' he says.

'But Mam says we have to live in a flat.'

'Don't sulk. There's nothing to be sulky about. Think of all the poor children who have nothing. No flat to live in and no shoes on their feet.'

'Like the ones in Africa?'

'Sure.'

'I'd rather not,' I say and I take the weapon card with the picture of the rope on it and show it to him.

He stares at it. 'And what does this mean?'

'Nothing,' I say. 'Do you want to play a game?'

'Not just now. Maybe later. We can all play tonight. Your cousins too.'

I hold the picture of the rope in front of him and I notice that, although I feel nervous, my hand is steady.

23

On Monday we go to church for a christening and we sit near the front in the same pew. I sit between Aunty Evelyn and Uncle Gerald, and Liam sits nearest the wall, which he kicks with his foot. Celia and Kay stare up at the Stations of the Cross and whisper in their private language.

When the priest comes out to the altar, his vestments flowing around him, it is as though an animal has come out of its cave. I want to see where he lives, to see behind the sacristy door into his cave and find out what it is like in there.

On the way home, my father suddenly stops outside a bookie's shop, with Turf Accountants written across the smoky glass. 'I'm just going to pop in here for a minute,' he says. 'You go on ahead.'

He goes inside and we stand on the street. Uncle Gerald shuffles his feet, embarrassed, and my mother's face and neck turn red.

'The bookie's the last place he should be,' says Aunty Evelyn.

'I'm not going to stop him,' says my mother. 'Let him do what he wants. Let him ruin . . .' She stops what she is saying and looks instead at a passing bus.

'What's being ruined?' I say. 'What's he ruining?'

She looks through the window of the bookie's shop and then rubs the back of her soft fingers against my cheek. She opens her mouth, then closes it.

'What?' I ask. 'What were you going to say?'

'Never mind.'

'What?'

She takes a deep breath. 'He . . .'

'He what?'

'He hit your granny,' she says.

She looks down then, down at sheets of newspaper flying around by the lamp-post near my feet.

'And now we're out on the dirty old street.'

'What?' I say.

'You are *not* out on the street,' says Aunty Evelyn.

'Why did he hit Granny? When?'

My mother puts her hand on my shoulder and Aunty Evelyn takes hold of my hand and pulls at me, the way she did when we arrived in the night. This is weird, the two of them touching me, one holding me down, the other pulling at me. A bolt of shame travels up my spine, all the way to my face.

'Come on,' says my mother. 'It's time to be getting home.'

'I'm going to find out for myself,' I say. 'I'm going in there and I'm not coming home.'

I go inside. The Turf Accountant's is full of smoke and noisy with the sound of the horse races on the radio. I stand by the doorway for a few minutes and scratch at the scab on my head until I draw blood and then I go up to him.

My father has already untucked his white shirt and is in a queue for the cashier's desk. He stands near the back of the crooked row of men, all of them holding tickets and, like him, looking at the man at the head of the queue to see how long he might be.

I stand by my father's side. 'Da?' I say.

He doesn't seem surprised to hear my voice. He looks straight ahead at the counter, at the bars in front of the cashier's window and at the grille under the sheet of glass where the money is put before it is taken by the cashier. 'What?' he says.

'Is it true you hit Granny?'

Still he doesn't look at me.

'Well, did you?'

He clears his throat. 'Yes,' he whispers. 'Now go home. Get out of this filthy place.'

'We have no home,' I say.

The hand that hangs down by his side curls into a fist, and the red worms he has for fingers hide under his hairy knuckles.

'Go home,' he says.

'Why did you hit her?'

He looks at me. 'Because she wanted to be hit,' he says. He turns away again, to face the cashier. 'I hit her because she nagged me. She knew I was about to hit her and still she nagged me. And then she told me to get out of her house. And I hit her and she knew I would.'

'Did you fail the test at Trinity?'

The Adam's apple in his neck bulges and he stares ahead.

'Did you?'

He turns to me and there are tears in his eyes. 'Do you know? You even look a bit like her.'

'Like who?'

'Like your granny. You're like a pair of gargoyles keeping watch over other people's lives.'

I feel sorry for him and guilty and sorry for myself. I keep looking at him. If he cries, I'll say I'm sorry. Then, maybe, when he's finished in here we could go to the greasy spoon near Aunty Evelyn's for a piece of cake. But he just coughs, puts his hand in his pocket and turns back to the cashier's window.

'Go home,' he says.

I walk out.

On the way back to Aunty Evelyn's I buy a Mars bar with the

money he gave me yesterday to replace the one on the living room floor that Liam or one of the twins took.

When I get back everybody is sitting at the kitchen table. Uncle Gerald is at the end nearest the toilet, with the twins sitting close to him. He is playing with them. He whispers and smiles as he makes his hands into the church and the steeple. 'Here is the church, and here is the steeple,' he says. 'Open the doors, and here are the people.'

The twins laugh when Uncle Gerald's fingers poke up and wiggle like naked people and it makes me feel sick. He does it again and when he says, 'Open the doors', the twins open their mouths wide and show bits of mashed food and stretch the saliva between their teeth.

Liam is nearest the living room door, where he always sits. My mother and Aunty Evelyn are together, holding hands, in the middle. My mother has been crying.

They all talk about nothing. About weddings and the brides-maid who was eating a chewy sweet and had a choking fit during the ceremony and spat the sweet onto the bride's dress.

There is chicken pie in the cooker for tea and, even though everybody is hungry, my mother says we should wait for my father to come home.

When it is seven o'clock and he still hasn't come, we eat, except Uncle Gerald; he doesn't eat because he doesn't like to eat in front of people, not even in front of his own family.

I look at the placemat on which there is a picture of a foxhunt – men in caps on horses, dogs, and dead foxes hanging from a fence. My mother sees me looking at the foxes. She makes her hands into paws and puts a frightened look on her face.

I smile and she smiles back. I wonder if this means she is feeling better and, if she is, whether I soon will be. Liam lifts his plate, holds it close to his face, then, when he thinks nobody is looking, sucks off bits of pie.

'Liam,' says Aunty Evelyn, 'Go to your room and let us alone so we can talk.'

Liam leaves without argument and the twins follow him like puppies.

'Well,' says my mother. 'I shouldn't have told you what your father did, but now that it's out I might as well set things straight.'

She stirs her tea while she speaks and I don't hear the spoon hitting the side of the cup. She tells me that my father hit my granny during a row and she fell against the dresser. It was an accident and she was taken to hospital to have stitches. When I ask why Da doesn't apologise so we can go back, she says, 'He's already made his apology, but it hasn't been accepted yet.'

She tells me we won't be here long; that we might live in a hotel for a while until we find our own flat.

'What kind of hotel?' I ask.

'A cheap one,' says Uncle Gerald from his place at the end of the table near the toilet door.

'There's a nice hotel near the gates of Phoenix Park,' says my mother. 'Right near the zoo and the elephant. We can take him peanuts.'

'Is Da going to go to prison?'

'Your granny isn't pressing charges,' says Aunty Evelyn. 'She knows it was an accident.'

The telephone rings and my mother rushes to answer it. 'They hung up,' she says.

The telephone rings again. She answers it.

'They hung up again,' she says.

The telephone rings one more time.

I answer it. 'Hello,' I say.

'It's your da. Is your mammy there? Is she all right?'

'Yes. Mam's grand. We just had chicken pie and now we're having some tea and cake.'

'I'll be home soon. Can you please tell her that?'

'OK. Bye-bye.'

I stand by the phone, expecting it to ring again.

'It was Da,' I say.

'Why were you yelling down the phone?' asks my mother.

'Because he was breathing so hard. It was like talking to a tractor or something.'

'He's probably just hoarse and choked up from all the cigarette smoke in that filthy place,' says Aunty Evelyn.

I take my piece of cake into the living room.

My father goes missing for two days, and I spend two days believing that he's in Mountjoy gaol. I have nightmares about him being in a cell with a toilet in the corner and a man with tattoos and a shaved head in the bunk above him.

He returns home on Thursday morning while I'm down in the bookshop with Aunty Evelyn. He is wearing a new brown coat with furry black cuffs and collar and he has the beginning of a moustache. 'Good news,' he says, as he reaches out for me with his cold red hands, 'we've got ourselves a new home.'

'Where?' I ask.

'Ballymun. Emergency housing high up on the twelfth floor of a fifteen-storey tower,' he says.

'The twelfth floor!' I say. 'We'll be living in a skyscraper?'

'Yes. And a swimming pool is being built and should be ready in a few weeks. And from your bedroom window you can watch the jumbo jets flying overhead on their way to America.'

'When are we going?'

'We move in first thing tomorrow morning.'

Aunty Evelyn turns the sign on the door that says Back in 5 Minutes.

'We'd better get moving,' she says. 'Let's go up and find Helen.'

We go upstairs and find my mother sitting in a straight chair under the window in the living room. The television isn't on and she isn't doing anything with her hands.

'You've got a flat, Helen! A brand new Corporation flat and you can move in tomorrow,' says Aunty Evelyn. 'And you can take the furniture from the junk room upstairs and the beds in the spare room.'

My father stands by the fire and plays with a box of matches. My mother nods but says nothing.

'Some of the neighbours are sure to donate a few odds and ends. But we don't have much time. I'll start the door-knocking right now.'

My mother frowns.

Aunty Evelyn gets up from the settee and goes to her. She holds her hand out to my mother, as though reaching out to help a cripple to stand. But my mother doesn't take her sister's hand. She thanks her and leaves the room.

'Don't go chasing her,' says my father.

I stay and turn on the television.

24

At eight o'clock in the morning, I stand with the blue suitcase at my feet and watch my father and my uncles load a dirty truck with furniture. My mother helps by giving directions and by putting small things on the trolley. I offer to help but she tells me to sit and wait by my suitcase in case errands need to be run. 'Like what?' I ask.

'Like fetching somebody a cup of tea or a glass of water when they need it.'

I sit on the kerb with a packet of plasters. I put one on below my knee, leave it for a few minutes, and then peel it off again. The pain is good when the plaster is ripped away and I like the way it pulls at the hairs and leaves a clear, soft patch of skin.

Uncle Gerald sees what I am doing. He wags his finger at me, making a cross face. I smile and wag my finger back and, as usual, he doesn't know what to do. He stands back and looks at me, his hands by his side, and then he turns and goes back to the truck and moves a chest of drawers a few inches for no good reason. Sometimes it is as though Uncle Gerald doesn't take life very seriously; he tries things out, sees that nobody has noticed him, changes course, does something else, and seems not to care about the difference.

A group of neighbours has gathered. There are five women and two men. They stand on the footpath in front of number 17, in a mob. The way they stand close together makes it seem that they are all from the same family. They stare as though they have only one mind between them; when one stares at me, they all stare at me, and when one stares at my mother, they all stare at my mother. When one watches my Uncle Jack light up a cigarette, they all watch.

One of the women holds a wooden spoon with cold porridge glued to its end, and another holds a dishrag. They say they have come to wish us *bon voyage*, but it is plain that they have come to see what a ruined family looks like.

My mother looks across at them and waves, and suddenly they move in towards the door of the truck and surround her. She steps back to stop them getting in the way.

'I hear there is central heating in every flat,' says a thin woman with red hair.

'And there'll be a swimming pool in a wee while,' says the one with the wooden spoon.

Uncle Jack and Uncle Tony are in the back of the truck with the furniture and I am happy to sit in the cab between my father and mother. I like being up high and my father's arms look strong when he turns the steering wheel to get us around tight corners.

We drive in heavy traffic, and there's a good view of all of the shops in North Circular Road. I look down at the children on their way to school and feel free. I hold my mother's hand.

But, as we get closer to Ballymun, my mood changes. The streets here are narrow and the gutters are full of rubbish. The houses are small and grey and nobody has painted the doors or windowsills. And as we pull into the car park at the base of one of the Ballymun high-rise towers, it is clear that nothing good can happen here.

My father jumps out of the cab and I climb down after him.

I feel heavy and tired. I look around at the seven towers and the dozens of smaller blocks of flats that surround us, the busy road at the edge of the car park, the big school across the busy road, and the roundabout.

My mother stays in her seat, her hands on her lap. My father lets Uncle Jack and Uncle Tony out of the back of the truck and then puts his hand on my shoulder.

'Each tower is named after the men who signed the proclamation of the Irish Republic in 1916,' he says.

'Which one is ours?' I ask.

'Plunkett,' he says. 'That one there. The one in the middle.'

It's not possible to see all seven towers in one glance. There are too many and they make it dark as night. To see them all, it is necessary to turn in a full circle. How can they be new when they are so soiled and dirty? They are like rotted teeth, decayed and brown and stained with tar, teeth pulled from an awful and dirty giant.

'How will we get everything up the stairs?' I ask my father.

'There are lifts, stupid.'

We go up to our new home. Unlike the dirty lifts and the dirty stairwell and the dirty corridors, the walls of our flat are white and clean and once inside there is no smell of urine or wet cigarette butts.

But it's a small flat with everything in it small: a tiny kitchen and a tiny living room with just enough room for a settee, the television and a few chairs. And the toilet is the smallest I've ever seen, with a bath only fit for a midget. And there are two small bedrooms, both with windows that can't be opened and which look down twelve floors to the car park and tarmac below.

Like everybody else who lives in the towers, we must send our rubbish down a chute, and the chute is at the top of the stairs, near my bedroom window.

'I don't want to sleep near the rubbish chute,' I say.

'Well, there's nowhere else,' says my father.

We go to the biggest bedroom. It has a built-in wardrobe covered in dark, tinted mirrors.

'If I'm going to sleep in here,' says my mother, 'I'm going to cover those.'

'First we need to finish moving,' says my father and so we go back downstairs in the lift.

Although we have more to move, my father insists that Uncle Jack and Uncle Tony should leave us. But Uncle Jack comes back soon after with five bags of hot chips and we all sit on the small patch of grass near the truck and eat together.

'All right, so. You'll leave us now,' says my father. 'We can manage the rest on our own.'

They leave after my father gives Uncle Tony a few quid for a taxi.

The central heating is turned up high in the flat. We are too hot inside, and then feel the cold like a shower of icy water when we go outside. After each trip my father puts his head under the cold-water tap. We stand in the empty kitchen and watch him drench himself as we fan ourselves with pieces of cardboard torn from boxes.

'Right, so. We'll talk to the Corporation about getting that heat turned down,' he says. 'We can't live in the tropics.'

My mother looks out the window to the dark block of flats behind us and sighs.

'I've already spoken to our new neighbour, Mrs McGahern, and she says the thermostat is set by the Corporation and can't be changed by the tenants.'

My father shakes his head.

'We'll get used to it,' she says. 'We'll just have to wear our summer togs.'

My father's rage is too ready. 'That's a fine attitude so early in the piece. Since when do you give in just like that? On the word of a nosy old woman?'

'I didn't say anything about an old woman or about anybody being nosy.'

'I've seen her standing out there peering inside every box we carry up. And you! The word of a stranger and you cave in?'

'Michael, I don't think . . .'

'I'm going to see some neighbours of my own and find out if there isn't a better explanation.'

'Waste your time getting a second opinion,' says my mother. 'I know what the answer will be.'

He storms out and slams the door behind him.

It is strange to be standing with my mother in an empty kitchen behind a door slammed shut with such echoing noise, standing with nothing to do, and so strange to have no choice but to leave by the same door without speaking.

Although it is dark when we finish unpacking and putting furniture where we want it, my father says we must take a walk around before we eat and go to our beds.

'We'll explore for a while and then we can have tea in a public bar. How's that?' We take the lift and I hold my nose all the way down and so does my mother. My father presses the button to take us to the basement.

'Let's have a look,' he says.

'What's there?' I ask.

'It's the activity centre. There's one in every tower, I think.'

But when we get there, the centre is closed. There's a sign on the door with the opening hours: it should be open on a Saturday night. There is also a sign listing free activities. There will be guitar lessons tomorrow for boys aged between ten and sixteen.

'There you are,' says my father. 'Music lessons.'

'That's great,' I say. 'But I'm starving.'

'Let's look around a while longer. Then we can eat.'

As we come out of the lift, I look up at the tops of the towers, which poke out of the concrete ground and reach high, higher than any other building in all of Dublin, straight into the sky as though desperate to drink from the white clouds, or to get washed by the rain.

We walk between all of them, and all over the brick walls are stains of darker grey, like weeping sores. The only colour comes from peeling green paint on windowsills, and black and red graffiti on the ground-floor walls. The concrete balconies are strung across with damp washing, and the long corridors and stairwells are full of the broken things that people have thrown away.

There are no trees, and only one narrow stretch of grass at the back of the flats. Along the edge of the grass, a tall barbed-wire fence separates the flats from the council houses in the blocks behind.

There are so many people making so much noise, more noise than I have ever known, and people everywhere with plastic bags of shopping, up and down the dark passageways or on the darkened stairs.

'Everybody here is ugly compared to Mammy,' I say.

She stops walking. 'That's not a very charitable thing to say.'

My father keeps walking and, when he is a few feet ahead of us, he stops and looks back at her. 'You're right, John. Your mother is very beautiful. She makes them all look ugly.'

She puts her head down and we keep walking. We walk across the car park towards the school, which my father wants me to see, and we pass a pub. The smell of frying chips makes my mouth water. 'I'm starving to death,' I say.

'Hold your horses,' says my father. 'Let's finish looking.'

'No,' says my mother. 'We need to eat.'

We go into The Slipper, which is one of three pubs within two minutes of the towers. It is noisy inside, with music and men and women talking, and the walls are covered with pictures of aeroplanes. I ask my father how many engines a Jumbo 747 has and he says, 'Enough,' and we laugh with him.

25

Our first day is spent putting things in drawers and cupboards and deciding where the furniture should go. The second day we shop for groceries. We must buy everything from scratch; salt and pepper and custard powder and semolina; saucepans, lightbulbs, batteries and tools for repairing some of the broken things people have given us.

In the supermarket my father drops a bottle of tomato sauce on the floor and it breaks; some of the sauce splashes onto my mother's white trousers.

'Michael!' she shouts. 'If I didn't know better I'd say you did that on purpose.'

'Well,' says my father as he walks away from the smashed bottle, 'you don't know better, and that's no surprise to anybody.'

'Don't you dare talk to me like that!' she shouts at him, not bothered at all that two old women by the frozen food section are staring at her.

'I'll talk as I want to talk,' says my father.

My mother folds her arms across her chest and looks squarely at him. 'I'm at the end of my rope, Michael, and it wasn't a long piece of rope to start with. So I'd be grateful if you'd find a damp cloth to wipe this mess off my britches.'

My father smiles at her then, a warm smile, and she smiles back at him as though all is forgiven. I don't know why she does this. What is it that passes between them? What way of knowing each other do they have? Why does my mother look at him so warmly?

My father goes away in search of a damp cloth, and when he comes back to clean her trousers, she is no longer cross with him. They kiss on the lips for a long time and then we pay for our groceries.

On the morning of our third day in Ballymun, I wake with a sore tooth. The pain is very bad and it pierces like cut glass into the left side of my jaw every time I take a breath.

My mother tells me to get dressed. 'Let's get you to the dentist,' she says. 'I'll take you to the community centre.'

The community centre is around the corner, next door to the shopping centre. We walk through the arcade with its walls painted with blue and red stripes. It is bright and clean and, compared to the flats where there is no sun, no light, not inside or between them or behind them or within a hundred feet of them, the shopping centre is like another country. Even though my tooth beats at me, I feel like I've gone on holiday. Inside the shopping centre, there is light and the good smell of doughnuts from the bakery.

Inside the community centre, there's a doctor, a dentist, and a chemist, and the waiting room is full of people reading magazines.

My mother tells the woman at the desk that I am in agony and we wait for only five minutes.

The dentist's name is Dr O'Connor. He is tall, with broad shoulders, and wears a dark suit with a red handkerchief sticking out of his top pocket.

I tell him about my tooth and he takes a look in my mouth with a stick that has a mirror on its end. Then, without warning, he pulls my lip down and sticks a needle in my gum.

'That will stop the pain. Now, relax here in the chair a minute while I pull this tooth out,' he says.

There is a big painting on his ceiling that I look at while he is removing my tooth. He tells me the painting is by Bruegel. I will remember. I memorise the faces of the peasants, women and children dressed in brown, picking potatoes in the snow. No gloves or hats or scarves.

'There's no point staring at a white ceiling,' says Dr O'Connor. 'Better to see somebody worse off than you are.'

'I didn't feel a thing,' I say when he has finished, and he shakes my hand and smiles at me for a long time.

'Good lad. I was worried you might need an extra shot.'

I like him and I wonder what I would be like if I had a different father.

At home, I lie on the couch. My mother is busy in the kitchen. I don't know where my father is.

As soon as I can eat again, my mother makes a fry-up with mushrooms and sausages and we eat while we listen to the radio turned up loud enough to cover the sound of slamming doors and an argument in the neighbouring flat.

At half four my father walks in. 'I start work in two days,' he says.

My mother pats him on the arm, and he looks at her hand.

'I'm not dying,' he says. 'It's not all over yet.'

'What work?' I ask. 'Have you got into Trinity?'

'No. I've got a scholarship in a metalworks factory.'

'But will you still sit the exams at Trinity?' I ask.

'Not just now,' he says. 'Right now I have to win some bread.'

'What?' I say.

'Oh, figure it out,' he says, 'and while you're at it, go to the shop and get some milk and a pack of purple Silk Cut.'

'How much money will you get paid every week?' I ask.

'Go and get the fags and I might tell you when you come back.'

I stand up and, as though my mother can read my mind, she says, 'Why don't we go into town tomorrow? Let's be tourists for a day.'

My father takes my mother's hands and kisses each in turn, then gives them back to her as though they were something he had on loan and, as she returns her hands to her apron pockets, I notice that they are shaking.

I go to the shop to buy my father's cigarettes and when I come back the lift has broken again. I take the stairs that smell of urine.

The sun is out over Dublin and it is warm. My father is wearing sunglasses that make him look like a car windscreen and my mother is wearing a knee-length pink dress and white boots. They look like movie stars again.

We walk slowly along the wide footpaths of O'Connell Street to Grafton Street, which curves and ends at Stephen's Green and the Dandelion market. The streets are busy with people shopping and eating and there are hundreds of buses, one behind the other, like tin elephants, with dozens of small eyes inside, each one keeping watch on the world.

There are people wearing good clothes getting in and out of taxis and people with suitcases coming and going from hotel foyers. Everybody is busy with something to do.

We eat lunch in Bewley's and afterwards we walk through Stephen's Green. We stop for ice-cream, which we eat while we watch the ducks being fed by little children. When it's dark we walk back along Grafton Street. The round streetlamps glow white like pickled onions and as we pass Moore Street we step over gutters running with soapy water used to wash away the vegetable scraps from today's market. I wish that we could live here, in town, near these lamps and the people singing for money in the street.

I hold my mother's hand and my father whistles as we walk once again to the top of O'Connell Street. We pass by the cinema and I stop. 'Can we see a film? Can we see what's showing?'

My father shrugs. 'I see no reason why we shouldn't.'

Butch Cassidy and the Sundance Kid is showing, but children under sixteen are not supposed to go in.

'Just walk in behind me,' says my father. 'Just walk in.'

My mother agrees. We get our tickets and give them to the usher and although the screening started twelve minutes ago I sit between my mother and father in the seventh row from the front and it's the best film I've ever seen.

After the film, we eat our fish and chips on a bench inside the grounds of Trinity College. Although it is dark and cooler now, there are students sitting on their coats beneath the old, tall trees or on the neat lawns or walking and riding bicycles along the paths paved with cobblestones.

Even though they are strangers to him, my father smiles at the students as they come and go. His head turns to watch them as they come down the stairs near our seat, as they come in and out of the door behind us, and as they take their bicycles and head for the street in pairs and threes and fours, sometimes holding hands. Then he looks up at the lighted rooms and nods his head.

'You'll be here one day,' I say.

'That's the strong hope,' he says.

My mother kisses him on the cheek and holds his hand.

'Fish and chips are good,' I say, 'but the smell is better. I wish you could eat the smell.'

They laugh.

'Time to go home,' says my mother and as she stands she tries to pull me up with her. But I'm far too heavy for her and she stumbles. I catch her before she falls.

My father laughs. 'Strange pair,' he says.

We are sitting on the upper deck of the bus on the way home. Four drunk men get on and they shout as they come up the stairs. I turn in my seat to watch them. They can barely walk. They holler and swear and sing and bash against the seats and, as they pass us on their way to the front, one of them drops a glass on the floor. My mother brushes her leg clean of the spray of liquid but says nothing.

The men sit in the row in front of us and for a while they talk about their night. Then one of them turns to look at us. He stares too long at my mother. My father folds his arms across his chest and his knee jumps up and down.

My mother stands and so do I.

'What's this?' says the drunk. 'A family of giants? And look here. A very pretty giantess'

My father stands and a second drunk says, 'Going off for a game of basketball, are ye? What's your team called? The beanstalks?'

'Come on,' says my father. 'We're going downstairs.'

He pushes me in the back as we walk and tells me to hurry. We go down and sit near the driver, who turns to us. 'A bit rowdy up there. It's the same every night.'

We nod and agree and he smiles at us in the rear-vision. Even though the drunks are upstairs, the smell of alcohol is so strong it is as though the men have leaked whiskey and beer from their skin, leaked onto the floor.

Without any warning, my father hits me hard across the back of my head.

'For feck's sake!' he shouts. 'Stop scratching your head.'

'Sorry,' I say, but I'm not. The drunks have made him angry, not me. My mother looks out the window. If my father was not with us, she would tend to me or at the very least say something. But she shakes her head as though to say, 'How stupid.' But who does she disapprove of – him or me?

It's our second Saturday in Ballymun; more than a week here now and I'm returning from the shops with two bottles of milk, a pound of sugar and two pans of bread.

As I get closer to our block, I see one of the Ballymun gangs at the bottom of our stairwell. They are teenage boys, a few years older than me. They lean against the wall and smoke; laughing and swearing and waiting for people to pass so that they can say something obscene. Even though none of the boys is as tall as me, I head for the lifts, in spite of the terrible smell, to avoid them.

I wait for the lift. I know the walls will be sprayed with vomit and urine. It is sometimes several days before the stinking mess is cleaned up with a bucket of water and mop or licked clean by dogs.

The urine is usually sprayed in the corners of the lift walls. It is thick and sticky, so it doesn't travel very far. I have never before seen urine so orange, so sticky, so thick.

When the lift arrives, I pick the shopping up and get in. There is a girl in the lift, squatting on the floor as though she means to go to the toilet. She is my age, about eleven or twelve, and she looks up and smiles at me. I expect her to stand, pull up her pants, get out, but she stays where she is and continues to squat.

As we travel up to the twelfth floor, I look down at her white underpants, stained with brown marks, stretched around her bruised knees. I wonder if she'll know that I have looked at the stains in her pants and I'm embarrassed; more embarrassed, I think, because she is not.

She smiles at me as she lifts herself up and presses the button, and I smile back. She runs from the lift on the eleventh floor, leaving behind a small black piece of shit.

My mother is in bed even though it is not yet night-time, not yet dark. She's not asleep, but on her back, looking up at the ceiling. I stand by the door and tell her about the girl shitting in the lift.

'What did she look like?' she asks.

'She had very white teeth,' I say.

But perhaps I think her teeth were white because her lips were so red.

'I see,' says my mother, as she closes her eyes.

During tea, we hear the sewing machine upstairs. There are three young women who live in the flat directly above ours and one of them runs a sewing machine from five o'clock often until after I go to bed.

My father laughs as he says, 'Those three up there. They're almost blind.'

'Are they?' asks my mother.

'Yes, and they're sisters. They can barely see past the end of their noses.'

'But if they are nearly blind, how can they use a sewing machine?' asks my mother.

'That's the one who can see the most,' he says, 'and she only sews tablecloths, which doesn't take much skill.'

'How do you know?' I ask.

'I work with a man who told me about them,' he says. 'They're quite well known around here. Some say their parents were first cousins.'

'How do they make their living if they're blind and don't have husbands?' I ask.

'How would I know?' says my father. 'How does any woman get on in this world that people allege belongs to men?'

My mother hits the side of her cup with a spoon and he clears his throat.

'Only joking,' he says. 'Only joking.'

But later, when we hear them making noise, my father calls them 'the three blind mice' and he sings the nursery rhyme while looking up at the ceiling.

The next morning, as we are having breakfast, we hear the women above, and it sounds as though they are beating the floor with broomsticks.

'Ah, the three blind mice walking about with their canes,' says my father.

But I'm sure I saw them yesterday getting out of the lift. Three women in their early twenties, with long dark hair and dark eyes, and who reeked of strong perfume. I didn't see them using canes or wearing dark glasses. They looked normal to me, and two of them were wearing high heels.

I frown. My mother stops eating.

'They're not legally blind,' he says. 'If they were legally blind they'd be in a home with spastics and seeing-eye dogs.'

It is the afternoon, and I am with my father. I see the three women again, near the stairs outside our flat. We are painting our front door. I stand on the mat and help him by holding the tin of paint.

He stops painting and grabs my shoulder. 'Three blind mice at twelve o'clock,' he says.

'What?' I say.

'Up ahead,' he whispers, 'three blind mice at the end of the hall.'

As my father whistles the tune of 'Three Blind Mice', the women walk towards the stairs on the other side of the tower.

'Let's follow them,' I say.

One of them hears me and turns. She doesn't look annoyed; she looks amused, and she stops walking for a moment. I look at my father. He keeps on whistling and he stares at her until she turns and walks away with the others. He watches them until they are out of sight.

Aunty Evelyn comes to visit. She brings a box of cream cakes and a poster for the hallway wall.

She takes a close look at everything in the flat and, and when she has finished, she stands by my parent's wedding photograph, which sits on the dresser near the kitchen door.

'I see you brought the glamour of the past with you,' she says.

'Don't you keep your wedding photo out?' asks my mother.

'Not at all. It's too much like seeing a pair of ghosts.'

Aunty Evelyn puts her hands on her hips. She will not leave without a fight.

'The wallpaper's a lovely shade of pink and with those little bits of yellow and those . . . those sticking-out yokes.'

'Stamens,' I say. 'They're called stamens.'

We go into the kitchen and sit at the table with a pot of tea. My father has a book on his lap, *The Science of Understanding the Depressive Mind*. It looks like a prop there, nothing more than a place for him to rest his hands. I haven't seen him read anything since we arrived.

My mother yawns and Aunty Evelyn goes on talking.

'Did you hear that Dr Behan died last week? He's gone to God.

Oh, he always respected the modesty of his patients. He never saw a female patient under the age of sixteen without the company of the mother, and the same for the little boys.'

My mother says nothing and, instead of speaking, she yawns again.

'John, stop scratching your head,' says my father.

The shouting from next door starts; a woman screams, and Aunty Evelyn looks at my mother.

'When you're used to that kind of noise, I think it'll be nice,' she says. 'Maybe it's a bit too warm with the heat coming up through the floor, but, overall, it's really very cosy. I think you've made it very nice.'

I can see by my mother's frown that she knows, as I do, that Aunty Evelyn is lying.

For the first time I wonder if I have inherited my gift from my mother, who sees what I see: Aunty Evelyn shrugs in the middle of the words, 'It's really very cosy', and her body language doesn't match what she is saying.

I have begun to sharpen my skills, master them. When I detect lies I get hot, around my ears and throat mostly, but I don't feel sick. Eventually I will become a wizard. I have memorised more passages from books. Here is one of my favourite:

'Most people will never recognise the signs and expressions of the liar. These facial expressions and gestures are involuntary and appear and disappear so rapidly that unless you have a very good eye – an instinct, a gift – you will never see them and you will never be able to detect lies.'

Aunty Evelyn goes on talking and seems too interested in my father's job at the factory, where all he does is wear overalls and solder bits of metal together.

'Just as well it's only a temporary thing,' says Aunty Evelyn, 'something to tide you over.'

My father stands up. 'Nobody is going to die of a bit of manual labour,' he says. 'You make it sound like working in a factory was the curse of a stinking fistula.'

'What in heaven's name is a fistula?' asks Aunty Evelyn.

Everybody looks at my father, but nobody speaks. I rush out and get the dictionary from the coffee table and take it back to the kitchen. 'Wait, I'll tell you.'

I read the meaning once, close the dictionary to my chest, and repeat it from memory. 'A fistula is a hole in your rectum that bleeds foul-smelling pus and faeces all day long,' I say.

My father laughs and keeps on laughing. 'Oh, at times like this I'm so glad of you,' he says.

Aunty Evelyn turns red. Her ears and neck are as red as cough medicine. 'Oh,' she says. 'I said the wrong thing when I was only trying to show an interest and now I've been ganged-up on.'

'I know it,' says my mother. 'Not to worry.'

Aunty Evelyn takes a deep breath; she will try one more time to have the fight she came for.

'Well, Helen, it's a blessing in disguise that you couldn't have more. I mean, a blessing that you could only have the one, isn't it?'

My mother frowns. 'What do you mean?'

'Better that you only have John, no other kiddies to worry about. I mean, in this place, and all.'

My mother gets up from the table and goes to the sink where, with her back to Aunty Evelyn, she rubs a wet cloth over the draining board. I silently count with her. She rubs the cloth back and forth exactly ten times.

My father leaves the room without excusing himself. Once again, nobody speaks. Aunty Evelyn fiddles with her teaspoon and turns her empty plate round and round. According to the clock next to the window, there is silence for only three minutes but it is as though nobody on earth will ever speak again, and my throat feels full of dry dirt.

'Well,' says my mother, turning to face her sister, 'it's time to get the tea on.'

Aunty Evelyn looks at her watch. 'Goodness! What happened to the time?'

'The same thing that always happens to it,' says my mother.

'We will see you on Sunday, then?' asks Aunty Evelyn as my mother shows her to the kitchen door.

'Yes. Sunday, then.'

The front door slams and I am alone with my mother. 'Why did she say that?' I ask. 'Why did she say, "It's just as well you could only have the one child"? I thought you only wanted one.'

'She had no right to say that. She was angry with your father and she couldn't think straight.'

'But still she meant something terrible by saying it.'

'I don't care if she did.' She holds out her arms and I walk to her body and we hug. 'Good. Now, go and wash your hands for tea.'

There is a picture on the news of starving African children.

'Awful,' says my mother, 'when those poor babies die they'll just be carted away in wheelbarrows.'

'Do you want me to turn the telly off?' I ask.

'No,' she says. 'Leave it.'

When the news is over we sit down to our tea at the kitchen table, and after a few minutes' silence my father says, 'Listen up. There go the three blind mice.'

From upstairs comes the sound of the sewing machine and, a moment later, somebody walking across the floor in heels.

'Walking sticks,' says my father. 'Listen.' He starts to whistle the tune, 'Three blind mice, Three blind mice, See how they run . . .'

'There they go again,' he says.

'Meeces to pieces,' says my mother, her eyes watery.

'What are you talking about?' I say.

'Ask no questions, and I'll tell you no lies,' says my father.

'But you do lie,' I say.

He ignores me, I can't believe it, and my mother pushes a chip into the yolk of her fried egg. I hate him for ignoring me and the blood filling my neck throbs and makes it hard to swallow.

Something is wrong, and I want to know what it is. I get up from the table and leave my food. They don't scold me and I'm not surprised. I go to my room and write another letter to the *Guinness Book of Records*. But when I'm finished, I worry that they might hold the Ballymun address against me and I add a final note:

P.S. *I am giving you our temporary Dublin address in Ballymun where we are living for a few months while my father builds our new house in Donnybrook.*

It's Sunday and we've been to mass with Aunty Evelyn, Uncle Gerald, the twins and Liam. We've eaten our dinner, and now my mother and I are alone in the kitchen listening to the radio.

'Mam, I was wondering if I could have a radio in my room?'

'What for?'

'To drown out the sound of the rubbish chute. I hate the noise and the smell.'

'You're like the rich people who always insist on living upwind of the mill smoke,' she says.

My father comes into the kitchen from behind me. He must have been lying on the settee. He didn't come to mass. 'We can't afford another radio,' he says.

'But I hate the noise and the smell and I don't want to sleep in there any more.'

He looks at my mother.

'All right,' he says, 'You can sleep with your mammy, if you want.'

'But where will you sleep?'

'I'll sleep on the settee. I'm getting quite attached to it.'

'Good idea,' I say.

'There'll be nobody sleeping on the settee,' says my mother.

'All right then,' says my father as he scratches his beard, which has grown back even blacker and thicker than before. 'Until we find ourselves a house, you'll sleep with your mother, and I'll sleep in the bedroom with the smell of rubbish.'

He winks cheerfully at me, but my mother isn't sure. 'Why don't we talk about this a bit more?' she says. 'Maybe later.'

'It's not so complicated,' says my father. 'I'll sleep in the small room and you two can share the big bed.'

'Wouldn't it be better if somebody slept on the settee?' she says.

'I'm not sleeping on the settee,' I say.

'Nor am I,' says my father.

My mother gives my father a mean and cold look. 'For heavens' sake, Michael! You're only after saying you've become quite attached to the settee.'

'I wasn't serious,' he says.

'Well,' she says as she walks away, 'that's that then.'

Last night my father slept on the settee after all, and now the three of us stand before breakfast in the living room in our pyjamas looking down at the mess of blankets and pillows, tissues and toffee wrappers he has left on the floor.

My mother reminds him that he must tidy up and put his

bedding away. He says, 'What the hell difference does it make to this death-hole whether or not it's tidy?'

My mother shakes her head and tries to smile. 'It's not that bad,' she says. 'It has its good side.'

'Where's that?' I ask. 'Has this tower got a fifth side I don't know about?'

My father punches me on the arm as though to say, 'Good for you', and my mother sighs.

Last night I slept soundly in the bed with her. It was warmer and, since she stayed over on her side and hardly moved at all during the night, my dreams were long and clear. And I liked sleeping with her because we talked before she turned out the light and when she's sleepy her voice is soft and gentle.

When my father gets home from work I ask him what it's like in the factory.

He shrugs. 'It keeps me out of trouble,' he says, which is not at all like the kind of thing he used to say.

'I suppose you can read on the bus though,' I say. 'You can study for your exams at Trinity.'

'And that's exactly what I do,' he says.

But this is a lie. I checked in his bag while he was in the bathroom; there were no books. Maybe he reads at night when my mother and I have gone to bed, but I don't think so. I think he watches television.

I make myself stay awake and when it is midnight I leave the bedroom and go in search of my father. He's not in the bedroom. He's in the living room sitting up on the settee watching the television.

'You're up late,' he says.

'I couldn't sleep.'

'Did you have a nighthorse?'

I laugh. 'No, just wide awake.'

'Sit with me and watch this.'

'But there's nothing on.'

The television finishes at midnight with the Angelus bells.

'I know. But staring at the blank screen helps me to think. Besides, Crito likes looking at her reflection in the black glass.'

I jump up from the settee. I can't believe it. 'Crito? Is Crito here? Did somebody bring her?'

'No, sit down. Crito's not here.'

'Then why did you talk about her as though she was here?'

'I imagine she is,' he says. 'Here. Watch.'

My father begins to stroke the air between us, soft, curved, cat-size strokes, as though Crito were sitting here. Then he taps his leg as though to invite her onto his lap. He says 'Ooph' when she jumps on and then he continues to stroke her back, this time, longer, flatter strokes.

'You see, it's as though she was here.'

I swallow twice, until my throat is dry again and look at the curtains.

'That's really mad, Da. I didn't know you were such a lunatic.'

'You should go back to bed. You don't want to fall asleep at school.'

I stand up. 'I haven't even started school yet. Mammy's trying to get me out of having to go to the Ballymun school.'

My mother wants to find me a place in a good convent school, like the one near Aunty Evelyn's bookshop, which is surrounded by a high brick wall, and has a grotto and a statue of the Virgin Mary and a holy water font in the front garden.

'Yes, of course. Still, you need your sleep. I'll see you tomorrow.'

'G'night, Da.'

'G'night, John.'

He kisses me on the hand for a joke and I laugh.

* * *

We have been in Ballymun for nearly two weeks, and I want to go to school. I want to make new friends and I'm tired of wandering around the flats. I've read all my books and I've nothing to put in the new Gol of Seil and I've even made a new puppet stage out of an apple box for my mother. There's nothing else to do, so I walk up to the top of all seven towers. I'm tired of walking up and down the stairs, I watch Ballymun life from the window, or lie on my mother's bed and read. The bedroom we share is better now that she has used leftover wallpaper to cover the tinted brown mirrors.

In three days I see four ambulances and eight Garda cars. Sometimes the injured person is in the back of the ambulance with the person who has hurt them. Sometimes women hurt men, sometimes women hurt each other, and sometimes drunk men hurt women after long bouts of screaming, but the women scream more than the men.

I see an unconscious woman on a stretcher being put inside an ambulance. The way the doors open, and the ambulance officer in a white coat adjusts the stretcher to make it straight before he slides it in, looks just like a chef putting food on a tray into a cooker.

I see washing falling off the clotheslines people rig to their ground-floor balconies and, when the washing doesn't fall, or get blown off by the wind, children steal it. The ground-floor flats are the ones nobody wants and nearly half are empty and boarded up.

26

A letter arrived yesterday announcing that I must go to Ballymun National School across the road. It will take me less than two minutes to walk there and I will probably be able to see Plunkett tower from the window of my classroom. I start tomorrow, and so this is my last free day. I get up late and go to the kitchen for breakfast. My mother is still sleeping but somebody has left two new exercise books on the table. I get a knife out of the drawer and cut squares out of the flock wallpaper in the gap between the cupboard and fridge and I use the wallpaper to cover the books. Then I see a note that has fallen from the table. It's from my father and has five pounds Sellotaped to the back.

Dear son,
  Have a great first day tomorrow. And here's some money to buy yourself a present. I hope this will make things up to you a bit.
  Love, Da.

I walk across the road and down two blocks to the toy shop in the big shopping centre. I've never been in a toy shop so big, so bright. I look around for an hour before settling on a remote-control racing car called Johnny Speed, The Most Fantastic Racing Car Ever Made, by Topper Toys. I turn the box over and read every inch of it and I gaze for ages at the big colour photo on the cover.

The car is a bright red convertible Jaguar XKE and there's a little cream-coloured plastic driver in the front seat and the car goes forward and reverse and the wheels can be steered so it also turns around. Nobody else will have one, and I can drive it around behind the flats and if, people stop to ask me about it, I can give them lessons. If I had the money I took from Granny I could also buy some of the accessories. I could buy a racing track, the pit-stop men in overall and caps, the grandstand for the spectators and the man who holds the black and white finish flag.

I get enough change to buy batteries, a Mars bar and a bottle of Fanta and I sit for a while on a big bench in the warm shopping centre and read the instructions. When I'm sure I understand how the car works, I take it and the control box out of the foam compartments and do my first test-run on the shiny, flat floor of the shopping centre.

The car works and it's fast! Two ladies come and stand by me and watch. There's a cord connecting the control box to the Jaguar but it's thirty feet long, so the car can go quite far.

'Isn't it magic?' says one of the ladies.

'It's grand,' I say. 'I just got it for my birthday.'

'Happy birthday.'

'What a lovely present.'

'Thanks, I love it,' I say.

'Ta-ta, now,' says one lady.

'We've got more shopping to do,' says the other, and off they go.

I wish other people would watch and I make the Jaguar go around the bench. The cord gets caught, but I unravel it and try again. The second time, I get it just right.

I walk back to the flats.

The boys in the gang are huddled in a pack near the lift.

I decide to take the stairs. If any of them speak to me, I'll pause before I answer, and take deep breaths so that I don't sound nervous.

As I reach the landing of the first floor one of the gang members comes running up behind me. I keep walking along the balcony, but he catches up.

'Get out of the feckin' way!' he says.

I'm not in his way so I stay to the left of the stairs and keep walking.

'I said get out of the feckin' way!' he shouts.

I keep walking up to the second floor and then turn right, pretending that I live on this floor. The rest of the gang has come up behind me.

I stop and turn around. I will put on a Dublin accent. 'Howya? I've just moved here from Gorey.'

'I'll show you Gorey,' says the tallest one, and then I count them: there are only five, not the dozen or more I've imagined.

'How old are ya?' one of them asks.

'Eleven,' I say.

'So, why aren't you at school?' asks the boy from the stairs, who has one blue eye and one hazel eye.

Now we're all standing on the balcony outside number 29. I hope that if anything happens the people inside will hear us.

'I didn't feel like going,' I say. 'What about youse?'

They tell me they didn't feel like going to school either. I wonder how they can get away with such a thing, but I don't ask. They all look about thirteen or fourteen. None is as tall as I am and I'm not as scared of being beaten as I was, but I'd still prefer it if they let me alone so I could go home with my new car.

'What's in the big bag?' asks the tallest boy, whose hair is blond at the top, with small greasy tails hanging out the back.

'Shopping,' I say.

'Doesn't look like shopping.'

'Looks like a colourful box.'

I move back a little so that I'm against the balcony wall and realise I'm only making them more curious.

'It's a remote-controlled car,' I say.

'Give it here,' says the boy with different coloured eyes.

'All right,' I say. 'But let me get it started first. I'll do a demo for you.'

I take the car out of its box, and try to make sure they don't see my hands shaking. I put the batteries in and think about what I'm going to do. I make the car drive along the balcony, all the way to the other end, and make it turn around when it reaches the stairs. They watch.

'Give us a cigarette,' I say. 'I'll show youse something.'

The boy with greasy tails gives me a cigarette, which I put in the passenger seat of the car, and then, from about ten feet away, I drive the car over to him.

'Fuck,' he says. 'I'm after having my fags delivered!'

'Yeah,' I say. 'Fuck.'

I wish I hadn't said it. They stare at me and then tell me to go down the other end of the balcony. I take the cigarette out of the car and put it in my pocket and make sure they see.

They call me back.

'Wanna join?' asks the boy with tails.

'OK,' I say.

'But you have to give us your car,' says the shorter boy. 'For keeps. It'll be instead of the membership fee.'

I crouch down to put my new car back in its box. I try to stay calm and I stall a while by making the batteries fall out, so there's time to stop myself from crying. I swallow a few times before I look up.

'Does your gang have a name?' I ask.

'Yeah,' says the one leaning against the railing with a smoke behind his ear, 'we're called The Fangs.'

They all laugh and I laugh too, even though I know they are laughing at me: they are not called The Fangs. I give them my new car and we shake hands.

They tell me their names. The leaders are Mark, the tallest one with the greasy tails, and Colman, the one with the different coloured eyes.

'One more thing,' says Mark, 'you gotta do a job before you are a fully fledged member.'

'What?'

'You've gotta go to the new housing estate and bring us back a brand new sink.'

'Yeah,' says Colman. 'And by five o'clock tomorrow.'

They ask me to swear that if I am ever caught doing anything I'll say I don't know them, and they promise that they'll say they don't know me.

'Sure,' I say and we shake hands again.

My hand is no damper than their hands.

They ask me which tower I live in and the number of my flat. I tell them the tower, but give them the number of Mrs McGahern's flat. I should have given them a random number from a different floor.

'But you better not come around,' I say. 'Me mam's deaf and blind and she gets very upset with surprises.'

I am getting better at lying. My face doesn't feel hot and my body doesn't shake. I am steadier on my feet and stronger. Mark tells me about how the building sites work. First the surveyors come and then trenches are laid and then the concrete is poured into the trenches.

'Has anybody ever got stuck in the wet concrete?' I ask.

They laugh and pass looks. 'We better leave you to it,' says Colman and, at his signal, they all turn and walk away.

A few minutes later Mark comes back. 'Better not forget,' he says. 'See you at five tomorrow at the bottom of the stairs.'

My brand new car is in its box under his armpit.

I'm not afraid of them. I'm only afraid that they'll humiliate me. I will do what I've agreed to do. I will steal a sink from an empty house that doesn't belong to anybody.

I go across the road to the new housing estate, and after the workmen have gone I walk along the half-finished walls for a while. When I'm ready, I go to the back of one of the new houses and climb through a window wet with white paint, which I get on my trousers and hands. The fresh paint smells like marzipan and so I breathe through my mouth to stop it getting into my head.

I go into the living room and sit on the soft, new carpet. There's so much clean, spare room. I lie on my back and roll around for a while. I take off my trousers to see what the carpet feels like against my bare legs and then I take my underpants off to see what the new carpet feels like on my bum.

I get dressed and go to the bathroom and sit on the new floor and play with the tap fittings, which are in the shape of dolphins. It's a nice, big house. I'd like to live in a house that hasn't been used.

I pull at the sink, but it's fixed to the wall with bolts. I leave. It's getting dark and walking though the trenches is like being in a maze. I write in the wet concrete, and break a piece of string that builders have set to mark where the rooms of the new house are going to be. All the time I half hope the gang is watching me.

I fantasise about living in one of these new houses, bigger and cleaner than our flat, with bigger windows. And they have stairs. I miss the stairs in my grandmother's cottage that led up to the bedroom where my mother and father slept.

It's nearly six o'clock and I haven't found a sink. I'm hungry and tired and so I go home. I'll get the sink tomorrow.

My mother is in the kitchen. She sits on the floor, her legs crossed, her arms on her knees. There are bits of broken plate on the floor. She looks as though she's been crying; strands of wet hair stick to her face.

'What happened?' I ask.

She looks me up and down. 'What happened to you?'

'Nothing.'

'You've got paint all over your trousers.'

I want to tell her. I want to tell her everything, about the new houses and the gang, but not now. I want to know why she's been crying.

'I was just helping to paint a wall downstairs. With some people from the community centre.'

'You should soak your clothes.'

'But why are you sitting on the floor? Why've you been crying?'

'Sit and I'll tell you,' she says.

Although she probably means for me to sit at the table, I move some bits of broken plate and sit on the floor.

'I was squeezing a lemon and it was so dry I felt like I'd just finished strangling somebody trying to get the little bit of juice out of it.'

I look carefully at her eyes, and she looks away.

'I was furious at nothing. Furious at this tiny thing. I picked up a plate your father left on the sideboard this morning and threw it against the wall.'

'Do you want me to do anything? Do you want me to help?'

She holds my hand. 'Yes, you can help. You can study hard, pass your Leaving with flying colours, become a dentist or a pilot

225

or something useful, marry a woman who has a brain and have at least four children. And sing "Auld Lang Syne" at my funeral.'

'But I can't sing,' I say.

'Play it on a record then,' she says.

'The record player wouldn't fit in the coffin.'

And then we are silent until she says, 'I love you more than I should. No matter what you do, I'll love you and that's something you'll never understand.'

'Yes I will,' I say. I fold myself over and rest my head in her lap.

'Get up, John. I'm going to get into bed. I'm very tired.'

'Again? You're always tired and sleepy.'

She yawns as she stands and I watch her go.

27

It's my first day at the Ballymun National School. My mother comes with me to the zebra crossing and points at the grey school building. We are only fifty feet from home. 'There it is,' she says, smiling, and waving her long, thin arm.

This gesture of hers, pointing to the concrete building as though it were splendid, reminds me of the day we visited the big house in Gorey together.

'I could've found it myself,' I say.

'I know,' she says. 'But I wanted to see you off.'

'OK, then. Bye-bye.'

Suddenly, her face collapses, as though she is crying dry, and she leaves me without saying goodbye I cross the road.

The teacher makes me stand at the front of the class while she introduces me.

'This is the new boy I told you about yesterday. His name is John Egan and he's moved to Dublin all the way from Gorey. I hope you'll make him feel very welcome.'

'Good-morn-ing-John-E-gan,' they say flatly and in unison.

I don't say anything. I want to, but since I can't think of anything good to say I don't speak at all. I look at them and let them look back at me.

The class is bigger than my class in Gorey and, while the teacher tells them where Gorey is, I count them: ten girls and seven boys. There's an empty seat in the middle row and the desk it sits behind has been scrubbed clean of graffiti.

I take my seat and spend the first few lessons of the day as though half awake. There is a small window to look out of but the room is too hot. My new teacher is a short, fat woman, with the cropped brown hair of a man. She wears glasses and whenever she asks a question she takes them off and dangles them in her fat hand.

The only pleasure I get from being in her class is catching her in lies. She comes to our desks and looks over our exercise books. When she lies to a pupil her voice lowers.

She tells the slow boy with the desk next to mine – who has obvious mistakes all through his work – that he is 'doing a splendid job', and her voice is so low it is barely audible.

At break-time, three crates containing small bottles of milk and a crate of jam sandwiches are delivered to our classroom. The milk is warm and the jam in the sandwiches is dry and crispy. I stay in the classroom and read.

At lunch I look for somebody to sit with and I see two boys, both of whom wear glasses, sitting under a classroom window, their heads lowered, their faces in their food. I sit down next to them. 'Hello,' I say. 'Do you mind if I sit here?'

They move over even though there's plenty of space, and after I sit they put their sandwiches down on their laps and wipe their hands clean on their trousers. They must be short, because they have to crane their necks to look up at me.

I ask them about school and what they did for the Easter holidays. I easily catch one of the boys telling a lie. He says he went to London at Easter and that his father took him for a drive in his uncle's red MG. He says they went seventy miles per hour and his mother's hat came flying off. He wasn't lying about being in London, or the sports car, but he was lying about his mother.

Either she wasn't in the car or she was and she wasn't wearing a hat.

I remember what one of the books said. 'One of the hardest parts of lie detection is when only a part of a statement contains the lie. It can be very difficult to separate the lie from the truthful part of the sentence.' All I know is that his voice faded and he gulped when he said 'and my mother's hat came flying off'.

I've noticed that when somebody lies it is almost as though something passes across their face, like a cloud; as though they fade from view slightly, become less real, less like the person you are used to seeing. It is hard to say exactly what it is that happens. But whatever it is, I can see it.

At the end of the day, my teacher tells the class that next week at school there'll be a delousing. All of us will line up (boys and girls in separate rooms) with only our underpants on and get sprayed with the stuff that kills lice and nits, and we'll be checked for ringworm too.

After school, I have an hour and a half before I'm due to meet the gang, in which time I have to get the sink I promised them. After walking around the new estate for half an hour, I decide that I won't meet them. I don't care about them.

I walk through the dark streets around Ballymun, past the tenements with green doors and small windows, and I walk by smouldering bonfires in the fields, the charred remains of mattresses and prams, and I memorise the names of the streets and car registration plates. A group of friends is not as important to me as my gift.

I go home and make a ham sandwich. My father isn't home and, although it's not yet dark, my mother is asleep. I don't wake her.

I eat half of the ham sandwich, put my pyjamas on and then get into bed. I read the section about prison escapees in the *Guinness Book*. I like the sound of James Kelly, who escaped from Broadmoor on 28 January, 1888, by using a key he made from a corset spring. Kelly spent thirty-nine years a free man, in Paris, New York, and at sea. In 1927 he returned to Broadmoor and asked to serve the remainder of the sentence he had been given for murdering his wife.

I think about how to attract the attention of the *Guinness Book*. Maybe this time I should send them a tape recording of an experiment. I could do the experiment with my mother. Perhaps they have written to me, and the letter is waiting for me in Gorey. After an hour of contemplation, I can't stand the quietness any longer. I tap my mother on the arm to wake her.

'I'm asleep,' she says. 'Get back over to your side of the bed. You're crushing me.'

'How will I get my post?' I ask.

'What post?' she says, covering a yawn with the back of her hand.

'I'm waiting for a letter from the *Guinness Book of Records*,' I say.

'What letter?'

'I told you already. I wrote to them about my gift for detecting lies.'

She sits up and puts a pillow behind her head. 'Make me a cup of tea and then tell me about it again.'

I make a pot of tea and bring it in to her on a tray with a packet of Digestives.

I sit on the end of the bed and tell her. She won't forget again.

'Oh, yes,' she says. 'But do you not think that these lies are harmless? Can't you see them for what they are? They're white lies. Your father was just embarrassed to admit that the cards were bought in a batch on the cheap. And Granny lied because sometimes it isn't polite to talk about money. Besides, money is a sticky topic at the moment.'

It isn't polite to talk about money? She is telling the truth but I hate that this is what she believes and I hate it even more that she sounds like a robot. Only her lips move, the rest of her face is stiff.

'I don't care why they lied!' I shout. 'Don't you get the point of this? I have a gift.'

The bed shakes and the ham sandwich slides off the plate; the bread and ham fall apart, and the ham sticks to the eiderdown.

'John, there's no need to shout. I think perhaps you are just more perceptive than most boys of your age, and that's a good thing, a really excellent thing. But maybe you should keep this in perspective. There's no point being a bull in a china shop, is there?'

I jump up from the bed and go to the bedside table so that I'm nearer to her.

'Do you think I should stop, and be like everybody else?'

I pick up a book and wave it around as I shout at her. I wish I had something else in my hand, but there's nothing else I can hold, and nothing that will calm me. I feel empty and want things to hold and touch. I want something in my mouth.

'Do you want me to pretend I don't have a gift?'

She sits up and puts her arms around her knees. 'Calm down.'

'No,' I shout. 'You're a dumb fool. Dumb, dumb, dumb!'

'Please calm down. You don't have to shout at me. I'm not deaf.' She is nervous.

I want to know why she doesn't take me seriously, but I won't talk any more. She will see for herself.

I go to the door. 'I'm going to watch television.'

'What about me?' she asks. 'Have you practised on me?'

'Yes. You turn red even when you tell white lies.'

'Is that so, Sergeant Egan?'

231

If I don't calm my body down, if I don't stop my body from being angry, I'll do something bad. I have to stop and be calm. I swallow and try to smile.

'Yes,' I say. 'I'm sorry I yelled at you.'

'Come here,' she says and I go to her.

She pinches my cheek.

As I kiss her, I notice a hole in the elbow of her nightdress and another larger hole under her armpit. I can see her skin and part of her breast under the hole. I look away.

'I could become famous,' I say.

My voice is like my da's and I wonder if this seems strange to her. I wonder what it will be like when my voice deepens still more. When my father speaks and I speak, it will be like the same person speaking.

'You could,' she says flatly.

'I'll make enough money so we can go to Niagara Falls together,' I say.

'You could.'

She hasn't eaten any biscuits, so I break one in half and hand it to her. She chews on it as though it is made of wood. I take another half and dip it in the tea. The biscuit is soft now and she eats it as though she has no teeth, her lips parting a small fraction and coming back together with a wet clicking noise.

'How will you prove you have this gift?' she asks, finally showing interest.

'They'll do experiments and conduct tests.'

She smiles. 'And then they'll pay you a fortune in gold and we'll fly to America on first-class tickets.'

'You don't believe me, do you?'

'It's a strange thing. A bit hard to take in, that's all.'

She isn't convinced; she thinks I am foolish. Well, then, it's only a matter of time.

She'll see.

I won't live with things this way, they can't stay as they are.

'Let's eat,' is all she says.

I hate the way people can eat no matter what has happened.

We go to the kitchen and she makes chips and eggs and for a while we don't speak, but it doesn't matter. My father isn't home and she doesn't say anything about it. She tells me that she is going to do some volunteer work at the Ballymun National School. She is going to help deliver the milk, and make jam sandwiches. I tell her that the jam sandwiches today were too dry and she agrees to put more butter on them.

'I'll wave at you as I pass by your classroom,' she says.

'And I'll wave back,' I say.

We stop talking again. We eat our eggs and chips and listen to the radio and then we go in to the living room and sit down together on the settee. She keeps her arm around me while we eat our cake and watch a film, and the happiness I feel is odd and makes every part of me seem liquid.

When she kisses me on the cheek I say sorry three times because I called her dumb three times. She tells me I'm a good boy and not to worry.

'I'm just upset,' I say, 'because we are underdogs now, and in Gorey we were over dogs.'

She laughs and doesn't cover her face with her hands. This is good.

We wait for my father to get home, but he is late again, working, and he comes home when *The Late Late Show* is nearly finished.

He smiles when he sees us sitting together under the blanket on the settee. He messes my hair. 'All right?' he says.

'Yes,' I say.

'Cup of tea?' says my mother.

'I'll get it myself,' he says.

'Hungry?' she asks.

'No, I had a steak sandwich in the cafeteria.'

I go to my room and get the new apple-box stage with the curtains drawn on the side.

When my father has settled down on the settee with his cup of tea, I stand in front of him. 'Da? I'd like to put on a puppet show. It only takes about five minutes.'

He smiles. A happy mood tonight. 'All right, son. Let's see it.'

'Youse have to turn off the television first.'

'Don't say youse,' says my father. 'It's common.'

I set the stage up on the coffee table, cover my head with a black cloth and crouch down. 'Welcome, lady and gentleman, to our special puppet show. It's called Puppet Philosophers of the World.

'One by one, you will meet four famous philosophers who are in disguise and you have to guess who they are. If you guess correctly, you get a piece of chocolate.'

I start with a hand puppet, a white sock with a face drawn on, wearing a toga. The sock puppet says to another sock puppet, 'You smell. You're annoying. You're an eejit.'

I ask, 'Can any member of the illustrious audience guess who this philosopher is?'

My father laughs and shouts. 'I've got it! I'd recognise that fat sock-face anywhere!'

His voice is so loud it is as though he thinks I won't be able to hear properly under the black cloth, or as though the puppets won't understand.

'It's Socrates!' he shouts.

'A-ha,' I say. 'Very clever deduction: Sock-ra-tease.'

I do three more philosophers, including Plato; a cardboard toe playing with a soccer ball made out of a piece of cotton wool

234

with a small stone inside it. My father gets two right and my mother gets one.

I am pleased and excited about the final philosopher I have prepared, and I got his name, like the others, from one of Da's books.

The final philosopher in disguise is a Lego man holding a shovel. I make the Lego man perform a digging motion into a small pile of straw.

'Who can guess the identity of this final philosopher?' I ask.

There is no answer.

'Do you need a hint?' I ask. 'He's digging.'

Silence.

'Come on, lady and gentleman!' I say. 'Can't you figure it out? Just think. All the clues are here.'

'We give up,' says my mother. 'Just tell us.'

'No,' I say, getting hot under the black cloth. 'It's not that hard! You have to think. Just think a bit longer. Just think!'

My father turns the television on.

'Not yet,' says my mother.

'I've had enough thinking for one night,' he says.

I come out from under my black cloth. 'It was Heidegger,' I say, as I kick the box across the room. 'Hay digger.'

My father looks away from Gay Byrne's face on the television, and smiles at me. 'Very clever,' he says. 'You get the last piece of chocolate.'

I go to my room so they won't see my disappointed face.

28

After school the next day, I see the gang at the base of the stairs. They are huddled together, rummaging through a shopping trolley full of somebody's groceries.

I turn back and walk around the block a few times and, when I return, they have gone.

My mother is sitting in the living room darning socks, and she is wearing one of her good dresses, the pink and black dress she wore to mass on Easter Sunday. She looks beautiful, darning and listening to the radio.

I say hello and then go to the bedroom, where I lie on my stomach. I need to think about the gang and what I'll do next.

At teatime, she comes in to ask me what I'm doing. I tell her I'm thinking about some of the things I've read in *The Guinness Book of Records*.

She puts her long hair into a ponytail. 'It's time for tea.'

'Can I stay here? I'm not hungry.'

'If you want.'

She leaves and I scratch my head, the same place I always scratch. But I have gone too far again and there's blood on my fingers. I wipe the blood away on my trousers. I go on thinking and scratching and then I close my eyes.

My mother comes back a few minutes later with a ham sandwich and sits on the end of the bed. 'Here, you have to eat something.'

I take the plate but don't eat the sandwich.

'Is everything OK?'

'Everything's fine.'

I would like to tell her about the gang; about how I owe them a sink and about how I will need to avoid them on the way home every night.

She stands next to the bed and looks down at my head. 'You're bleeding!'

'I didn't realise.'

'I'm going to put some Dettol on that.'

She returns with the bottle and a ball of cotton wool and sits next to me on the bed as she puts the Dettol on the hole in my scalp.

'Are you troubled by something?' she asks.

'No, I'm just thinking. I've been thinking a lot.'

'You're in the amusement park again? The one you told me about?'

At least she can remember this.

'Yes.'

Then, as we lie on the bed, looking up at the ceiling, we both hear it: an aeroplane flying low, on its way down to Dublin airport. The noise of the groan of the landing gear, the low moan of the engines.

I go to the window. 'I can see the tip of the wing,' I say. 'It's very low.'

I get quite excited when I say this, even though I'm lying. I can't see the plane. I'm a better liar than I was in Gorey. It seems likely that I will become both a great lie detector and a gifted liar. I have no intention of lying in any bad way, and I won't be a criminal or a cheat, but it will be a crucial second stage of my art to be able to sit through a polygraph test and win. Surely this combination of talents will bring more fame.

I keep looking up at the sky, at nothing but grey clouds. And I say, 'I can see the plane, Mam!'

I imagine being on that plane, the dinner on my lap and a blanket to sleep under. I tell my mother about the headphones, slippers and eye-masks first-class passengers are given on aeroplanes.

'You seem to know a lot about what happens on planes for somebody who hasn't been in one.'

'That's because I know I'm going to go on one. Unlike some people, like Da, I know I'm going to do the things I really want to do and not just talk about it.'

She pulls the eiderdown up under her chin. 'John, if you can't say something nice then don't say anything at all.'

'Even if it's the truth?'

'You're not being fair. I think you need to learn some tolerance. Do unto others as you would have them do unto you.'

The Bible! I can't speak so I make a loud and long growling noise, like a dog shouting.

'John? What's got into you?'

She didn't sound like this in Gorey. She read books and used witty and interesting words and talked about making puppets, and now she is sad and weak for no good reason.

'How can you not realise how dumb you sound?' I shout. 'You're a dummy all of a sudden! A dummy lady with the voice of an old hag at the bus stop. Why do you only talk to me with these sayings all the time? You're a dummy!'

'That's not fair.' She closes her eyes.

'Yes, it is. It's fair and it's true. You're like a zombie since we moved here.'

She opens her eyes. 'We're all going through a very trying and difficult time.'

I don't know what happens to me but I am suddenly on the bed, on my knees, and I have my hand over my mother's mouth, like a gag, to stop her from speaking. To stop her from being a weak person. Repeating what she hears and making herself dumb.

'Shut up, shut up, shut up! Don't say any more.'

I can't stop screaming at her to make her shut up. She struggles, which makes me frightened, but I am strong, and I keep my hand over her mouth while she tries to speak, while she struggles to get my hand away from her face.

'Shut up!' I scream. 'Stop trying to talk!'

When, at last, she is silent, I take my hand off her mouth and sit on the bed next to her. She moves away from me, but doesn't get up from the bed. She looks at me. There is no expression on her face, a blankness. Empty.

'Just don't talk to me,' I say. 'Just stay quiet.'

She looks at me. No tears, not afraid. Blank.

'Don't do that. Don't just stare at me. I just want you to be quiet.'

'I am quiet,' she says.

She closes her eyes, as though waiting.

I am quiet too and my heart stops thumping, but there is a strange taste in my mouth; like dirt, like soil. I want her to open her eyes. 'I'm going out to watch television now,' I say.

She opens her eyes and stares at me again.

I leave the bedroom.

I don't feel bad about what I've done, only surprised, as though I have been somewhere else, or asleep for a few minutes; in a film or a play.

I go out into the living room and my father isn't there, and I'm not very interested in where he is.

I eat some biscuits and then I sit at the kitchen table with a pad and pen and compose another letter to the *Guinness Book of Records*.

At ten o'clock my mother comes into the kitchen. She stands

awkwardly in the doorway. I think she was hoping I wouldn't be here.

'I'm sorry about before,' I say. 'Could I please have a stamp?'

She is tense and nervous; her posture is stooped and her pupils are black and too big. She looks shorter and her mouth is smaller, tightly shut, not as red as it is supposed to be.

'I've a good mind to smack you,' she says, her voice pinched and small. 'I've been trying for hours to calm myself down so that I wouldn't.'

I go and stand by her. 'Go on. Smack me now.'

She doesn't hesitate. She brings her hand up over her head and then she smacks me hard across my face. It stings the way a football does when it hits my leg on a cold day.

She goes to the table and sits down.

I follow her and sit too.

'Don't you ever lay a hand on me again, John. Not ever again.'

'I'm sorry. I won't. I promise.'

We sit for a minute, both of us looking at the kitchen table. She goes to the fridge and takes out some corned beef. She slices it and then she boils brussels sprouts and carrots. I watch her. She offers me a sandwich. I tell her I'm not hungry.

'Is the stamp you need for your letter to the *Guinness Book of Records*?'

'Yes.'

'I think we should forget about this lie-detection business. Don't you?'

'That's what you say every time we talk about it. Don't you understand? I've had to tell you twice and both times you've said exactly the same thing. Can't you understand anything?'

'I'm tired,' she says. 'I'm very tired.'

She licks the stamp for me, and her tongue looks swollen, too fat and red.

'Thanks,' I say.

'I'm going to sleep now. Tell your father when he gets in that his tea is in the oven.'

29

Two days later, it's the weekend and the sun is out, but I can't go outside because of the gang. They are probably still waiting for me. They might want to bash me. But I'm still more afraid of being shamed than of being hit. I don't want to be laughed at and humiliated.

I stay inside the flat and tell my mother I feel sick. She asks me if I'd like to go to the zoo, testing perhaps, to see if I'm lying about feeling sick.

'No,' I say. 'I feel sick.'

She offers to take my temperature. I tell her not to worry about it.

'Well,' she says, 'I'm going for a ride on a bus to Stephen's Green and then I'm going to walk for a while and get a big dose of fresh air. I might even see a film.'

'Where's Da?'

'He's working. He's got a job with Uncle Jack today. He'll be home for tea.'

I lie on the settee and eat poached eggs on toast. There's a film on television that's set in a boy's school in England and the well-spoken voice of the actor playing the teacher makes me think of Mr Roche.

After the film, I decide to see if I can find Mr Roche's telephone number. I remember that the headmaster said that Mr Roche was from Dublin, so I look in the Dublin directory. There are too many people called Roche and I don't know his first name. I find the number for Gorey National School instead. I don't expect anybody to be at the school of a Saturday, but a woman answers the phone after two rings.

I tell her who I am, an ex-pupil of Mr Roche's and that I'd like to speak to him.

'You're Helen Egan's boy,' she says.

'Yes, I am.'

She gives me Mr Roche's number in Gorey. When I thank her, she says, 'How is your mammy?'

'She's grand,' I say.

'You're lucky you caught me here. I was just about to lock up. Will you tell her I was asking after her?'

'Yes, I will,' I say. 'I have to go now. Bye-bye.'

I hang up and take a few deep breaths before I dial the number.

I dial and he answers. When I hear his soft, slow voice, saying, 'Hello, David Roche speaking', I get nervous. My throat dries and my hand trembles.

I don't intend to play a practical joke, but that's what happens. 'Hello,' I say, 'this is Mr Roche.'

He says, '*This* is Mr Roche.'

I say, 'I think I am a distant relative of yours and wonder if you might invite me to your abode for a cup of tea.'

He hangs up.

I don't understand what I have done. I call again straight away. If I wait, I'll lose my courage. I speak in a rush. 'Hello Mr Roche. It's John Egan, sir. I was in your class at Gorey National School.'

There is a long pause. I hear some papers rustling and then, when he finally speaks, he seems to have food in his mouth. 'Oh, the boy who left in the dead of night?'

'Yes,' I say, pleased that he remembers. Perhaps things will work out between us after all. He will help me do what I need to do to become famous. He will help me get the attention of the *Guinness Book*. 'We moved to Dublin. To Ballymun, sir.'

Another long pause, while my heart races.

'Did you ring this number a few minutes ago?' he asks.

'No,' I say. 'No. I just called now. For the first time.' This is a lie told badly.

'Well, whoever it was sounded as if it could have been you.'

'Well, it wasn't, sir. It must have been somebody else. It must have been a coincidence.'

I notice the sensations caused by lying: what lying does to my temperature, my voice and my body. I notice that my left hand is in a fist but it is hard to know what my right hand might be doing if it were not occupied holding the telephone receiver. I also notice that I am speaking faster than usual.

'You live in Ballymun now.'

I am not sure if this is a question or a statement. 'Yes,' I say. 'It's pretty good when you get used to it.'

He's definitely eating. I wait for him to chew and swallow. 'I'll pray you never get used to it. I'll pray you'll leave the very first chance you get.'

'Yes,' I say, 'that's exactly right and . . .'

'Well, young John, remember to be good and, more importantly, good luck.'

He hangs up.

I have never been on the phone with somebody who didn't bother to say goodbye. I say goodbye to the beeping tone, and then I look around the living room, embarrassed.

I pace the living room floor behind the settee for a while and then I call him again. 'Sir,' I say. 'It's me again.'

'Yes.'

'I forgot to tell you that I have a gift.'

'I don't think there's any need to be sending me a present.'

'Not a present, sir. A gift. I'm gifted. I have a gift.'

He breathes heavily but doesn't speak.

I wait.

'What kind of gift?'

He sounds bored. I'm no longer sure that I should tell him. 'I can't say yet. But it's a real gift and I was wondering if you could help with a letter I need to . . .'

'Why mention this gift if you can't tell me what it is?'

Why don't I say what I set out to say? Why can't I control what I say and how I say it? How can I have been thrown off course so easily? I hate myself.

'Well, sir. I'm going to be famous one day. I think I'm a human lie detector. I'm pretty sure, but I need help with . . .'

He clears his throat. 'Yes? Go on.'

I tell him about my father's and grandmother's lies. I tell him about The Gol of Seil, and the books I have read.

'Tell me more,' he says. 'Explain it to me.'

I have a chance now to prove that I have a gift and to show off some of what I have learnt. 'I have an instinct and I know that lying stirs up emotions that are involuntary and I know these emotions can't be completely hidden.'

I continue. He has stopped eating.

'And I can see these emotions in people's faces and in what they do with their bodies, how they fidget with their hands, and other things. I can even tell when a good liar is lying because "one of the most important clues to a deception is the mismatch between what the person is saying and what his face and body are doing".'

'That's quite a mouthful. You've obviously done your homework. But how do you know these sensations of yours are not simply feelings like hurt and shame? Emotions you feel when you believe somebody close to you is lying?'

'Because there is proof. I tested it on Brendan and I've made notes in my Log of Lies.'

He laughs. 'As long as this goes no further,' he says, 'I am happy to tell you that Brendan is one of the worst young liars I have ever encountered, both with respect to the number of lies he tells and their alarming lack of credibility.'

'Oh,' I say. 'But . . .' I'm angry and short of breath, as though I've been running. I make sure that I don't sound angry.

He begins to eat again. 'You might want to test this gift of yours on some friends who are more practised liars.'

'Well,' I say, 'I met this gang. I could practise on them. Maybe next time I could . . .'

He coughs loudly to interrupt me. Is this a trick for getting in the way of a boring speech? Does he mean to cut me off? If I don't do something to stop it, I'll become too angry to speak. I take a deep breath and count to ten.

'Well, John, I'm intrigued. If you still have this gift when you finish your Leaving, please feel free to contact me.'

'All right, sir.'

'I do mean that, John. I'd like you to have something that will get you out of that wretched place.'

He speaks this last sentence with a warmth that is so sudden, and so strong, I feel the urge to cry, to laugh, to clap my hands. He doesn't hate me. 'Me too,' I say. 'I hope so too.'

I go to the dresser and get the permanent black marker Mammy uses for writing my name on the labels of my new clothes. I take my jersey off and write Mr Roche's phone number on the inside of my left arm, just under my armpit; if the number fades when I wash it, I'll write over it again. I will keep the number with me every day.

30

It's the middle of the same night and my father stands by the bedroom door and whispers my name. I pretend not to hear him but he tiptoes over to the bed and shakes my shoulder. 'Get up,' he says. 'And don't wake your mother.'

He is wearing the same dirty yellow Aran jumper he has been wearing nearly every day since we moved to Ballymun.

'I'm too sleepy.'

'Get up,' he says. 'I've something to tell you.'

I put my dressing gown on and go with him into the small bedroom that used to be mine. The smell of the rubbish chute is strong, and it crunches and churns.

It's 3.15 am and the clock on the wall beside the bed looks strange, with both hands together, back to back, thick and black.

He lies down and I sit at the end of the bed. The artery in his temple is pulsing in time with the clock; the blue worm throbs once every second. I turn away and hope that when I look back his fringe will have fallen down to cover him.

'Are you properly awake?' he asks.

'I'm wide awake.'

'Good, because you'll need to concentrate.'

'Why?'

'Because I've got to tell you to stop peeling all the wallpaper off. Your mother says you've been very bold.'

'I haven't been bold.'

'Well, I hear you have and I'm the one who has to tell you.'

'Why?'

'Because I'm your father.'

'OK,' I say. 'Is that all?'

He puts his hands behind his head. 'It's late and your da's a bit tipsy. Just felt like taking a look at his only child.'

The artery in his temple is pulsing faster. Two worm-pulses per second.

'Where've you been?' I ask.

'Just went for a few pints after work down at the local pub.'

'Who with?'

'Some of my pals from work.'

He's lying.

'Where did you go?' I ask.

'The Terminal.'

'How come you stayed so late?' I ask.

'We had a lot to talk about. The boss is getting on our goat. You've never met such an old fecker. Today he made us clean the kitchen; five men down on their hands and knees scrubbing.'

The sheer mental strain of having to fabricate is showing on his face.

'So, how are you, fish-face?' he asks.

'Don't call me fish-face.'

He is my father, and he should think I look well, even if I don't.

'You are a fish-face,' he says, slurring fish and face together so that it comes out more like fliss-lace.

He puts his hand on my knee and I let him leave it there.

'Sorry, fish-face, you don't really look like a fish. It's only 'cause you eat so many fish fingers that I call you that.'

'You eat them, too,' I say.

'All right. Don't get your knickers in a knot.'

We are quiet for a while. He closes his eyes and I stay where

I am sitting on the end of the bed. And then, as he moves his arm up over his head, I smell perfume.

'Da? How come you're always making fun of the blind women upstairs? Do you know them?'

'No reason,' he says. 'I just like to make fun.'

'But do you know them?'

'No, why would I know them?'

His face is frozen, just as though paralysed. Now I will play the part of a detective. 'Do you really not know them?'

'No. I've seen them just as you have. But I don't know them.'

'Are the other flats here all the same as this one?'

'Mrs McGahern's is the same. So, I suppose they are all more or less the same. Just slightly smaller or larger.'

'Have you ever been up to the thirteenth floor?'

He sits forward and reaches out to touch my face. 'No, son. I've no reason to go up there.'

He never calls me son and he never touches my face.

'Have you really never been up in their flat?' I ask. 'The flat of the three blind mice?'

'Why do you keep on hounding me with these questions? Why these questions?'

'You seem to know a lot about these women.'

He thinks now. He's taking his time. 'Well, the answer is no. I've no reason to go up there.'

He's lying. I am certain he's lying. He is getting ready to get up off the bed.

'So you haven't been upstairs?'

'Yes, I've been up to Mark's for a cup of tea after work. He's on the fifteenth floor. So, yes, I have been upstairs.'

'Can I ask you one more important question?'

'Of course you can, son. You can ask me any damn thing you like.'

'Have you ever done anything dirty with them?'

251

He stands up. He stands up right next to me and his legs are close to mine. His face is red and he is panting. I think he's going to belt me. But I'm not afraid. I'm in the right, and he's in the wrong. I know he's been up there with those women. His lie has told me the truth.

But he kicks the bedroom door instead of kicking me and I worry that he'll wake Mammy. I expect him to storm out but he turns around to face me and stands with his hands dangling by his side as though waiting. I look at him and say nothing and he opens his mouth but makes no sound. He walks to the wall and back twice, head down.

'I give up,' he says. 'I give up.'

And then, without another word, he leaves.

I get back into bed with my mother and pull myself up next to her body and lie close to her. Although I'd like to stay like this, and fall asleep with my chest against her warm back, I move away to my side of the double bed and that's where I sleep.

At night, instead of watching television after school, I go outside. Every night, for five nights, I tell my mother that I'm going down to the basement to take a guitar class.

Instead of going to the basement, I walk upstairs to the flat above ours, where the three blind mice live. I loiter near their doorway and pace up and down the hall until after nine o'clock. When my father comes out, I'll catch him.

But he doesn't come out and I can't hear him through the door. At ten o'clock I go back down the stairs to our flat.

On the fifth night, I decide to wait at the bottom of the stairs on the twelfth-floor balcony. I sit on the bottom step and look up. And when I see him, I can hardly believe it. He is coming down the stairs from the thirteenth floor, carrying the black bag he takes to work, wearing his ugly blue overalls.

'Hello there,' he says when he sees me, as though nothing at all is wrong with the world.

I grip the rail and stare up at him. 'Where've you been?'

'Not that it's any of your business,' he says, 'but I've been up to Mark's flat for a cup of tea.'

'No you haven't. I saw you coming down from the thirteenth floor.'

He pushes past me and his foot knocks my knee. 'Your problem is that you see what you want to see.'

I wait until he has been inside for a while before I go in. I get to the bathroom just in time, and vomit until there's nothing left. I haven't been sick for a long time and his lie must be the worst kind to cause this reaction. My heart thuds with anger when I hear him in the kitchen, talking in a normal and innocent way with my mother.

It is teatime, the day after I caught my father coming down the stairs, and he hasn't come home. I'm in the kitchen making semolina and my mother is at the table drying her hair with a hairdryer that has a tube connected to a plastic hat. She plugs the contraption in and the tube fills the plastic cap full of hot air until it expands like a balloon on her head.

'What do you think of this?' she asks. 'What do you think about this old-fashioned hairdryer?'

'I think it's good,' I say. 'It has personality. Just like you.'

She laughs and takes the plastic cap off and puts it on her knees.

'My mammy used this hairdryer once to dry a chicken. Did you know that?'

'No.'

'She kept chickens, and one day one of them fell in a big puddle of mud and she decided to wash him. She gave the chicken a bath and then she brought him into the living room and used this gizmo to dry him off.'

'Did it work?'

'Wait there,' she says.

She comes back a few minutes later with a black-and-white photo of a chicken inside this hairdryer with its head and beak sticking out.

'So,' she says, 'that's something else you can think about. You can add it to your amusement park.'

'Thanks,' I say.

'Gimme a kiss,' she says and, when I give her a kiss on the forehead, I feel like I'm her husband.

'Mam? I have something really, really important to tell you.'

'Stop scratching your head.'

'Can I tell you?'

'Yes.'

'I'll wait till you're ready and you're listening properly.'

'Tell me now. I'm listening properly.'

'I think Da is doing something funny with them upstairs.'

'For goodness' sake!'

'No, Mammy. Listen. I think you should know. Just listen to me for a minute.'

I tell her that Da came into the room at 3.15 am and that he was drunk, that he lied about where he'd been. I tell her that he's been upstairs with them.

'This is crazy business,' she says. 'Who are you?'

'I'm telling the truth.'

'Not this time, you don't. Your father would never do such a thing. Not ever. He might have fibbed about where he was, but I know this for sure: he wasn't upstairs with those women.'

'How can you not believe me? Why can't you just listen?'

'I don't like this talk one bit.'

'If you don't believe me, why don't you go up and talk to the

254

women yourself? Ask them if Da has been up there.'

She stands up. 'I'll do no such thing. And you should wash your mouth out.'

I protest and beg her to believe me.

She puts her head in her hands. 'OK. You'll go back to your own bed tonight. A boy as filthy as you can put up with a bit of stink from a rubbish chute.'

'I'm not filthy. I'm the opposite! I know the truth!'

'You weren't filthy in Gorey, but you are some filthy now.'

I get my anorak and go downstairs.

I hope I might run into the gang. I don't care now what happens, and I feel the urge for something to take the place of the trouble and drama I wanted but didn't get with my mother. But I don't see the gang, so I go alone to the new housing estate and walk around in the concrete trenches. There's a small red wellington boot stuck in one of the newly laid cement slabs.

When I get home, my father is at the kitchen table with my mother, eating corned beef, carrots and mashed potatoes.

'Yours is over there,' says my mother.

My plate is being kept warm on top of a saucepan filled with hot water.

'Where've you been?' asks my father.

'Just went down to the basement to see if there were any activities.'

'And were there?' asks my mother.

'Only a bit of painting and little kids making stuff like snakes out of egg cartons.'

'That's funny,' says my father. 'I was down there not so long ago and it was closed for cleaning. There's a sign on the door saying so.'

I've been caught but he lets me go.

'Anyway, you're a bit old to be making snakes,' he says, smiling, and patting me on the hand.

'I s'pose.'

'Remember, Michael,' says my mother, 'how much John used to love those colour-by-number books? Oh, and Fuzzy Felt. Remember how he loved that?'

'I didn't love Fuzzy Felt,' I say. 'I hated it.'

They laugh.

'I know what I liked and what I didn't like. You must be confusing me with somebody else.'

They are still laughing, and my mother is trying to make me feel jolly by tickling me under the armpit.

'Don't!' I say.

After what she has been told, I don't understand her happy mood.

I leave as soon as I've cleared my plate and go into the living room to watch television. I have the volume on low so that I can still hear them talking.

They talk about the central heating, about the flat being too hot, the fact that the fridge always stinks, the cost of petrol, whether oil might run out one day, and the size of Phoenix Park; whether it is the biggest city park in the world.

I know it is. 'What are we having for dessert?' I call out.

'Peanuts!' shouts my father and they both laugh.

I go back into the kitchen. 'I have to go to the dentist again next week,' I say. 'I have another sore tooth.'

I want his sympathy. But I won't get it.

'Jesus,' says my father, 'you'd be the only child on the face of the earth volunteering to go to the dentist.'

'I don't mind,' I say. 'I like the dentist.'

'I think he likes Dr O'Connor because the man wears a fancy suit and speaks so nicely,' says my mother. 'He's like a lawyer who gives advice to teeth.'

They laugh at my mother's clever joke, and I pretend to laugh too. I will never be a person who is left out of things.

'Yes,' I say. 'A lawyer who gives advice to teeth and who makes you pay through the nose.'

My father grins and holds out his hand for me to shake it. I hold out my hand and we shake hands for a good while. It's an odd thing, and I've not noticed it before, but he has skin as soft as my mother's.

I go to the bedroom with its smell of rubbish and lie on the bed. On my stomach, on my side, on my back, it doesn't go away. There's a sad sickness in my stomach when I think of Brendan and I miss him and can't stop myself from imagining him with Kate and laughing together, laughing at me, and I lie on my back and it's the same thought over and over ... in the darkness and the sadness with the blackness on my backness ... in the darkness and the sadness with the blackness on my backness.

I turn over onto my stomach and my father knocks on the door. I tell him to come in and he sneaks in on tiptoe as though he is a cat burglar. He closes the door quietly behind him and sits on the end of the bed.

I close my schoolbook and sit up cross-legged.

He sits next to me, his legs over the side. 'Hey, fish-face,' he says. 'We haven't had a good chat for a while. How are you?'

'What?' I say. 'But we talked in the middle of the night.'

'Well, I'm sorry about that. I'd had a few drinks and you know how I am. I'm not an expert at drinking. I'm sorry I woke you. I shouldn't have.'

'That's OK.'

'I remembered your present this time.'

I see no sign of any gifts.

'But when I give it to you, I want you to forgive me for

forgetting your presents so many times in the past. Will you do that? Now that I've remembered, will you forgive me?'

It's too late, I think, but give me the present and let me see how good it is. 'OK,' I say.

He takes a pair of enormous brown socks out of a paper bag. 'Well, son, here you are! I've a pair of famous socks for you and you can make a puppet out of them or whatever you want.'

He is grinning and so pleased.

I hold the brown socks. They are huge, have several holes in both left and right toes and a big hole on the left heel and are thin and almost see-through in places around the foot.

'I don't get it.'

He speaks slowly.

'These socks belonged to the tallest man who ever lived. These were a pair of socks worn by the tallest man in the world.'

I am amazed. My mouth falls open and my eyes water. 'Robert Pershing Wadlow? These belonged to Robert Pershing Wadlow?'

'Yes, thats the one. They're a size 37AA foot. Eighteen and a half inches long,' he says. 'He wore them in the last year of his life. They were among his final possessions and kept by his father.'

I sit up straight, happy, astonished, but mostly happy. I hold the socks up and examine them. The foot of one sock runs almost the length of my arm from elbow to the end of my index finger. The whole sock is as long as my arm.

'How about that?' says my father. 'They are very old, so a bit crusty and worn out. But that just goes to show that they're authentic.'

My happiness is smashed to pieces. I didn't notice it before. I was too busy in my excitement. But I notice it now: he is lying.

I am almost too sad to test him. I cannot believe what he has done again. I want to go to bed, get under the covers, sleep, and have him gone.

'Yes,' I say, forcing a smile. 'What a wonderful present.'

'Not easy to get but, as I say, the holes and general shabbiness show that they are the real thing.'

I have a choice, to cry or to think. I will think.

It is common for the liar to back up his lies with expressions like, 'Scout's honour', 'Cross my heart and hope to die' and 'On my mother's grave'. My father saying that the shabbiness of the socks goes to prove that they're authentic is an example of what some books call 'telltale oath swearing'.

'How did you get them?' I ask.

'I've been hunting them down for months. And I finally met a man at work who knew another man in America who bought them in Illinois at an auction a few years ago.'

My father has lied not once, but several times in quick succession, like somebody who has pepper in his nostrils and sneezes uncontrollably.

I am angry and ashamed. 'They must have been very expensive,' I say.

'Yes and no. I wanted to get his shoes. But they would have sent me broke for two lifetimes.'

'I like the socks better,' I say. 'Thank you.'

'You're more than welcome, my only son.'

I will need to be more careful this time not to 'contaminate the scene' because the lie detector should not create an atmosphere that makes the liar more likely to show signs of stress. Signs of stress might be confused with signs of lying. The lie detector must be neutral and patient.

I must not give him any clue that I know he is lying. I will leave the counterfeit socks alone and turn to something different. I put the socks down.

'I'm glad they make you happy,' he says. 'I'll leave you to your homework now. All right?'

I sit up with pillows behind my head. 'Wait, Da. I want to ask something for school.'

'Go ahead.'

'Did you come the top of your class in your Leaving? Next week we're doing an IQ test at school and the teacher said if we know our parents' IQ, it would be helpful.'

'Yes,' he says, 'I knocked my opponents to the ground so swiftly there wasn't a fleck of dust disturbed in the arena. Just like Milo of Croton, I was the winner without dust.' I smile at him to keep him confident. 'But what's your IQ? What IQ did you have to have to get into Mensa?'

'You know this. You were there when I got the news.'

He rubs his leg, the same way he rubbed his leg when he lied to me about my Easter card.

'Just tell me again. I've forgotten and I really want to know.'

'One hundred and forty-five,' he says, his voice harsh and croaking. 'Over one-forty anyway. And I only need one hundred and thirty-three to get into Mensa.'

He hasn't even enough intelligence to be silent; to realise that I am setting a trap.

Does he not realise what I can do?

'It's been a long time since I had it tested,' he adds, 'and it might be due for re-testing.' This is the liar clarifying and amending until the deception is obvious.

I can hardly believe how bad he is at lying. I don't understand at all how he can expect to get away with it and why he can't stop himself. I don't understand him. He must think I'm stupid.

Being in the room with him is like being alone, like being completely alone, but not as peaceful.

'Thanks, Da. I'm going to get some milk.'

I get up from the bed, and he follows me into the hallway, the way Crito used to.

'You're all right, son,' he says, patting me on the shoulder, but his face looks tired and sad.

I am afraid he will tell me that he loves me.

31

When I don't see my mother at school the next day, I know that something terrible has happened. She usually goes past my classroom window at half ten with the other mothers, carrying the milk crates and jam sandwiches, and I usually wave to her from my desk.

I drink my milk and remove the waxy paper from my jam sandwich, but I don't eat. I decide that I will go home and see what has happened to her.

During maths class, I don't bother putting my hand up: I walk straight to the front of the classroom and say, 'Miss? I feel very ill and I have to go home.'

I leave the classroom before my teacher can respond. Unfortunately, she catches me up just as I am about to leave the main building.

'Young John Egan!' she says, in her deep, man's voice. 'You can't just walk out of school like this. Come back at once and see the nurse.'

I turn my back on her and double over, as though I'm dying of the pain, and I put my index finger down my throat and produce a reflex strong enough to vomit.

I'm surprised to see how much bread there is in what comes out of my gullet, since all I had for breakfast was a bowl of Ready Brek. 'I have to go,' I cry out and I run from her as fast as my legs will carry me.

'God love you!' she cries after me, suddenly full of sympathy.

* * *

When I get home, the door is wide open and my mother is sitting on the floor in the hallway. The phone has been pulled from the hall table and it lies next to her legs on the floor, the receiver out of its cradle.

She's wearing her nightie – the one with the big holes in the armpit and elbow – and her hair is messy. She looks up at me when I walk over to her, but doesn't speak.

My face feels very cold.

'Well,' she says at last, but without looking at me, 'you've told the truth, and now you have no father.'

I am frozen; the blood has rushed from my head and is pummelling through my arms. My arms tingle from my shoulder all the way to the tips of my fingers. This shaking blood terrifies me; it is as though my arms might come loose and fall to the floor.

'So, you're not talking now?' my mother says, her face crazy. 'Has the cat finally got your tongue?'

I am frightened and want to stop this. I want to sit down on the floor and do something to comfort her. I swallow and try to wet my dry mouth so that I can speak.

'What's happened?' I ask. 'Where's Da?'

She wipes her nose with the sleeve of her nightdress. 'I rang him at work.'

She tells me that she called the factory and that the foreman told her he could only reach a man on the factory floor in case of an emergency. She had to say that there was an emergency.

'What kind of emergency did you say there was?' I ask. 'What did you say?'

'Never mind what kind of emergency. I had to embarrass myself and invent something and then listen to the foreman call for your father on the loudspeaker, 'Michael Egan. Michael Egan. To the office for an urgent telephone call.' Then your father came to the phone puffing and panting and I told him what you told me yesterday, and do you know what he said?'

'No.'

I don't want her to be on the floor like this. I want her to stand up. She shouldn't be on the floor in her torn nightie.

'He said, "Well, do what the boy says, then, if you believe him. Go ask them yourself." And then he hung up in my ear.'

'So?' I say.

She thumps her fist on the floor and her fist makes a dull sound because of the carpet.

'And so, I went up there. I went up there in my nightdress. I could smell the booze when the women answered the door. And I asked her about your father, and do you know what she said?'

'No.'

'She laughed and said, "He's a good screw, yer one!"'

I almost fall. I can't focus. She shouldn't say this to me. She shouldn't say this. I reach out for the door behind me, to get away from her crying, angry, horrible voice. I am afraid of what she will say next. 'I'm going back to school,' I say.

'You are not going back to school! You will have your nose rubbed in this. Go and pack your father's things. He'll be here for his suitcase at three o'clock.'

'Why?'

'Why?'

We are silent. The baby crying in the next-door flat seems to get louder and more panic-stricken. I look at the phone next to my mother and want it to ring. I want the woman upstairs to say she was only messing. I want this to be over. I want to be right and I want to be wrong.

'Why?' I ask again. 'Why do I have to pack his suitcase?'

'Because I've asked him to leave. You wanted me to believe you, and now I do. You should be happy. Now that you're after having your way.'

I need to go to the toilet. 'But I only meant the truth to come out.'

'And what did you think would happen when the truth was out?'

'I don't know,' I say, wishing we could sit in the kitchen and talk in a normal way, instead of doing this in the hallway.

'You don't know?' she says. 'You don't know?'

'I'm sorry.'

'You're sorry?'

We are silent again and somebody outside kicks an empty can all the way along the corridor.

'Go pack a suitcase for your father, and a suitcase for yourself, if that's what you feel like doing.'

She lifts herself up from the floor, walks into her bedroom, and shuts the door behind her.

I go to the toilet and then I walk around the flat for a few minutes. The wedding photograph on the dresser has been removed and in its place there is a box of tissues. I still have something like a feeling that if I wanted to I could make everything go back to how it was; I could change things back. I think about calling my grandmother and asking her whether she will come and live with us a while, patch things up with my father, or let us come back to Gorey.

On the way, we could stop at a fairground or Duffy's circus. And there might be a miniature steam-train and pony rides and people dressed up as animals. I wouldn't want to leave.

All four of us could stop in at a circus and eat candy floss and watch the lion tamers and tightrope walkers, and I could sit between my father and grandmother. When they put their hands on my lap, I could make it so that they held each other's hands instead.

I go to the phone and ring Granny's number in Gorey. There is no answer. I put my hands over my eyes and then I pace up and down. I keep my eyes covered and lean against the sink, and when I feel calmer, I walk out to the hallway. I stand outside my mother's bedroom door and I wonder if she wants me to leave with my father. I go to my room and sit on my bed and I bash my legs with my fists so that I will have bruises there tomorrow.

The apple box for puppet shows has gone. I rush to the kitchen to see whether it's in the rubbish bin and there it is, and on the kitchen table there's a note from my mother to my father, written on airmail paper:

Michael

Take the things belonging to you and leave. And when you've a place to stay, make sure you tell your son where you are.

Helen.

I take the note with me and go back to my bedroom. The baby crying in the flat next door is louder. I put my fingers in my ears and lie face down on my bed. I want to leave, but I also want to stay. I want to be in two places; here with my mother, and away with my father, and I want to travel with him wherever he goes. Perhaps we could go back to Gorey together and I could see Mr Roche again.

I close my eyes and fantasise about living with my father in that hotel near the gates of Phoenix Park, the hotel near the zoo. Or we could stay together in a fancy hotel, like the Shelbourne; a hotel with a concierge who wears a coat and tails and I could go down to him and ask questions whenever I needed to. We could order dinner from room service and eat on our laps in the big bed in our hotel room and have breakfast brought to us on a trolley, and go downstairs at night and sit in the bar and eat crisps and I could drink red lemonade and we could watch the big television there.

But isn't he the bad party? Isn't he the cause of this trouble? Yes, this trouble is my father's fault and I won't go with him. I'll stay right here, where I am, with my mother. It's not her fault. He should leave us alone and cause us no more trouble.

At three o'clock, my father comes home. I hear him before he opens the front door, talking to somebody outside. I get up and go out to meet him. He's with Uncle Jack and Uncle Tony and they're all wearing blue overalls. I don't like seeing my father in overalls; I prefer him in his black suit jacket and a white shirt. Without a suit jacket, some of his personality is lost, because then he can't do his buttons up the wrong way, and wear one sleeve turned up and the other down.

'You're here,' he says. 'Shouldn't you be at school?'

'I was sick,' I say. 'I came home early.'

'He's always sick, isn't he?' says Uncle Jack to Uncle Tony, as though I'm a dog that needs putting down.

'I'm not always sick,' I say.

My father leaves and goes into the bedroom. Uncle Jack comes to me and hugs me. I look over his shoulder at Uncle Tony, who is putting the phone back on the hall table.

'Let's go into the kitchen and make ourselves a nice strong brew,' says Uncle Jack.

'All right,' I say.

I sit down at the kitchen table. When Uncle Jack has finished making the tea, he comes and stands over me. He puts his hands on my shoulders and stares down. I hate it when people tower over me like this. He could just as well have sat beside me.

'Get off me!' I say.

'Easy does it,' says Uncle Tony. 'He's only trying to help.'

'I don't need help. I know what's going on. I'm the one who told Mammy the truth.'

They look at each other. They know about my role in this. They must know about my gift for lie detection.

'Well, then,' says Uncle Jack, making himself at home in my mother's usual seat, 'you'll not be needing us to fill you in on the birds and bees.'

'No,' I say. 'I know all about it.'

'You'll be staying here, I suppose,' says Uncle Tony as he looks in the cupboard for something to eat.

'Yes. But I'll be able to change my mind and go with Da if I feel like it.'

'Sure you will,' says Uncle Jack.

'Any biscuits in this establishment?' Uncle Tony asks.

The front door slams. My mother has gone.

My father comes into the kitchen when it's nearly dark. Nobody has turned the light on, and he looks old and sad, his mouth turned down, his eyes smaller. 'Right, so,' he says. 'It's time I was off.'

'Better pack up this party then,' says Uncle Tony.

My father smiles and bends down towards me. He gives me a peck on the cheek and whispers, 'It's all right.'

His breath is rotten. I smile back at him but I want him to stand away from me. I've never smelt such rotten breath. What if this is the last time I kiss him? What if this is the last I see of him, and my final memory is of his rotten breath?

'Where are you going to live?' I ask him.

'With Uncle Tony, and there'll be a spare cot for you whenever you feel like visiting. So shall we not get maudlin in saying goodbye, because we're not really saying goodbye, and just . . .'

'Just what?' I say. 'You mean you won't say goodbye and just leave instead?'

My father stands back and looks me up and down. 'You're an odd mixture, you are, of little boy and a grown lad. Which am I speaking to now?'

I hang my head and feel embarrassed for feeling embarrassed and want him to go.

'What will your phone number be, then?' I ask in the toughest voice I have.

'It'll be the same as my number,' says Uncle Tony.

'Oh, yeah,' I say.

'Well, then . . .'

'Right, so . . .'

'Bye now, John.'

They leave.

I go to my room and get under the covers and wait there until I hear my mother come home. She goes straight to her room.

I make a fresh pot and bring it to her.

She is sitting up in bed with the radio on, the volume turned up loud. 'Has he gone?' she asks, although she must know he has left.

'Yes.'

'Well, what now then?'

'I don't know,' I say.

'I don't suppose your father gave you any money?'

It sounds to me like she said 'the fecker' and not 'your father' and so I feel confused and don't answer straight away.

'Well, did he?'

'He did. He gave me a tenner, and Uncle Jack and Tony gave me five more each. And Granny can send some money, can't she? So we won't be poor.'

'Being poor is the least of our worries.'

'That's good, then, isn't it?'

She shrugs, and smiles weakly. 'Will you go to the chipper and get yourself something? I'll not be cooking.'

'All right. What do you want?'

'Just go. And when you've had your tea, do your chores.'

In the morning my mother calls the school headmaster and tells him that I have a fever and won't be in for a few days.

'Stay in, please, but don't make too much noise. I'm going to bed for a while,' she says.

'But you just woke up.'

'I've been awake all night.'

I follow her into the bedroom and stand next to her by the bed. 'Did you know that if you don't sleep for eleven days in a row you will die?' I say.

'Yes,' she says. 'Not sleeping will kill you faster than not eating. Most human beings can last twelve weeks without food.'

She is like another person, her voice so flat, her face creased around her mouth.

'How many days without water?' I ask.

'I don't know.' She takes her dressing gown off, and closes her eyes. Her head falls and her teeth scrape together.

'You nearly fell asleep just now. Standing up!'

'I'll lie down then.'

'Maybe I should sleep in here with you again, and that will help you sleep.'

'I think I'd better be alone in the bed.'

'Will you let Da come back if he says he's sorry?'

'I'm too tired to talk about this now and you know far too much already.'

'But can't you tell me what's going to happen?'

'Enough, John. Please leave me alone. I'm going to try to sleep now.'

32

It's the middle of the night and my mother comes to my bedroom door. This is the fourth night in a row she has come to my door during the night and she says the same thing, more or less, each time.

'I didn't mean to wake you. I just came to see how you were. Just came to see whether you were having trouble sleeping too.'

'I was sound asleep.'

'Sorry. Go back to sleep then.'

The first two nights I got up with her and went to the kitchen and we made hot milk and, on the third night, we played backgammon for an hour or so, until she said she was sleepy enough and she went back to bed.

But tonight is different. She turns on the light and is leaning against the doorframe, as though she can't stand up.

'Mammy, what's wrong?'

'Oh, it's just the worry. I miss Michael.'

'Do you want me to come and sleep in your bed?' I ask.

'If you'd like,' she says.

'OK,' I say.

I get out of bed and go with her to her bedroom. I like the smell of her bedclothes now that my father has gone. They smell like the soil after it has rained.

'I'll keep my light on for a while and read my book. Will that disturb you?'

'No,' I say, and go quickly back to sleep.

In the morning, she doesn't wake me, and when I go into the kitchen at half nine she is there, sitting at the table, with a letter in her hand.

'It's from your granny,' she says. 'Your father has gone back to Gorey.'

'When did the post come?'

'It's from yesterday.'

'Why didn't you read it then?'

'I didn't have the courage.'

'But it's from Granny. You should have opened it. It's from Granny.'

'I know well enough who it's from. I don't need you to tell me.'

She hasn't been angry with me since the day I came home from school and found her sitting on the hallway floor.

'And who cares when it came? I've read it now and it says Michael has gone back to his mammy. And isn't that what you wanted? Did you not want to see the back of him?'

This doesn't make any sense to me and I begin to shake with anger. If anybody is going back to Gorey, it should be us, not him. 'Why is he back in Gorey?' I ask.

I am hardly able to breathe.

'Your father has promised your granny that he'll continue to work. They've made a truce.'

'So, then we can go back?'

'Come here to me a minute,' she says. 'Come and sit.'

'I don't want to.'

'Suit yourself.'

I take the letter from the table and read it.

'But Granny says she wants to see us. Doesn't that mean we'll be going back too?'

'I don't know.'

'But what does she mean?'

'Why don't you ring her and find out? Then I want you to go to school.'

'But I'll be too late.'

'You'll only be a bit late.'

It takes my grandmother a long time to answer the phone.

'Hello, Mrs Egan here,' she says.

'Hello, Granny? It's me, John.'

'Hello, John. How are you getting on?'

'I'm getting on fine.'

'And your mother? How is she?'

'She's fine too.'

'That's grand.'

'How's Crito?'

I have a picture in my mind of Crito sitting on my bed, looking out the window at the trees and chewing on her foot, her nose snuffling.

'Crito's fine. She's asleep by the fire at the moment, purring away.'

'Is Da there?'

'He is indeed. He arrived on Saturday night.'

'But he said he was going to live with Uncle Tony.'

'Well, he came here, and he's safe and that's the main thing.'

My breathing is short and shallow; to speak without sounding puffed I must go slowly, one word at a time.

'But ... did ... he ... tell ... you ... what ... he ... did? Did ... he. .. tell ... you ... what ... he ... did ... to ... me ... and ... Mammy?'

She sighs. 'You'll be wanting to talk to your father about that.'

I can't speak. The world has turned upside down. I want her to fill in the silence and ask me one simple question, a question like 'Are you all right?', but she is silent and I can hear my breath against the mouthpiece.

I sense she wants to say goodbye. I say 'Don't you know that I told Mammy the truth? Don't you know that I can tell when people are lying?'

'Now, now. This is not for us to talk about. This is not a soap opera where people blurt things out whenever they feel the urge.'

I hear a man's voice in the background. 'Was that Da? What did he say?'

'Yes, that was your father. He was only after calling out to tell me that the postman is here.'

'Does he want to talk to me?'

'I'll see. Wait a moment.'

She calls out to my father and says something else too, something about Dublin, all of it in Irish, so that I won't understand.

I wait and wait but the phone is quiet and I wonder if she has hung up. I wait and wait some more, and when she comes back, at last, she sounds out of breath.

'He says to say he loves you.'

'Doesn't he want to say hello?'

'He does sure, but he has something he has to do at the moment.'

'Oh.'

'Shall I tell you a story about a mouse in Gorey?'

'No!' I say. 'I don't want you to tell me a story about a mouse in Gorey.'

'I know you don't mean that, John.'

I don't answer. I can't speak.

'Bye now, John.'

'Wait. Can you see if there's a letter for me? I'm expecting a letter from the *Guinness Book of Records*.'

'I'll call you again if there's anything there. All right?'

'Are you sure no letters have come for me?'

'I'm sure.'

'All right.'

'God willing, everything will work itself out. Pray for me now, like a good boy, and pray for your mother and father too. And for yourself, if you can spare the time.'

I hang up without saying goodbye.

I tell my mother what my grandmother said and she looks upset, but she says nothing. She wraps her hand around her cup of tea.

'What will we do?' I ask.

'It's gone cold,' she says.

'Don't you care? Aren't you angry?' I ask.

'There's no point.'

'I'm going to school now,' I say.

But I don't go to school. I open and close the front door then go quietly to my room and sit on my bed. A half an hour later, my mother bursts into the room without knocking.

'I thought you went to school,' she says.

'I did,' I say. 'But they were going on an excursion and I didn't have a note from you so the teacher sent me home.'

She frowns. 'You're a poor liar for somebody who calls himself a lie detector.'

I'm angry again. My neck hurts and swells. It's hard to breathe. I move my feet and put my hands in my pocket and stare at her. 'I'll go tomorrow,' I say.

'Tomorrow. Tomorrow is the first day of the rest of your life.'

Is she trying to provoke me with another one of these dumb expressions?

'I might watch the telly now,' I say.

'I might go to bed,' she says.

'Again?'

'I didn't sleep at all last night. I'm very tired.'

'Why can't you sleep?'

'I don't know.'

I walk away and sit on the settee. Instead of turning on the television, I fold forward and rest my head on my knees and make my knees jump up and down. I want her back so much. I want her to be the way she was before. She can't stay the dull and dumb way she is now. This is a problem that must be solved before it's too late.

33

There's a comedy on the television, but I can't enjoy it. My mood is like it was the night in the caretaker's shed with Brendan; now, like then, there is no escape, and because there is no way to be distracted, and I am alone, it is as though I am exaggerated, and notice everything. I am too alive; too much of myself, all blown up.

I hear knocking at the door, and I get up and open it, but there is nobody there.

I thought it could be him. It would make sense for him to come back now.

I sit on the floor, close to the television screen, but bad memories come. They are the strangest kind of memories, things I thought I'd forgotten. I remember the time I was on the toilet at Brendan's house. I was in there for a long time because I was constipated. Brendan was standing outside, waiting. I could hear him shuffling his feet and sighing. Finally he said, 'Hurry up', and I said, 'I'm doing a big plop.'

I don't know why I said I was doing a big plop. I had to stay in the toilet like a prisoner until I stopped being red in the face. I couldn't see the humour in it, but he kept laughing and ran around the house telling his sisters what I said. He teased me about it all day.

I remember this and turn red even though there's nobody in the living room. It is as though my brain has decided to run its own dark film with the volume on high; a film of bad thoughts, of bad memories, and every thought is worse than the one before it, and nothing will stop the film from running.

I hear ringing at the door and go to it.

There is nobody there.

I call out. 'Hello?'

Is it him?

'Hello?'

I go back to the living room and turn the volume up and the television is much louder, but my brain is stronger and I can't control it. I go to the kitchen. There's nothing to eat, no milk, bread, biscuits or Weetabix.

I go to my mother's bedroom so I can take a few coins from her purse for the shops. I open the door quietly. She is awake, sitting up in bed, her back against the headboard, and staring at the wall.

'I thought you'd be asleep,' I say.

'I couldn't.'

'Why not?'

'It's been seven days now,' she says. 'Seven days and only a few hours of sleep. I've had it. Can you believe it? Your mother's had it.'

There are tears rolling down her face, but she doesn't make a crying noise.

'What do you mean you've had it?' My knees buckle and I almost fall.

'I used to be beautiful. But I've had my last beautiful day. I didn't even know when it was. Was it last month or last winter? Was it my last birthday or the one before?'

I fold my arms to have something to do with myself. I don't know why she's talking about the way she looks. She is not ugly and she is not old.

'My last day of looking beautiful is gone and there was no warning. And it has gone for good.'

She reaches for the glass of water by the bed and takes a small sip. Her lips are dry and bits of skin are flaking and peeling from them.

'And one day soon it won't matter what kind of mirror I look in, it won't matter what the light is like, bright or dark, I will look old.'

'But you aren't old,' I say. 'You'll never be ugly. It's just that lately your hair is messy, and a bit grey.'

'Come here to me for a minute.'

'No,' I say. I don't feel like being close.

'Do you miss your da?'

'Sort of.'

'I spoke to him today. I told him I forgive him, but he says he won't be coming back. He says we have humiliated him. He says he has been annihilated.'

'Why don't we go to Gorey, then?'

'We're not welcome there.'

'Yes, we are.'

'No. We are not. We are not welcome there.'

'Why?'

'Because we have brought shame to the good name of your father's family, and that will never be forgiven.'

'It was the truth. Would you prefer I didn't tell you? I was protecting you.'

She laughs. A strange laugh, like a bark or a dark cough. 'Protecting me from what? Syphilis? Gonorrhoea?' She laughs again. 'Look at you. An eleven-year-old in the body of a grown man who insists on the ridiculous truth and who has got into a bad habit of lying.'

I walk over to the bed and she straightens up and pulls the covers up to her neck.

'I'm not a liar. He is,' I say. 'You used to say that trust matters more than anything.'

'I care about avoiding misery wherever I can. I think that's all anybody cares about.'

281

'That's a dumb thing to think.'

'Of course it is. But pain is much harder on the mind than ignorance.'

'You're stupid,' I say. 'I didn't know you were so stupid.'

'Maybe I am. Why don't you make yourself a sandwich?'

'There's no bread,' I say and leave the room without remembering to take the money.

I don't go to school the next day. I stay at home and eat some spaghetti from the saucepan, and creamed rice out of the tin, and watch television most of the day. I go to the shops downstairs to buy some bread and tea. I bring my mother a pot of tea and a plate of toast and, when I tell her I'm worried about her not being able to sleep, she tells me not to worry for her, that she has a cold, a bad cold, that's all.

'But you never sleep. And you're tired all the time. Can't you get out of bed? Let's go out and do something.'

'What would you like to do?'

'Anything. Maybe go into Grafton Street or to the zoo.'

'Maybe tomorrow.'

'You used to want to do things. You used to want to go to the sea and go for drives.'

'And I will again. I'm just a bit weary with this cold.'

'You've never had such a bad cold before. And colds aren't meant to change people and make them so different.'

'Well, I'm older now.'

I want her to stop talking about being old. I want to break the vase on her bedside table and knock the lampshade over and drag her by the arm onto the floor and change her back to who she used to be.

'Who cares?' I say. 'Let's go to the zoo or get the train to Dún Laoghaire. And when we get home, maybe there'll be a film.'

'Maybe tomorrow. I might feel better tomorrow.'

'Why don't you say definitely tomorrow and then you'll definitely feel better?'

'All right. Definitely tomorrow. We'll catch the train to the sea.'

I go to sleep and in the morning I remember the dream I had about me and my mother. We are on a cruise ship and we're very happy together, on our way to Niagara to see Ripley's Museum.

We sit near the porthole in our cabin on the top deck and watch while a man dressed in green overalls loads our suitcases onto a chute and we watch the suitcases slide down.

But the chute becomes narrower and some of the suitcases slide down too fast, fly into the air, and drop into the water. People scream and cry but the man in the green overalls laughs. 'Some will miss,' he says. 'Some will miss.'

Then I see my suitcase, a small blue one with a leather strap, and I am nervous as I watch it slide off the chute. But instead of flying into the water to be lost forever, the case comes towards me. It flies through the porthole window and lands softly on my lap.

I feel happy. I don't know what happened to my mother's suitcase in the dream but it doesn't seem to matter.

I make tea and take it to the bedroom. She's awake; sitting up in bed, more or less the way I left her yesterday, wearing a pink cardigan over her nightie, staring at the wall.

'Room service,' I say. 'Did you order a cup of tea?'

'Aren't you sweet?' she says. 'I'd love a cup of tea. Why don't you sit with me a while?'

She drinks her tea and I lie down next to her. 'What will happen if you can't ever sleep again?' I ask.

'God help me, if that happens.'

'So, we'll go on the train to the sea today?'

She puts her arm around me. 'My darling, I think at the moment there's more chance vampire bats will take up drinking hot milk.'

She laughs at her joke, but I don't want to laugh. 'Are you saying no?'

'That's not what I said,' she says. 'This isn't a good time. It's a very bad time.'

She has cold blood like my father. And her hair, it's not only grey at the front, near her temples and her ears; grey strands hang down near her eyes, and it's greasy and dirty hair too. Dirty and grey.

I wait for her to finish her tea and when she puts the cup down on the bedside table I take a pillow from behind my head and rest it on my knee. I don't talk, and neither does she. I put the radio on to drown out some of my thoughts.

'Turn that off,' she says and, like most of what she says, it is as though she hardly cares, as though what happens next is none of her business.

I turn the radio off, get back into bed, and hold the pillow on my lap.

'You're taking up too much room there, John. Can't you move to the other side of the bed?'

I move across and, without my weight in the middle of the mattress, her body rises up, as though it were something light and plastic in the water. I must be much heavier than she is.

'That's better,' she says as she presses her fingers to her temples. 'But I've got a rotten headache. If only I could sleep. If I could sleep then we could be happy again.'

'You'd be yourself again? You'd be happy again?'

'I don't know, but I'd give anything.'

I wait for her to take two sleeping pills and, when she lies down on her side, I lie down too, and stroke her back.

'Thank you,' she says. 'It soothes me to have you here. Maybe I'll sleep now.'

I leave her and go to the living room. I want to be calm, but I don't know how. I sit and stand again. I fidget and pace. I try to sit but I can't. At three o'clock I go back to her, to see if she is sleeping. But she doesn't sleep. She is sitting up, fiddling with the seam of her torn nightdress.

'Come and sit with me,' she says. 'I feel shattered. I'm in pieces.'

She lies on her back. I get on the bed and lie next to her. She is quiet and her breathing is soft. I take her resting hands and fold them across her chest and I look at her. She is still and peaceful now. But I know she'll soon wake.

I climb on top of her. My legs straddle her stomach and hips and I want to stay here and look down at her calm face, but she moves and groans.

To stop her moving, I take the pillow and put it over her face and then I lay down on her, on top of the pillow, and I make myself heavy. When she stops moving, I put my head on the pillow. We are both sleepy now.

Suddenly she kicks. She kicks against me and her arms fly at my face. I am surprised by her violence, surprised by her strength. The pillow muffles her cries and moans but still I wish the radio could be turned on to drown out the awful noise.

With all my strength, I press down hard on the pillow and I hold her arms down with my hands and fight against her kicking. When, at last, she stops struggling, I take myself off her body and look at her: She is calmer again; she is prettier.

I get up off the bed. It is over.

*　*　*

But my feet are cold. Why are they so cold? I need socks. Something to keep them warm. Why are they so cold? What is wrong with my feet? I go to the drawer to find some socks. I must think about what I will do next, but my feet are so cold. I search in the drawers for warm socks. I cannot think.

I hear a rattle, a scraping noise, a faint but constant sound, somebody outside running a coin along the wall? I stop still and now I hear it, louder and clearer, the sound is in the bedroom. I close the drawer and as I straighten to stand I realise she is coughing.

I turn to face her. Her eyes are open and her hands are on her neck. I watch until she stops spluttering. I watch until she looks at me.

'Mammy?'

She lifts herself from the bed, puts her feet over the side, and stands, her arms held out, her hands up as though to stop me coming towards her.

'Did you try to smother me?' Her voice is uncaring, calm. 'Is that what you tried to do?'

'No, Mammy. You just went to sleep. You had a nightmare.'

She doesn't look at me, takes her dressing gown from the back of the chair and leaves, out to the hallway.

I follow her.

'Get out of my sight,' she says.

She walks into the living room and I follow her.

'Get away from me,' she says, her hands held out in front of her breasts.

'But why? What's wrong?'

I move towards her, but she backs away and stands hunched in the corner.

'Holy Mary full of grace, the Lord is with thee, blessed art thou amongst women and blessed is the fruit of thy womb Jesus.'

'Why are you praying?'

'Because my son tried to smother his mother. Oh, God. Smother his mother! Smother his own mother!'

'You said you wanted to sleep.'

'I didn't say I wanted to die. You could have killed me.'

'But you didn't die. I love you, Mammy. Won't you stop crying?'

I move towards her and she backs away.

'But I didn't,' I say. 'I didn't do anything.'

'Get out of my sight!' she shouts.

I go to my room and lie on my bed and listen to my mother on the telephone to the Gardai.

She gives our address. She repeats it three times and then she says, 'I think my son tried to murder me in the bed.'

34

My mother walks into the living room with two guards; a man with red hair and a short female guard with a big nose. They're both shorter than I am and they look at me but say nothing. I want them to go. I walk to the front door and open it. This is not their home and they should not be so casual about coming here.

'The front door's open,' I shout. 'You can go now.'

But nobody comes.

I go back to the living room and watch my mother. She stands behind the female guard as though for protection and wipes her nose with the pink handkerchief I gave her last Christmas. There is another knock at the door. My mother goes to answer it and I am left alone with the guards.

Nobody speaks and I am annoyed when the female guard looks at the photo on the mantelpiece of me making my first Holy Communion: I'm holding the white prayerbook against my leg and I'm not ready for the camera.

My mother is at the front door, crying and telling somebody what happened.

A man in his early twenties comes in, with his hand on my mother's shoulder. 'Hello,' he says. 'You must be John Egan. My name's Kevin McDonald. I'm a social worker.'

'Yes,' I say, looking at my mother while she wipes her eyes with the handkerchief.

I don't feel anything except tired, and annoyed with having strangers in my house.

'I'm going to take you into another room for a while,' says the social worker. He wears an earring and he has a tattoo of a bluebird on his neck. 'Shall we go to your bedroom?' he asks.

He reaches out to put his hand on my arm.

'You don't have to touch me,' I say.

We go to my room and he sits cross-legged on my bedroom floor.

'Your mother has made it very nice in here,' he says. 'These flats can be awful depressing.'

I lie on my bed and stare up at the ceiling and listen to the ambulance siren outside.

After a few minutes there's another knock on the door. I can hear the voices of the ambulance men and my mother who says, 'I'm feeling fine now, thank you.'

One of the ambulance men tells her that they should examine her nevertheless, and she says, 'I don't want to waste your time. There's no need to fuss.'

I stand up and move towards the door. I want to talk to her.

'You need to stay in here,' says the social worker.

'I want to talk to her.'

'You can talk to me if you want,' he says.

'Aren't the guards going to get a statement or something?' I say. 'Aren't they going to question me and make a tape recording?'

'Yes, that will happen later, but we can talk for a while first, if you like.'

'Will they fingerprint me?'

'Don't worry yourself about that now. Why don't we talk for a while? Hmmm?'

'But what if I tell you something, and then I tell them something different? What then?'

'What you say to me will be off the record.'

'That's a bit stupid. I think I'd rather just be quiet,' I say.

'Suit yourself.'

After a few minutes, I feel like I wouldn't mind talking, but the more I think about what I want to say, the less I'm able to get things clear, and then I become confused about what happened, and then I can't say it at all and it gets so that I wonder if I'll ever speak again.

The female guard knocks on my door. She smiles at me, as though she likes me all of a sudden. 'We've finished talking to your mammy and we're ready for you now,' she says. 'In the kitchen.'

I go to the kitchen and my mother waits in the living room, which seems strange. Since she'll be able to hear everything we say, she might as well come into the kitchen and sit with us.

'Would you like something to drink?' asks the social worker.

'No, thanks. There's nothing but water anyway. There isn't even any milk. Not that I'd want milk anyway. I'd only want Fanta.'

They look at me and nobody speaks for a minute.

'How old are you, John?' asks the female guard with the big nose.

'Eleven,' I say. 'Twelve in July.'

'You look quite a bit older,' says the guard.

'Yeah,' I say. 'I know.'

'Do you want to tell us what happened?'

'Hasn't she already told you?'

The guards look at each other and it seems they don't believe what they've been told. The female guard shrugs and the male guard shakes his head at her as though to tell her to keep her gestures to herself.

'Yes, but don't you want to tell your side of the story?' says the male guard.

'There's only one side,' I say.

'Did you try to help your mother to get to sleep by putting a pillow over her head?' asks the female guard.

'I helped her.'

'Yes, but how?'

'Didn't she already tell you?'

'Yes, but why don't you tell us? We're here now.'

'I helped her with a pillow.'

'Did you want to hurt her?'

'No.'

'What did you think would happen when you put the pillow on her face?'

'I thought she'd go to sleep.'

'Didn't you think that you might hurt her?'

'No.'

'But you did,' says the male guard. 'You did hurt her. That's what you did.'

'No I didn't. I just did what she wanted. She wasn't the same any more. I just did what she said she wanted, to make things better for her.'

'How so?'

'You don't understand anything. Why does nobody understand anything?'

'If you explain, we might understand,' says the social worker. 'Why don't you tell us? Help us understand.'

'Waste of time,' I say.

They ask more of the same sort of questions, but when I refuse to say any more they leave me alone in the kitchen and go into the living room to talk to my mother.

'Helen,' says the female guard, 'we need to take him with us now.'

'Yes. Take him,' she says. 'I can't stay here with that monster.'

Monster? Monster? Who is she talking about? I knock a kitchen chair over and rush into the living room, but I stop near the end of the settee when the male guard moves towards me. I stand with my hands folded across my chest and look at her over the top of his head.

'I only did what you wanted,' I say. 'It's not my fault you changed your mind. Is it? It's not my fault you changed your mind. You changed, not me.'

She looks at the female guard. 'Take him,' she says.

'Take me where?'

'You'll see when you get there,' says the male guard.

The social worker tells me to pack a bag with enough clothes for a week; some schoolbooks, a pen and something to play with.

'Like what?' I ask. 'Like a football? Like what?'

'Use your imagination,' he says.

The guards stay with my mother. The social worker and I leave the flat together and he doesn't speak until the lift arrives. As we get in, he puts his hand on my back. I cover my mouth because of the stench of urine, but he seems not to mind.

'Your mother is very upset,' he says, 'but she says she loves you still. You're lucky for that. She's a good woman.'

I look at the graffiti on the wall – *pigs are fucking animals* – and I smile and pretend not to hear him. But, in some way, I'd like to show the graffiti to the social worker, and say, 'This graffiti has a double meaning.'

'I'll be coming with you to the Children's Court in the morning,' he says. 'The judge will decide what to do with you until the hearing.'

'What's a hearing? Is that like a trial?'

'Maybe we should talk more when we get you to your room.'

'You're the one that mentioned the hearing. I didn't even ask.'

'That's true. I did bring it up. I'm sorry.'

The ambulance is parked downstairs outside the lift; one door is open, one closed. It says LANCE.

The social worker's car is blue and the smell inside is like the smell of new shoes.

'Right, so,' he says. 'The place I'm taking you might seem a bit scary at first, but it's not a bad place, and everybody there will want to look after you and see that you are all right. I know you must be feeling a bit overwhelmed after what's happened and maybe it won't sink in until later.'

'I'm not a baby,' I say. 'You don't have to talk to me like I'm a baby.'

He shrugs and lets a truck overtake us.

'Can I've a cigarette?' I ask.

'In the glovebox,' he says.

I root around and find a packet of Silk Cut. 'Matches?'

'Use the car lighter,' he says.

'Oh yeah,' I say.

I'm having fun. I shouldn't be having fun. I want to stay in this car; keep driving; take the car on a ferry across to France or England and drive all the way to Switzerland and go on a funicular, then drive to the airport and fly to America. Keep driving for the hell of it. It's warm in the car and there's a tape playing.

'I suppose this is jazz,' I say.

'Do you like it?'

'Yeah.'

He nods, but doesn't speak, and so we drive in silence while I smoke two cigarettes, lighting one from the other. As we get closer to the city I wind down the window and hang my head out like a dog does. I look out at the dark sky, and up at the fingernail

294

moon, and I feel happy. When we turn into a big square near the statue of Parnell, I look at the lights in the windows of the big terrace houses and hope that I'll be staying in one of them.

'We're here,' says the social worker.

He points to a four-storey house with a blue front door, bars on the windows, and stone stairs leading down to a basement. There are lights on in all the windows and a Manchester United football jersey stuck to the inside of a window on the top floor.

'Is this a boys' home?'

'Yes, it's a boys' home. Let's get you inside and see if they have the bed ready yet.'

There is a room for me at the end of the long, dark hallway. We come to a yellow door with a brass number 84 on it and we go inside. The social worker turns on the light, which flickers for a moment before working. It's a small room, with a round yellow rug – the same yellow as the paint on the door – in the middle of the floor, a narrow bed that is low to the ground, and there are racing cars on the wallpaper. The bed doesn't look big enough for me and, although I prefer to sleep flat on my back, I'll probably have to curl my legs up during the night.

'So, this will be your room for a few days,' says the social worker. 'Leave your bag in the cupboard and come with me to the interview room.'

I sit on the tidy bed. It's white, like a tablet, made tight, the sheets tucked in all the way under the thin mattress. There are three blankets in a neat pile on the end, orange, green and brown.

'What for?' I ask.

'You'll be interviewed by the housefather, just for a minute, and in the morning you'll be back with the guards.'

'I feel sick,' I say.

'That's understandable,' he says, as he fastens the button on his sleeve. 'What's happened is probably starting to sink in.'

'No, it's not. I just feel sick.'

'All right, I'll get you some aspirin, but we need to go. The housefather has got out of bed especially and we don't want to keep him up all night.'

'OK.'

The two guards who came to our flat are in the interview room and they sit in chairs against the back wall. The social worker pulls a chair out from the table and points at it. I sit at the table and then he disappears, or so I think, until I realise that he is standing behind me.

The room has nothing in it except the table, four chairs, a heater and some toys for small children: rings that fit over plastic sticks, and plastic shapes that fit into plastic holes. Somebody has tried to force a triangle into a square hole.

The housefather comes in. He is old and skinny, and he has messy black and grey hair. He sits opposite me at the table and holds a pen over a pad of writing paper.

'Good evening, John,' he says. 'My name is Mr Keating.'

'Hello,' I say.

He hands me a key and tells me it's for the cupboard in my room. The key must be made of plastic: it weighs no more than a cube of sugar. There are chocolate biscuits on the table but I don't want them. I feel hungry and full all at once, like there's too much air in my stomach.

Then we are silent and he looks at me. 'You're scratching your head quite a bit,' he says. 'Are you conscious of doing that?'

I wasn't, but there's no way now to hide the blood on my fingers.

'Does that not hurt? Does it not hurt to make your scalp bleed?'

'Not really. I just scratch because it's itchy.'

'There are better ways to stop an itch.'

I shrug.

'Do you feel the pain now? In the place where your head is bleeding?'

'No.'

He looks over at the social worker. 'Would you like me to get you a tissue or some cotton wool?'

'No. It doesn't matter.'

More silence.

'I hear you think of yourself as a bit of a lie detector? I hear you can tell when people are lying?'

'Yes.'

'I know a little of that subject myself. Did you know that there are other people in the world who can do this?'

'Yes. I've read about them.' I tell him a little of what I've read about the wizards, how they score between ninety and one hundred per cent in tests.

'Did you know that most lie detectors develop their super-sensitivity to emotion early in life? And this heightened sensitivity is often due to unusual childhood circumstances?'

I enjoy being spoken to as though I am an intelligent adult, but I don't get his point. 'So?' I say.

'Well, John, many people who claim to have this ability to detect lies have extremely irritable mothers, or alcoholic fathers, or some other force or presence in their early life that is, or was, unhealthy, unnatural, unpleasant or extremely upsetting in some way. Does that ring any bells, John? Did you have an upsetting experience?'

He is wrong. 'I feel sick,' I say.

As I move to stand, the chair falls out from under me. And that is the last thing I remember of my first night in the Parnell Square Home for Boys.

* * *

When I wake, the social worker and the housefather are standing by my bed. The room is stuffy and, although it must be morning, the curtains haven't been opened and it is still dark.

'We came to wake you,' says the social worker. 'But you woke yourself. How did you sleep?'

'Good,' I say. 'Fine.'

'You've missed breakfast,' says the housefather as he opens the curtains. 'It's eleven o'clock.'

I sit up and an insect lands on my face, and then on my arm. The room is hot and infested with midges. I've never seen midges inside. They shouldn't be here.

'Get dressed. We'll wait outside.'

I dress in the same clothes I came in and go out into the hall.

The housefather folds his arms across his chest. I do the same. But I feel stupid, unfold them, and lean my shoulder against the door.

'Your mother is coming for you later this afternoon. She came to get you at nine o'clock and was waiting for you but she didn't want us to wake you. And your father will be here on the afternoon train, but first you need to come with us to the interview room. Then you'll have some lunch.'

'If my mother is here, why can't I see her?' I ask.

'She was here but we sent her home for some rest. She'll be back later this afternoon. We need to sort out some paperwork first. We need to sign your discharge papers.'

'Does that mean I'm leaving?'

'Yes, but let's take care of that business somewhere other than in the corridor.'

They sit at one side of the wobbling table and I sit at the other. The housefather does all the talking. I don't have any thoughts about anything much except my nervous stomach.

'Your mother says she doesn't want to pursue any charges against you. She hasn't been to bed. She was with the guards most of the night, and came in here this morning.'

I stare at him.

'We need to sign you in, and this must be done quite formally, since you were unfit to sign anything last night.'

'But why should I be signed in when I'm about to be signed out?'

'Can you read?'

'Of course I can read.'

'Then read this, and if you agree to it, sign it, and then you'll be free to go home with your mother, if that's where she'd like to take you.'

'Back home?'

'Looks like it,' says the housefather. 'And you'd better stop rubbing your face. It muffles your words and you'll end up with acne vulgaris.'

'Acne vulgaris is . . .' offers the social worker.

'I know what it is.'

The two-sided discharge paper says that I was taken 'involuntarily into the custody of the Department of Justice' and that I am being 'discharged by order of the same'; today's date, a few names, something about 'indemnification against damage to property', and that's about it.

I'd like to keep it as a souvenir.

'So I can go now?' I ask. 'Back home?'

The social worker clears his throat. 'Well, you can see your mother and I'll be sitting in with you in the family room for a few minutes, just to be sure everything is ship-shape.'

'Oh.'

* * *

At lunchtime, I sit in the dining room, with the social worker. There are seven tables, with five or six boys at each. They are between ten and seventeen years old, and make so much noise that every few minutes a man in a brown and green uniform walks down beside them and bangs two frying pans together, saying, 'Who wants to lose their ears now? Who?', but they all laugh and go back to the noise, including the man in the green and brown uniform. I've never been on a school camp, the kind that Americans have, but this must be what it's like.

My appetite is back and I eat two helpings of mashed potato and sausages and two helpings of trifle. The social worker eats a cheese sandwich cut into triangles, and he takes small bites, the sharp, small bites that a rat might take. It is as though he is afraid of opening his mouth too wide.

'If you had stayed here,' he says, putting his sandwich down while he speaks, 'you'd have enjoyed the meal on the first Sunday of every month.'

'Why?'

'The trainee chefs for the big hotels come in and try out their new recipes. Trainee chefs for posh hotels like the Shelbourne.'

'I want to stay there one day.'

He ignores this.

'And on Thursday nights there's a billiards competition and on Saturday there are darts and table tennis.'

'But after here the boys go to prison, don't they?'

'Some do. Some don't.'

'Would I have been charged with attempted murder if my mam had wanted to press charges?'

'Very likely.'

'I'm lucky, then.'

'One of the luckiest boys I've ever met. Do you have any idea what your life might have become?'

'I'd probably have been in prison.'

'More likely you'd have spent a very long time in a psychiatric hospital for the criminally insane.'

'Children don't go there.'

He puts his sandwich down. 'That's true. But adolescents do.'

I stare at him.

'Well then, I wouldn't have gone there.'

'Just count yourself lucky you have such a loving mother.'

I don't want to talk about my mother, I want to see her. He doesn't continue with his cheese sandwich and it stays there on the tray like something in a cartoon, with his tiny teeth marks in it. He looks at me, waiting for me to speak and when I don't, he tells me to go my room to pack my bag.

I lie on the bed for a while, stare up at the ceiling, and hit the midges with the small softcover Bible that was in the bedside drawer.

At four o'clock the social worker comes in. 'OK, they're waiting for you.'

The family room is large, with three orange settees, a big television, a record player and two bookshelves filled mostly with magazines.

My mother stands up when I walk in. She has make-up on and her hair is plaited. She holds her arms out and I walk into her embrace, and she holds me and I smell the milky tea with sugar she must have had while she was waiting. I am happy.

'I couldn't do it,' she says.

She lets go and stands back to look at me.

'You're my son, and I love you and I can't see your life ruined. Your life will not be ruined. Your life will not be ruined. Not by you, and not by me. Your life will not be ruined. Do you understand?'

Her voice is strong and loud.

'Yes,' I say.

My father stands in the corner, holding two helium-filled balloons, both orange, the same as the colour of the settees.

'And you're sorry,' he says without moving. 'We know you're sorry. Aren't you?'

'Yes,' says my mother. 'You're sorry.'

They look at each other, and something seems settled. My mother collapses onto the settee and weeps silently. I stay standing; the social worker is standing behind me, breathing heavily but saying nothing.

I don't want to sit. I want to leave. I look at my father; it is easier than looking at my mother. 'What are the balloons for?' I ask.

'Something to hold me up,' he says.

This must be a joke, but he doesn't smile. 'Oh,' I say.

'The balloons are for the twins,' says my mother. 'It's their eighth birthday today. We're going around to Aunty Evelyn's house for tea. And we'll stop on the way to pick up the cake. And we'll not talk about what you did. And you'll not say that you've been locked up here. What you did is forgotten and forgiven. There's no other way.'

I smile at her but she doesn't look at me; she looks at the floor.

'It's forgotten and forgiven,' she continues, 'and we will forget, and you will drop the nonsense about lie detection. There's no point in ruining a perfectly good and promising life.'

I look at my father. I study his reaction to what my mother is saying. Maybe he has a punishment in store for me? His shoulders rise and fall with his breathing and, impatient but not angry, he moves the balloons from one hand to the other.

He looks at me. 'We're starting again,' he says. 'The three of us. We're starting all over again.'

'Are we going back to Gorey?'

'Yes. We'll leave tomorrow.'

'Good,' I say. 'I want to go back.'

My mother gets up to leave and the social worker steps forward and asks her if she is ready to go.

'Yes.'

'And you're sure?'

'Yes.'

He opens the door and takes us down the hall to the front door. We stand to say goodbye on the footpath outside, by the car.

'Thanks,' I say. 'Thanks for all your help.'

'You're very welcome,' he says, putting his hands in his pockets.

'Yes, thank you,' says my father.

The social worker nods and turns away without saying goodbye. He walks towards the door of the home.

My mother says, 'Let's go now,' and opens the car door and we get in, but my father stands by the car, and watches the social worker.

He calls out after him, 'Thank you.'

And when the social worker has not heard, my father calls out again, 'Thank you! Goodbye!' but his voice is too loud.

The social worker turns around and, when he sees my father still looking at him, he waves and my father waves, his hand beating too fast and too long in the deaf air.

35

We drive to Aunty Evelyn's for the birthday party and my mother and father talk about the traffic and the weather. But when I wind the window down and stick my head out, my father turns around in his seat and yells at me.

'What the hell do you think you're doing?'

I don't argue. I say I'm sorry, wind the window up and sit back, quietly, in my seat.

In the kitchen at Aunty Evelyn's my mother helps light the candles on the cake with a slow, steady hand, and my father starts the singing. He sings so well that Kay, who rarely speaks, unless it is in unison with her twin sister, says, 'You sound nice, Uncle Michael.'

After the cake, Aunty Evelyn brings out a tray of ham sandwiches. 'Beautiful leg ham,' she says.

My mother covers her nose and mouth with her hand. 'I don't know what's got into me, but I can't stomach the smell of those ham sandwiches.'

Aunty Evelyn laughs. 'Who ever heard of such a thing!'

My mother takes a sandwich but she doesn't eat; it stays in her hand, held down close to the table.

'I could make some cheese sandwiches instead,' I say.

Uncle Gerald doesn't lift his head, but his voice is loud and sarcastic. 'Put that boy in the *Guinness Book of Records* for being the first teenager to offer his mammy lunch!'

Aunty Evelyn laughs again. Alone.

✳   ✳   ✳

In the afternoon the adults go to the good room upstairs to drink port and whiskey. I'm in the living room with Liam and the twins watching the FA Cup final. I can't sit still. I am worried that Aunty Evelyn and Uncle Gerald will find out what has happened. I close my eyes for a few seconds, and by the time I open them again I can't remember what the score is.

Liam starts shouting, abusing the Man U goalie for letting a penalty through. The goalie didn't do anything wrong, it was a good shot, that's all, but Liam keeps on screaming at the goalie, 'You idiot! You mongoloid! You sissy!'

All the Man U supporters in the crowd are screaming at the goalie, their mouths wide open, most of them standing, waving their fists. When a close-up of the goalie's face comes up on the television, Liam moves in close to the screen and spits at him. The goalie is trying his hardest to block the balls. In the close-up he looks frightened.

I rush to the toilet.

I have diarrhoea. It floods out of me, and I get a sharp pain down my thighs. The diarrhoea keeps coming, so much of it, and as it rushes into the toilet some of the dirty water splashes up against the back of my legs. The smell is terrible. I flush the toilet three times, all the while holding my nose. I use a towel to wipe the back of my thighs and rinse the towel in the bath. After I have washed the towel, I wash my hands, and I run the hot water tap for a long time, hoping the heat and the steam will cover up the smell and stop me feeling sick.

Liam knocks on the door. 'What're ya doin' in there? Havin' a bath?'

'Yes,' I say.

He keeps knocking and shouting at me and I want to go out there and hurt his face. I picture myself going at his face with my hands.

But I stay where I am. I wait. Instead of going out to him, I run hot water in the bath again. While the tap is running, I can't hear Liam and I feel better. I stand in front of the mirror and the hot water steams it up so that I can't see my reflection. But I face the mirror and look at the steam on the surface of the glass.

'On the count of ten,' I say, 'you will come back and everything will be normal again.'

I wipe the mirror clean. When I can see my face again, I don't like how it looks.

I let the mirror steam up a second time. I wipe it clear once more and look at my face. I smile. The second time is better. I put my hand on the reflection of my hand and I say, 'You will be all right. You won't be a criminal. You will be better than other people.'

I wash my hands and scrub under my nails, then I get Liam's aftershave and splash it on my underpants and the legs of my jeans. I go back into the living room. The football match is over and Liam and the twins are eating more cake. I sit in the chair nearest the window and look down at the street. I watch a hunchbacked old man cross the road. He doesn't look to see if there are any cars coming.

At eight o'clock my parents come to take me home. My mother smiles without showing her teeth. My father looks at me properly for the first time since he came to collect me from the boys' home. I'd like him to hug me instead of looking at me.

'Time to go,' he says.

I fall asleep in the car and go straight to bed when we get home.

In the morning, my mother comes to my room. 'You'd better get washed. Uncle Jack and Uncle Tony are coming for breakfast. They've agreed to move the furniture.'

I want her to come and sit on my bed, but I don't think she will. She will stay in the doorway. 'Do they know?'

'Only Granny knows.'

'What about Aunty Evelyn? Did you tell her?'

'We told her what we've told your uncles; that we've decided to go back to Gorey because we like it better there.'

I stand up and move towards the door. She puts her hand across her chest and reaches for her shoulder. She holds her shoulder as though it is sore.

'John. Listen to me. You'll be seeing a doctor in Gorey. He's a child psychologist. I'll be taking you to see him as soon as we get back and you'll go for as long as he says you need to.'

I don't care about doctors. I want to know what she thinks, and I want to know why she is taking me back. But if I ask, things might change; things that aren't clear or certain might become clear and certain. She might decide to have me locked up; my father might leave again; I might be punished.

'Are you happy?' I ask.

She walks away without answering.

Uncle Jack and Uncle Tony come just before nine. They eat two helpings of eggs and rashers and black pudding, and drink three pots of tea. I eat only toast. I'm too nervous about diarrhoea.

'Why won't you eat?' my father asks.

'I have a toothache.'

Immediately after I say this, Uncle Tony distracts everybody by complaining about his gout, the swelling and soreness of his big toe. 'Even the weight of the sheet on my foot gives me pain,' he says.

My mother has no patience with him and talks to him the way she used to.

'Well, if you'd stop eating all those kippers and fatty foods you might not have the gout.'

My father smiles with the corner of his mouth.

'Fair play,' says Uncle Tony.

'Time to pack now, John,' says my father.

I open my cupboard drawers. All five editions of the *Guinness Book of Records* are missing. That's five whole years gone.

I go back into the kitchen. My parents are holding hands, looking at each other, whispering.

'Where are my books?'

'I've given them to charity,' says my mother. 'I'd prefer you to read something else from now on.'

'Like what?'

'School books.'

'But I needed them.'

'Let's pack and get out of here,' says my father.

I go to my room but instead of packing I sit up on my bed and throw my clothes out the window. My shirts and trousers and socks float down more slowly than I expect them to and they land on the ground-floor balconies; only one pair of trousers makes it all the way down to the ground.

I go back to the kitchen with an empty suitcase. I open it and put it on the floor near my father's feet. 'I'm packed,' I say.

'Where are all your clothes?' he asks.

'I threw them out the window.'

They look at each other and don't seem at all surprised. They don't protest. Then, suddenly, as though somebody has pressed a button, my parents start laughing and then the laughing stops.

'You were outgrowing most of them anyway,' says my mother. 'It's probably just as well.'

❋ ❋ ❋

309

At eleven o'clock, we are ready to go. Uncle Jack and Uncle Tony lean against the car and say how exhausted they are. My father hands each of them an envelope. They both refuse, but my father insists they take it.

'Something small. That's all. Please take it.'

'We're very grateful,' says my mother.

'Not at all,' says Uncle Jack, and then we say goodbye.

My mother sits in the back of the car and my father tells me to sit in the front passenger seat. 'There's more room for your legs in the front,' he says.

But I think my mother wants to sit in the back because she feels safer there.

It's a nice sunny day, no clouds, and the traffic moves quickly. We talk about Ballymun. My mother says she'd never have got used to the smell of the rubbish chute and the noise, and my father says he's never been gladder to see the back of a place.

And then all that they talk about is the roads and the drive. Talk about nothing. The kind of talk robots would have. It makes me nervous. It makes me think that there will be a sudden explosion when we get to Gorey.

And then, out of nowhere, my mother says to my father. 'By the way, I was right about Jack the Ripper and Sherlock Holmes. They were around at the same time. Jack the Ripper committed his murders in 1888 and Sherlock Holmes first appeared in 1887.'

'What on earth made you drag that up now?'

'I just saw a wee pub called The Sherlock. And then I remembered that I'd checked up on it in the Ballymun school library.'

'You win,' he says, and he pats her leg and they smile at each other.

We stop at a pub for something to eat and so my father can rest from driving and we sit in a booth near the back. The food comes from the kitchen to the bar through a service hatch. I like it that I can see the white sleeves of the person holding the plates but not his head.

There's a good smell of burnt chops and I like the heavy cutlery and the big plates. My father smokes. He lights one cigarette from another. My mother goes to the bar and gets three fizzy drinks. We sit for a while without speaking.

A little girl walks in and out of the bar and leaves the door open. Her brother gets up and closes the door after her and the people sitting nearest the door complain each time she leaves it open. I hate it when people leave doors open and cause draughts.

But this is almost exactly what happened when we stopped at the hotel near the Wicklow mountains on the way to Dublin. I'm sure of it! There was a little girl there, too, who left the door open and her brother had to get up and close it after her.

My heart is thumping so hard I can feel the blood in my teeth, and I'm very nervous, but I have to speak. 'What's going to happen?' I ask.

'Well, we're going home now, and your granny will be very happy to see you,' my father says. 'But first I have something for you.'

He gives me a small parcel wrapped in brown paper. I unwrap it. It's a cap, the kind of stupid cap farmers wear.

'It's yours,' he says.

'Why?'

My mother and father look at each other, wanting the other to say it.

'To stop your scratching,' says my mother. 'At least until your head heals and you get out of the habit.'

'I don't want to wear this.'

'You'll wear that hat,' says my mother. 'You'll wear it all day, every day, until I tell you not to.'

I put the cap on my head and I feel like a fool. It's a soft brown cap, not a hat, not quite a beret. I don't know what to call it. I take it off and look at it. 'This is stupid. I haven't even been scratching,' I say.

'You've been scratching that hole in your head non-stop since we left Ballymun,' says my father.

I didn't know. 'Where did you get it from?'

'It was your Uncle Gerald's.'

'Why did he give it to you?'

My mother laughs and looks happy, pleased with herself. 'He didn't,' she says. 'Your father found it yesterday down behind a chair and it was covered in fluff and cobwebs. So he took it.'

I put the hat on and then I realise what I have done: I have brought her back. I have brought her back. She is better now.

My grandmother is waiting outside the cottage when we arrive; standing on the doorstep, her hands on her wide hips. She's dressed in blue from head to toe and this usually means a special occasion. Blue jumper and cardigan and skirt and pale blue stockings and blue shoes.

I get out of the car first and walk towards her. I want her to be glad to see me and I had hoped she might be standing outside by the road, smiling, holding Crito in one arm, the other ready to hold me. But there is no sign of Crito, and her hands stay on her hips. She doesn't move towards me.

'Hello,' she says. 'You had a fine day for the drive.'

'Hello, Granny,' I say.

'Smart hat,' she says.

She stays where she is, on the doorstep, looking at me. 'Aren't you going to help your poor mammy and daddy with all those big, heavy cases?'

I go to the trunk and take out the last case, a small red one.

'You're big, enough and bold enough now to offer a helping hand.'

'Sorry,' I say. 'I wasn't thinking.'

I was thinking: thinking that I would like a better welcome home. But I don't deserve it. There'll be no understanding of what I have done. I will be given no forgiveness; there will only be forgetting.

'Better get you inside and unpacking,' she says. 'And I'll make us all something to eat.'

I go to my bedroom, close the door, and check under the mattress. The Gol of Seil and the money are still there. I'm very relieved to see my things: nobody should know where I keep them and what I do with them should be up to me.

I sit on the floor and make my decision. I probably won't keep the money and I might not keep The Gol of Seil either; it's full of mistakes of learning, mistakes of the past. If I find a way to return the money and get rid of The Gol of Seil, everything will be normal again. There'll be nothing in my way of setting things right.

At tea, we are all in our old places at the kitchen table, and we eat runny stew with more carrots than meat and mop it up with thick brown bread. Crito sits by my feet and when I lean down to stroke her I realise that she is fatter than she was when we left. I lift her and put her on my lap so that her face is near my belt buckle. She seems to remember who I am and curls into a ball before closing her eyes. Nobody tells me to put her back on the floor.

'Crito's purring is really loud,' I say. 'She must be happy to see us.'

'She must be,' says my grandmother.

'Are you, too? Are you happy to have us back?'

'Of course I am,' she says without smiling. 'It's good to have you home.'

'And it's lovely to be here,' says my mother. 'I so missed being here.'

My mother's cup shakes in her hand and I wish it wouldn't. I do something I haven't done since before Christmas, since before my father lied about the kittens. I take a Digestive biscuit from the packet and dip it into my tea. And I count aloud, to test how long it takes for the biscuit to dissolve and fall into the tea. I take another one, and remove the biscuit the moment before it breaks.

'Five seconds,' I say. 'A record.'

I laugh, and they watch this thing I used to do at the table after meals, before Ballymun, and I do it now because I think it is something they will remember; a bit of how I used to be. I will show them I'm the same boy.

My grandmother seems pleased and holds her cup up over her head. '*Slàinte*,' she says. 'Here's to being home.'

'*Slàinte*,' I say, standing up. 'And Hip! Hip! Hooray!'

36

I wake in the night. My arm is numb, as though all of the bones have been removed. When I lift my arm, it is limp and dead, like a chicken's neck after it has been broken. I'm scared that it may be paralysed as punishment. I get out of bed and turn on the light and keep moving my arm, hoping it will come back to life. And I chant the Our Father.

My mother comes in. 'Why are you up?' she asks.

'My arm was paralysed or something. I couldn't feel it.'

'And now?'

'It's still numb. I don't understand.'

She smiles. 'It's asleep,' she says. 'That's all. Your arm has gone to sleep.'

'But it feels like it's gone.'

'Don't worry. It'll come back.'

I sit on the bed, rubbing my arm. She stays by the open door.

'Da doesn't say much,' I say. 'He's gone all quiet.'

She takes a deep breath and looks down at a spot in the carpet somewhere between her feet and the end of my bed. 'He'll talk again. Just leave him be.'

'But he was reading last night. That's good, isn't it? And you're happy again. That's good too, isn't it?'

'Yes.'

She looks at me for a long time, and I look back. I've stared at her eyes before but this time is different. She stares at me as though she has never seen me before, as though she is nervously meeting a stranger. I want her to come closer but she steps away.

'We have to see your new doctor tomorrow,' she says. 'Go back to sleep.'

As I stand up, she leaves.

When I get up and go to the kitchen, my father is already at the table. 'Morning,' I say.

'Morning,' he says. 'Do you want some sausages?'

'Yes, please.'

He smiles and his fringe falls down over his eyes. He looks handsome and young. I want to talk to him. 'Are you glad we're back?' I ask.

'Yes. Are you?'

'Yes. Very much.'

'That's good, then,' he says.

'Why are you happy to be back?' I ask, hoping for more.

He turns around and folds his arms across his chest. 'There are too many reasons to name.'

'Just name one.'

He looks at the window. 'Well, it's nice here.'

'What do you mean by nice?' I ask.

He turns back to the frying pan and turns the sausages over. 'You wanted to be back, and we're back. You should be happy enough with that.'

He's not lying because he's not saying anything; he's not talking to me, not giving me a good reason. Does he have a plan against me? Is he hiding something? Does he mean to get rid of me? What does he suspect me of? I'm nervous and my stomach churns. I leave the table and when I'm in the doorway

I turn to him and say, 'I am glad. Thanks for bringing me back.'

'The hat looks well on you,' he says, smiling, his voice breaking.

I go straight to my room. Does he know that I stole the station-master from the big house? And if he knows that, what else does he know? I check under my mattress, and everything is where I left it.

I look at the stationmaster's face, his moustache, and his red cap with a visor, then I put him in my pocket. I take the money I took from Granny's purse and put it under the torn lining of my suit-case. I will find a way to return it to her. I'll do this soon, maybe bit by bit; she won't notice. Or perhaps I'll wait until after her next visit to the races, when she's not sure how much money she has.

I take The Gol of Seil and put it in my schoolbag. I won't destroy it, after all. I'll put it in a plastic bag and dig a hole under the tree where the doll is, and bury it there, so I can dig it up and read it, if I ever want to, on the way to and from school.

I'll leave no evidence that he might use against me; nothing he can use to get rid of me. I'll put things back. Everything where it belongs.

I go up the stairs. My mother is sitting on the end of the bed, elbows on her knees, her face in her hands.

'Oh, John,' she says. 'I was just catching my breath.'

'From what?'

'I've been up and down those stairs four times this morning.'

'Why?'

'I think I've got a tummy bug.'

'Is that why your hands have been shaking a bit lately?'

She looks at me and she looks beautiful and calm and as

though she loves me. I close the door and stand with my back against it.

She sits up. 'John, please keep the door open.'

'No. I want to talk to you privately. Please?'

She looks at me for a moment, not sure what to do and I go to her and sit next to her on the bed. But she doesn't talk. Not one word. I don't talk either. Suddenly she falls back and I fall back too and we lie together on our backs looking up at the low ceiling. I hold her hand and she doesn't mind.

'Are you happy we're back?' I ask.

'Of course I am.'

'Why?'

'It's good to be together again. This is where we belong.'

'That's good, because I've been thinking about making a model village. Like the one in the big house.'

'What model village?'

'In the nursery upstairs. I think I told you about it. Anyway, I want to make my own. It'll take a long time, but I really want to do it.'

She sits up and I sit up with her; our legs over the side of the bed.

'And I'd like to make my model village even bigger and better than the one in the big house. I'll have schools and churches and even a hospital and a cemetery.'

She smiles.

'So, can we go there again soon so I can take a photo of it? Then I could work from the photo.'

'Can we talk about it more later?'

'Can't we decide now?'

She stands up and puts her hand on her stomach. 'Oh dear, I need to go again.'

I follow her down the narrow stairs and watch the way her silky hair slides across her back.

She goes into the bathroom and shuts the door. I wait outside, but she is taking a long time. I'm worried.

'Are you all right, Mammy?'

'Yes, yes. Go and wait for me in the kitchen.'

I wait in the kitchen, and at half eleven, she drives me to Gorey, for my appointment with of Dr Murphy, the child psychologist. In the car, she tells me I must see him for at least six months. I don't mind. That guarantees six months in Gorey.

She speaks in a bored voice, in the flat way she did all the way home from Dublin. She drives at fifty miles per hour on the winding roads, as though she thinks she can get rid of thoughts by going too fast for them.

We arrive at the car park of the shopping centre and Dr Ryan's surgery.

'Isn't this the same building as Dr Ryan?' I ask.

'Yes.'

'But I don't want Dr Ryan to see me here.'

'Why not?'

'He'll think I'm crazy.'

'Well, you are.'

She opens her mouth and throws her head back. She wants me to think she's joking, but she's lying about how she feels; faking a laugh.

I get out of the car. 'Don't come with me, then,' I say as I slam the door. 'You might get killed or something.'

Dr Murphy sits behind a big, glass-topped desk. His long face is reflected in the glass on his desk and a bit of the blue sky from the window behind him.

He introduces himself and I look at the paintings on the wall;

two of them are of peasants in the snow. The dentist in Dublin had the same kind of paintings.

Dr Murphy tries to get my attention by moving suddenly. But I keep looking at the paintings.

'Do you like them?'

'I like Bruegel,' I say, hoping like mad I'm right.

'Well, well. Nobody mentioned that you were an art expert.'

'I am,' I say. 'I'm very interested in art.'

Lying like this makes me want to laugh. I pick the big stapler off his desk and move it around on my knee to stop myself from grinning.

'Perhaps we can return to that later. First I'm going to ask you some questions and when we've done what needs to be done we should have a much better picture of . . . a much better idea of your state of mind. Is that all right with you?'

He seems nervous; maybe he thinks I'll throw the stapler at him. Maybe I should make him smile by telling him about the world's fastest psychiatrist, Dr Albert L. Weiner, who treated more than forty patients in a day in his rooms and used electroshock and muscle relaxants. But the needles he used were not properly sterilised and in 1961 he was imprisoned on twelve counts of manslaughter.

I put the stapler back on the table.

'First of all, how do you feel today? Are you a little better than you were in Dublin? At the time of the incident?'

'I feel good,' I say.

I don't know how I feel, except that I feel very awake, as though I'd have no trouble recalling anything I've ever read. And I feel better than I did when my mother left my room in the middle of the night. I feel good about the fact that I lied about being an art lover and that Dr Murphy cannot control me even though he thinks he can.

'How do you feel now about what happened with your mother?'

A few thin hairs stick out of the balding pink circle at the top of his head, and I can hear his breathing, raspy and wet. 'I think I feel like ... I feel like it wasn't real. I feel like somebody else did it. I feel like I was in a film. I feel like she wasn't my mammy and she was somebody I didn't know.'

Dr Murphy sits up and moves into a position so different from the first that it shocks me. He leans back in his chair, as far back as the chair will allow, his arms behind his long, narrow head, and I am woken by this sudden change as though the curtains have been opened in a dark room. And I see him as though for the first time. This must be a technique of some kind.

'Are you aware that you tried to kill your mother? Were you conscious of your actions then and are you conscious of them now?'

I don't move.

He moves forward again.

'No,' I say. 'I just said. None of it felt real. I felt like I wasn't me. I felt like I was somebody else.'

'Who were you, then, if you weren't you?'

'Somebody else. I didn't know who, just not me.'

'But you felt you were human nevertheless. You were a human boy.'

'Well, I wasn't an animal. I wasn't a dog or a sheep, was I?'

'I can hear that you are angry. Do you think my questions are unfair?'

'No.'

He stands up. 'Would you like a glass of water? Or a fizzy drink?'

'OK. Please.'

'Which? The water or the fizzy drink?'

'A Fanta.'

'I only have Club Orange, will that do?'

He opens the fridge (its door is behind a wood panel) and

takes out a bottle of Club Orange, then he offers me a box that contains hundreds of paper straws with bendable tops.

I choose a blue one.

'Blue for a boy,' he says.

I frown.

'While you drink your fizzy drink, I'm going to ask some questions and the most important thing is that you should answer them truthfully. Can I ask you to give me your word that you will answer truthfully?'

'Yes.' And I will.

He sits down behind his desk, this time in a normal position, legs under the desk, pen in hand poised over a blank sheet of paper. 'OK. Are you ready?'

'Yes.'

'Are you able to ignore physical pain?'

'Yes. Sometimes.' I think of making my head bleed and not feeling it.

'Are you ever not sure whether you have done something or only thought about it?'

He is in a hurry and doesn't seem to care about the answer. If I wasn't telling the truth, his lack of attention would bother me less, but since I'm telling the truth I don't understand why he seems so uninterested.

'Yes. Sometimes I'm confused like that, especially during the night.'

'Do you spend time staring into space?'

'A lot. But I'm thinking, not just staring. I'm always thinking when I'm staring.'

'Are you ever not sure whether an event happened or was a dream?'

'No,' I say. 'That's never happened.' Now I have been inconsistent.

He looks up from the desk and coughs. 'Do you ever not remember important events in your life?'

'I can't remember being born or when I was a baby.'

'What about events in the past six or seven years?'

'I don't remember my first Holy Communion. I only know what happened because there are photos and because Mammy tells me what happened.'

Suddenly he is interested. He stands up and walks to the smaller desk near his filing cabinet and the fridge. He stands with his back to this smaller desk and puts his clasped hands in front of his belt buckle.

'Could something bad have happened that day that you don't remember?'

'How would I know, if I can't remember?'

I stand, too, and offer him my bottle of Club Orange, but he refuses it by waving his hand.

'Please, John. Sit down.'

I sit and he sits, back behind his big, glass-topped desk.

'Do you ever find notes or drawings that you must have done but don't remember doing?'

'Yes,' I lie.

'Do you hear voices inside your head?'

Shouldn't he want to know more about the drawings before he moves to the next question? 'Only my own. Is that what you mean?'

'Do other people and objects sometimes not seem real to you?'

This is a good question. I need to think about this for a while; about what 'real' means. 'No. Yes. Sometimes people. Like my mother. She didn't seem real before it happened or during, but after she did. After it happened, she seemed real again.'

I swallow and stop talking.

'Do you want to say any more about this?'

'No.'

'It might help. To say more might help. This is important.'

I lower my head and don't speak.

'Well?'

'No.'

'Do you ever feel as though your body is not your own?'

'That's a bit stupid.'

'What's your answer?'

'No.'

'Do you ever not recognise your own reflection in the mirror?'

'No.'

He stands up and I hope it's time for me to go home. I'm very hungry.

'All right, John. You did well. You thought about your answers and you were very patient. I'm going to leave you alone now for a while. I'm going to go into another room and chat to your mother. Are you happy to sit here for a few minutes?'

'Yes.'

He leaves and locks the door behind him, and then I notice the bars on the windows and my stomach turns. It seems unfair somehow; he ought to have told me he was going to lock me in and, because I know I'm locked in, I want to get out.

When he doesn't come back after ten minutes, I look for something to eat in his fridge. There's a pat of butter and an apple and nothing else. I eat the butter while I sit and read some pamphlets and articles about child suicide, but none of the notes say anything about the ages of these children, and I wonder how old the youngest suicide was, and how they did it.

I get bored. He has me waiting for half an hour. I would like to talk to somebody.

I take off my shirt and look at my arm. There it is — Mr Roche's phone number.

I dial the number but I don't expect anybody to answer.

'Hello?'

'Hello. It's John Egan.'

'Well now! Hello.'

I whisper. 'I'm back in Gorey and I still have my gift. I want to use it but they all want me to keep it a secret.'

'Who wants it to be a secret?'

'Everybody.'

'And why must it be a secret?'

'They think it's destructive and dangerous.'

'And is it?'

I hear footsteps outside. 'I have to go,' I say and hang up.

But the footsteps disappear and nobody is coming. I am alone again and, although the silence is as heavy in the room, I feel lighter.

Dr Murphy returns with my mother. The pat of butter has made the roof of my mouth feel slippery, but otherwise I feel well.

My mother smiles and puts her hand out for me to hold, and Dr Murphy raises his eyebrows, not in an obvious way, but I see it clearly enough and so does my mother.

She looks at him, grins, then gives me a good long kiss on the cheek. 'Come on, darling one. Let's get you home.'

It's a sunny, warm afternoon. She takes my hand and we walk to the car.

'What did he say?' I ask.

'I don't care.'

'You don't care? Why not?'

'It occurred to me while he was prating away to me about disso-ciative disorders and borderline personalities and medications and ECG . . . well, it struck me that I don't care what he thinks. He's only met you once and he's after giving you every disease of the mind known to mankind.'

I spin around, and laugh. I grab both her hands and raise them up. 'So I'm free?'

She stops dead and lets go of my hands. 'Don't get too carried away.'

She walks on and I follow her.

37

At half eight in the morning, I wake to hear my father talking outside to another man. And then somebody leaves by the front door. A few minutes later my mother knocks on my door.

'There's somebody here to see you,' she says.

'Who is it?'

'It's your old class teacher, Mr Roche.'

She closes the door and leans against it. She tells me that Mr Roche no longer teaches at Gorey National School and that he has work as a private tutor now.

'He seems to have heard that you're back and wanted to pay you a visit. But he doesn't know about anything. And, as we've discussed, there is no need for anybody to know what happened.'

'I want to see him.'

'Good. Now, get dressed. And don't forget your hat. You father has gone out for a while and when he gets back he'll want to see you wearing that hat. And don't come out until you've made your bed.'

'Can't I make the bed later? It's rude to keep visitors waiting.'

'I'll tell you what's rude and what isn't,' she says. 'Make your bed.'

She watches while I make my bed. Then she tells me to dress (with the hat) and wash up before going out to the living room.

✻ ✻ ✻

Mr Roche is sitting in my grandmother's armchair by the fire. He's wearing a suit and he's holding a present; a small box wrapped in silver paper. 'Hello, young man,' he says, smiling.

His shoulder-length hair has been cut short, and he looks fatter and has a melted face, especially around his mouth and chin.

'Hello, sir,' I say.

He looks at my mother, and she leaves, but she doesn't shut the door; she leaves it slightly ajar. Mr Roche stands up and hands me the box.

'What is it?'

'Just a small gift. Open it later.'

'All right.'

'Shall we catch up on your news first?'

'Thanks for coming,' I say.

'My pleasure. So, how are you?'

I don't like that he has come without warning and he sits too far back, and too relaxed, in my grandmother's armchair. I sit on the edge of the settee. And, even though I am lonely, I regret that I phoned him yesterday.

'I'd like to hear your news,' he says.

I cannot speak. I don't know what's wrong. There's no way to begin. I don't know why he's here. I feel clumsy and ugly and don't want to be looked at the way he looks at me.

But he stands and comes and sits by me. He sits close and puts his hand on my sleeve. I should be happy that he's here; after all, I wanted him to like me.

'So, tell me how you are. I can see that your mind is racing.'

Can he? Can he see that?

'It looks to me like there are so many things you'd like to say that you don't know where to start. It looks to me like that charming face of yours is trying to hide a multitude of fascinating things.'

I look over his shoulder at the door. Surely this will make him be quiet.

'Why don't you start by telling me what it was like in Ballymun? What about your gift for lie detection?'

I look at the door again. 'I don't have it any more,' I say.

'But yesterday you . . .'

I put my finger over my mouth to shush him, but he goes on.

'Perhaps you never did have a gift,' he says. 'Maybe you're as commonplace as the next boy.'

My heart pounds with hurt and anger. 'But I thought you believed me?' I say.

Mr Roche reaches out and touches my hand. I look at it, curious.

'Talk to me about the gift, then. What was it like when you could tell somebody was lying? By what means did you know it?'

I sit up straight. And then I realise what he is trying to do. He is trying to trap me into talking about my gift by making me defend myself. I think this is clever but it also makes me angry. My anger surprises me. I feel calm and suddenly I hate the person who has tricked me so much I would like never to see them again. I want to leave the room. 'I just knew it,' I say.

'But how, John?'

'It's not like the books say. The police know a criminal is lying about a crime "because his mouth gets dry, because his face gets flushed, and his carotid artery throbs". But I didn't ever see these things. I could tell from the little things. Facial expressions, and hands and voice mostly.'

'But you were detecting lies within your own family and these are people you know very well. Aren't you just reading them from your knowledge of them? Did you ever detect others lying?'

I stand up. 'But, anyway,' I say, 'I don't have it any more.'

He says nothing for a while and neither do I. We are silent for several minutes and the clock above the mantelpiece ticks so slowly it is as though it is trying to make my heart stop.

I am agitated and restless. I tear at the paper around the present until I have it opened. I throw the shreds of paper onto the floor. His present is a fancy gift-set containing a razor, a bar of soap, a shaving brush and aftershave lotion. There's a card too, which probably has money in it. I'll open that later.

'I hope these things aren't premature,' he says.

'No. I like them. Thank you.'

I move towards him because I think I should hug him or show some gratitude but he also gets to his feet and we are standing too close. I start to sweat. 'So, thanks,' I say.

'My pleasure.'

'Thanks.'

My mother comes in. She has make-up on and looks well. 'I have to take John away now,' she says. 'He hasn't had any breakfast and we've a thousand things to get done today.'

'Right, so,' says Mr Roche. 'I'll be off.'

'Yes, sir. Thank you, sir.'

We walk outside with him. When he gets to the front garden, he stops, puts his hands on his hips, looks down the road, and then at his watch. He doesn't have a car. I wonder how far he will have to walk, and so does my mother, but she doesn't offer to drive him.

At breakfast, my mother and father both read while they eat their porridge, and my grandmother stands by the range, peeling carrots.

Suddenly, my father puts his book down and clears his throat. 'John? Would you like to go to the big house today? Your mammy said you'd like to go and look at the model village there.'

'Really? Today?'

'Yes,' he says. 'It's a nice sunny day and we think making a model village sounds like a very good project.'

'I'd like to go very much. I'd love that.'

'Well, then. As soon as we've finished breakfast.'

'The people might be home from Dublin,' says Granny. 'You might not be allowed in.'

She drops a potato and it rolls under the table. I pick it up and hand it to her. I stay standing by her and she says, 'Now that I think about it, I don't think the people are home from Dublin. I think you'll be allowed in.'

'All right,' says my mother. 'The four of us will go.'

We all look at Granny. 'No, no,' she says. 'You go on. I'll stay here. You won't be long.'

We arrive at the gates of the house as the gardener is leaving in his van. My mother leans across my father and beeps the horn. The gardener sees her, and she waves at him. He stops and gets out of his van. She gets out of the car and runs over to him.

My father and I stay in the car and watch. My mother stands close to the gardener and he looks at his watch. He shakes his head, but she puts her hand on his arm. She must be saying 'please' because her face is smiling.

He looks at his watch again, and then he nods.

She comes back to the car. 'We have five minutes. That's all. I told him John had six weeks to live.'

'Did he remember us from last time?' I ask.

'It seems not.'

My father looks at my mother.

She nods, 'Let's go in, then.'

'I'll stay here and wait,' he says. 'You'll only be five minutes.'

'You're coming too,' she says. 'And bring the camera.'

* * *

My father gives me the camera and we walk for a while through the downstairs rooms and then I tell them I want to go up, alone, to the room with the model village.

'Why must you go alone?'

'Can I tell you later? I swear I'll tell you. You'll be happy and pleased when I tell you.'

'Be right back here in two minutes,' says my father.

I look at my watch. 'I promise,' I say.

I go into the nursery room, and it is as it was before, only this time there are more bottles filled with sand and there is a second rocking horse between the two small beds.

I go to the model village by the window and look at it. Everything is just as it was. There are trains and shops and plastic people and shrubs and dogs. And the train to Pigalle has a balcony at the back for passengers to stand on.

And then I see it: there is a new stationmaster. And, just like the stationmaster in my hand, he has a moustache, wears a red cap with a visor, and he stands on a flat piece of green plastic.

The stationmaster at the station for the train to Pigalle has been replaced. There he is, identical to the one in my hand, a little less dusty, but the same. And now there are two; two of the same.

I put my stationmaster next to the substitute. They stand side by side. It's a strange but happy sight, the twin stationmasters. But they might not be twins; they might be brothers, or friends, or just two men who look very much alike. Or, they could be the same person.

I take a photograph of one stationmaster standing alone and then I take a second photograph of both stationmasters standing together.

I stand back and smile.

* * *

I put the camera in my parka pocket and leave the nursery. I go to the landing at the top of the stairs, where I stop and look down, and I see my mother. There she is, there she is waiting.

I walk down to greet her and, as I walk, I make loose fists of my hands and put them by my side. I shout 'Ahoy!' when I'm half way down, and she turns around to look up at me. When I get to the bottom, she smiles and I smile back. My father is standing by the front door, his hands in his pockets.

'Are you finished?' she asks.

'Yes,' I say. 'And I got what I needed.'

'What have you got there?' she asks.

'Where?' I say.

'In your hands?'

'Nothing.'

'It looks to me like you've got something in your hands.'

'Well, I haven't.'

'Then open them.'

I stand back and bump against the banister. 'Why?' I ask.

My father steps forward, comes towards us.

'Open your hands!' says my mother.

I say nothing and she puts her hands over mine and tries to open them.

And now my father is by my left side and he is pulling at my fingers, 'What are you hiding?'

I keep my hands shut tight.

My mother struggles with my right hand and my father takes hold of my left. I use all the strength I have to stop them, but both, at last, succeed, and my hands are open, and empty. Both empty.

'See?' I say, laughing. 'Nothing there. Just like I said.'

My father grins at me and says, 'Just as well.' But he's not angry.

'Yes, just as well,' says my mother and she's not angry either.

*　*　*

We leave the mansion and walk side by side to the car. I sit in the back, near the middle, and I lean forward so I can see their faces. My father drives away slowly, with one hand on the steering wheel, the other resting lightly on his thigh. My mother looks out the window, calm, I think, and happy. It's a perfect day for the beach and perhaps, if I ask, that's where we will go.

The stationmasters are together. The train is arriving and the boom-gate bells are ringing. When the last passenger gets on board, the stationmasters wave their white flags in unison and they watch the train as it pulls away from the platform. The driver waves at them from his cabin window, but they pay no attention. They are too busy talking.

When they get cold or need a rest, or when they need something sweet or warm to eat, they can go into the station buffet together. They can sit at a table near the window, eat tea and toast and cake, and watch the people come and go. And the fire inside will warm their hands and faces.

The door is open.

Acknowledgements

I thank my editor, Michael Heyward, whose excellent work made *Carry Me Down* a better book. I also thank — for the same reason — Stewart Andrew Muir, Carolyn Tétaz, Jenny Lee, Marion May Campbell and David Winter. Thanks also to Jamie Byng, whose steadfast confidence makes it possible for me to write every day. Special thanks to my Irish proofreader, Anne McCarry in Wexford, for her painstaking and patient help. Thanks also to Mark Monnone, Rosalie Ham, Sue Maslin, Helen Bleck, Karen McCrossan, Polly Collingridge, Jessica Craig, Barbara Mobbs and David McCormick. And for his generous last-minute fact checking, my grateful thanks to Colin Brennan.